the PROMISE of AMAZING

the PROMISE of AMAZING

ROBIN CONSTANTINE

BALZER + BRAY

An Imprint of HarperCollins*Publishers*

Balzer + Bray is an imprint of HarperCollins Publishers.

The Promise of Amazing

Copyright © 2014 by Robin Constantine

All rights reserved. Printed in the United States of America.

No part of this book may be used or reproduced in any manner whatsoever
without written permission except in the case of brief quotations embodied
in critical articles and reviews. For information address HarperCollins
Children's Books, a division of HarperCollins Publishers, 10 East 53rd
Street, New York, NY 10022.

www.epicreads.com

ISBN 978-0-06-227948-4

Typography by Erin Fitzsimmons

13 14 15 16 17   CG/RRDH   10 9 8 7 6 5 4 3 2 1

First Edition

For Ruth and Leo,
one of my favorite love stories

"NONE OF YOU ARE GOING TO HARVARD."

Mrs. Fiore paused for effect, scanning the faces in my Honors Lit class with a smug smile. She'd delivered the words with such conviction, it was as if the dean of admissions called and told her that no girl from the entire junior class of Sacred Heart Academy would even be allowed to apply to Harvard.

This was supposed to be a pep talk.

It was a rainy, miserable Friday in November. The kind better suited to burrowing under a comforter watching a *Gossip Girl* marathon than being dissed by your guidance counselor. My chances of going to Harvard, or any college for that matter, were on the fringes of my mind. The future was a faraway idea that came after more pressing ones, like Thanksgiving break or the gamble of putting a deposit down for junior prom by the December deadline without a date prospect in sight.

I surveyed the class, wondering if anyone else found this speech irritating. Resigned eyes stared straight ahead as Fiore droned on. Next to me, Jazz took notes. Across the room in the back corner, Maddie had her head down, pencil in hand. It looked like she was taking notes too, but I could tell she was sketching. I hoped I wasn't her subject this time, because the look on my face was anything but pretty.

Honestly? Harvard had never been a passing thought, even as a reach school, but to hear someone, a guidance counselor no less, tell me it wasn't a possibility made my mind reel. Was this some sort of Guidance 101 mind trick? Didn't Mrs. Fiore realize she was insulting us?

I imagined recording her little speech. I'd strap her into one of our ass-numbing desks and demand proof of her guidance degree, since it was painfully clear she must have skipped the How to Inspire Your Students seminar in favor of the Dowdy Floral Prints and the Many Ways to Rock Them workshop. Then I'd force her to listen to that condescending drivel over and over again and see how inspired she felt afterward.

Fiore's proclamation added another depressing dimension to what was fast becoming my semester of discontent. My current class rank was an unimpressive forty-nine. Forty-freakin'-nine out of one hundred and two, which technically put me in the top half of the class but *barely*. And my application for the Sacred Heart National Honor Society was a total fail. Nominated but denied. To add to the humiliation, the teachers felt compelled to let you in on the reasons why you didn't get in, so you could improve and work harder to make it the following semester.

Wren Caswell. Doesn't participate in class.

Bright but quiet.

Quiet. Quiet.

Too quiet.

I tried not to let the evaluation bother me, but it did. Being quiet was not a conscious protest. It was my nature. And once that sort of "Wow, you're quiet!" klieg light was forced on me, it drove me deeper into my shell. If I had something to say, well, yeah, I would say it, but I never went out of my way to call attention to myself. In school this had always been a good thing. Applauded, even. The NHS evaluation made it sound like a character flaw. Something I could improve.

That's just not how it worked.

"What was up with Fiore today?" Jazz asked, peeling away the plastic wrap from her baby carrots and fat-free dip. Jazz was training to run her first half marathon with her father in January and had adopted a clean-eating philosophy. Lately she ate the same lunch—lean protein on sprouted-grain bread, a Vitaminwater Zero, baby carrots and fat-free dip. It had never bothered me, but today, after the No Harvard speech, I resented its wholesome overachieving perfection.

"*Thank you.* You thought she was out of line too?"

"Oooh, who's out of line? What did I miss?" Mads plopped down her lunch tray on the table.

"Fiore. Last class, or were you dozing again?" Jazz asked, pointing at her with a baby carrot. Mads leaned over, grabbed the carrot out of Jazz's fingers with her teeth, and chewed as she shimmied her chair closer to the table. With her close-cropped platinum hair and devilish grin, she looked like a naughty, private-school Tinkerbell.

"Not dozing, doodling," she said, grabbing a sketchbook from her pile of books and sliding it to me.

"You were doodling Ben Franklin?"

"No." She grabbed the book and flipped to a different page. "That was yesterday. Here, from before."

"Oh, um . . . who?" I asked, handing the book to Jazz.

"You can't tell?"

Jazz peered at me over the sketchbook, brows raised in question.

"Some guy from a boy band?" I guessed.

"No! Zach," Mads said, taking the book from Jazz.

"Ah, should have known, very Cro Magnon–like," Jazz said, dipping another carrot.

Mads scrunched her face but smiled. "I suck at noses. It's all in the shading. So what about Fiore?"

"You know, that whole 'none of you are going to Harvard' thing," I said.

"Oh, *that*? What's the big deal?" she asked, popping open her bag of baked chips and offering me one. I waved them away.

"I don't like to be talked down to," Jazz said.

Mads shrugged. "She's a realist, that's all."

"I can get in to Harvard if I want," Jazz countered.

"Okay, so maybe *you* can, Dr. Kadam, but what about the rest of us? Harvard is like a million miles away from here, metaphorically, at least. Why are you both taking it so personally?"

"Because it feels personal," I said, pushing my brown-bag slacker lunch away. "It was like she was telling us we're stupid, so why bother?"

Neither of them responded, and instead shared a knowing look. Mads crunched a potato chip extra loud between her teeth.

"What?"

"This is about NHS, isn't it?" Jazz asked with the same doe-eyed face of pity she'd given me when I'd shown her my rejection letter.

"It's okay to be pissed, Wren," Mads added.

The pressure of backed-up tears made me blink fast and look away. Sometimes I hated my friends and how well they knew me.

"That's not it."

"Screw NHS, it's not a big deal," Mads said.

"It is a big deal," Jazz protested.

"Jazzy Girl, not helping."

"You'll be nominated again next semester. It's a great thing to have on your transcript."

They bickered back and forth about the importance of NHS while I zoned out. I knew NHS was a big deal. It was the academic elite of the school. What bothered me most was that damn evaluation that summed me up as the average, quiet girl.

I'd always thought of myself as smart, had no problem making first or second honors, but in a small, competitive school just making it didn't translate into anything spectacular. My rank had slipped because my brain refused to comprehend higher math. Even with tutoring, I'd taken home my first-ever Cs in Algebra II and Trig earlier in the semester. As I sat across from my NHS-accepted pals, I felt like an imposter. Like maybe I'd be better suited to being friends with Darby Greene, who sold her mother's Xanax for ten bucks a pill in the back of the classroom and didn't seem to be bothered with less-than-stellar grades. Then again, teachers liked her. She spoke up in class.

"Forget it, really, I'm okay," I finally said.

"And why should we be taking guidance from a woman who buys her hair color off the shelf at Duane Reade?" Mads asked. "Come over after school. I've been dying to practice those ombré highlights on your hair. Zach and his friends can drop by. We'll hang in my basement."

Zach was Madison's overgrown pup of a hook-up buddy. They had about zero in common, except they couldn't keep their hands to themselves when they were within three feet of each other. She'd been trying to share the wealth by setting me and Jazz up with his pals, but so far Zach's friend pool was about as bland as the baked chips Mads was noshing.

"If 'hang in your basement' is code for fighting off whatever soccer teammate Zach has with him this week, I'll pass, but I'll take a rain check on the highlights," I said.

"How 'bout a movie night?" Jazz suggested. "I reserved *Pretty in Pink* at the library. I could pick up something else too, make it a double feature? Big bucket of air-popped popcorn? I'll even splurge with peanut M&M's."

"That sounds great, but—"

"Wait," Mads said, "so both of you would choose cheesy, canned romance and junk food over flesh-and-blood, six-packed-out-the-ass soccer guys?"

Jazz's dark eyes turned incredulous. "Cheesy? Canned romance? *Pretty in Pink* is a classic—"

"—that I've seen chopped up on basic cable about umpteen times."

"Guys, I have to work," I said, trying to snuff out their fantasy-versus-reality debate.

"What's the fun in being the owner's daughter if you can't skip out now and then?" Mads asked.

"We're booked solid this weekend. Besides, the Camelot may be my future."

Jazz looked between Maddie and me. "Since when?"

"Weddings are big business. It wouldn't be a bad thing, right? I wouldn't need major math skills to run it. I could hire someone for that."

"Sure, and then you could hire me fresh out of Pratt to give the place an overhaul," Mads continued. "And Jazz could have her huge Bollywood-style wedding there, and we'll all live happily ever after."

"Why am I the one getting married in this scenario?"

"Because I'm the architect, and Wren is the business owner, and I wasn't sure how a pediatrician would fit into the whole thing. Besides, I want to wear a sari."

"Four years of medical school plus a residency, ha, I'll never have time for a real romance."

"It's just an option I'm tossing around. Not everyone has such a clear picture of their life after high school," I said, balling up my uneaten lunch. The PB&J squished like Play-Doh in the brown paper bag.

"What about after work, Wren? You're usually done by eleven, no?"

"Dunno. I think I'm just gonna lie low this weekend."

"You've hooked up with someone like, what, once, twice, since the Trevor hump-and-dump? Come on, ditch work for one night. You're overdue for some fun."

"Madison," Jazz reprimanded her in a whisper.

I gathered my books and trash and pushed back from the table. "Stop telling me what I need, 'kay?"

"Wren, wait, sorry. Trev's the idiot. All I'm trying to say is it's time to get your feet wet again . . . well, among other things."

"Mads, really," Jazz said, chuckling.

"Use it or lose it. Zach's friends are hot. You never know, you could be cozying up with the next David Beckham."

"Yeah, I'll give that some thought . . . *not*," I said, walking away before either of them could say anything else.

One slight mention from Mads and—*zap*—Trevor DiMarco was back in my head. I was over him, but I wasn't exactly over *us*. He was my first. My only. My cautionary tale.

He'd been a friend of my brother, Josh. One of the many guys that hung around our house, playing basketball in the driveway or sitting around our living room watching Comedy Central and wasting time until they figured out what sports event or party they were hitting that night. The revolving door of cute boys was a perk of having an older brother at St. Gabriel Prep, and I took full advantage during Josh's senior year. Inventing reasons to be in the kitchen. Doing my homework on the deck. Anything to inconspicuously put myself in the middle of the action.

Trev called me Osprey. Seagull. Raven. Every bird name except Wren. But I never took his teasing to be anything more than that. Until the night I looked up from *Wuthering Heights* and saw that Josh and the others had left. Trev stood in front of me, hands in pockets, shoulders hunched to his ears, his blue eyes slightly timid, unsure. Something I'd never seen in him.

"Hey, Wren," he said, taking the book out of my hand as he leaned against the island. My stomach knotted up when he said my name. I hadn't even had the chance to bookmark my page. "I was thinking, maybe . . . would you . . . how about . . . wanna hang with me tonight?"

"Here?" My voice was tight as I drummed my fingers on the counter. He'd never made me nervous before, but now that we were one-on-one, it hit me upside the head. *He* was the reason I hung around so much. Trev, with his perfect sandy hair and laid-back attitude had gotten to me. He cupped his hand over mine to stop the drumming.

"Why don't we just, you know, roll where the night takes us?"

"Roll where the night takes us" was Trev's life philosophy, and I couldn't get enough. Our relationship was a dizzying blitz of prom, graduation parties, and endless nights rolling wherever life took us, and while sometimes it only led us to the lumpy futon in his family room, it was exotic to me. I was gone, gone, gone—caught up in the rush of being in what felt like my first serious relationship. With Trev starting SUNY Purchase in the fall, I knew we had an expiration date, but it wasn't something we talked about. Part of me even held on to the hope that maybe we wouldn't have to end.

None of that was on my mind, though, as we rolled into Belmar one gorgeous day in mid-July. The sun was warm, the breeze was cool, and I was having my first-ever hand-in-hand walk down the beach in the surf with a guy I truly cared about. Then we had *that* conversation.

All Trev said was that he couldn't believe he'd be at orientation in less than a month. All I said was that I couldn't wait to visit him in the fall, how I'd work it out somehow, take a bus or a train or hitch a ride with Josh when he went up to see him. Then we walked in silence. His grip loosened slightly, and he kept looking at me like he wanted to say more. The longer the silence, the more I realized I'd said too much, but I never thought he'd dump me right then as a biplane with a banner that read One-Dollar Shots and Half-Price Apps—D'Jais! sputtered by overhead.

"Baby, no, I thought . . . well . . . I want to be free when I go to school. You should be free too. I thought that was sort of . . . understood." The tone in his voice was sweet, almost concerned. I knew this breakup wouldn't bother him—this was something he was just rolling with, like everything.

That was the last day I saw him.

I tried to be casual about the whole thing, worldly, but . . . hump-and-dump, well, yeah, that felt about right.

With my mom already at work and my dad stuck on a case at the prosecutor's office, I had to walk the ten blocks crosstown to the Camelot. I raced down our front steps, bracing against the raw dusk air, and stared wistfully at my sister Brooke's Altima, which sat idle in our driveway since she was away at law school. Four more months until my road test, and then it was mine. Tonight I didn't mind the walk. At least the rain had stopped, and the exercise helped shake off my grumpy mood.

The Camelot had been in my mother's family for forty-five years. Every celebration, from my grandparents' golden wedding anniversary to my sweet sixteen, had been held in one of the Arthurian-inspired ballrooms. When the Camelot opened in 1967, it was *the* place to have a wedding. Now only the lobby retained the kitschy medieval charm, with dark wood, burgundy drapes, and an oil painting of King Arthur (which insiders knew was my great-grandfather posing as him) over a working stone fireplace. One suit of armor, a six-foot mono-lith Josh had named Sir Gus, presided over the entrance to our main ballroom, the Lancelot.

None of us were ever forced to work, but there was an unspoken expectation that we would pitch in when we hit high school. Brooke had worked around her studies and social life. Josh, on the other hand, had turned the Camelot into his social life when he was on, recruiting friends and transforming the back room into a party between courses. I filled in here and there through sophomore year, but now, since both Brooke and Josh were away at school, I took on a full weekend schedule when necessary.

As I breezed through the front doors, the chaotic energy of wedding prep gave me an instant lift. I'd been joking with Jazz and Mads, but maybe it wouldn't be so crazy for me to take over in the future. I already knew the business from shadowing my mother, and I definitely had opinions on what worked and what didn't. I'd even helped choose the color scheme when we gave the ballrooms much-needed makeovers. Since Brooke was in law school and Josh was . . . well, doing whatever he was doing at Rutgers, it was a sure bet that neither of them was interested. The Camelot, right under my nose, might be my calling. I knocked on the doorjamb to my mother's office before strolling in, ready to share my recent epiphany.

She slammed down the phone and fumbled with a bottle of ibuprofen before shaking out two little orange pills.

"You were supposed to be in twenty minutes ago," she said, popping them into her mouth and washing them down with a swig of water from the bottle on her desk.

"I'm sorry. I had to walk," I answered, whipping off my coat and pulling down the sleeves of my starched white work shirt. My underarms were damp. I did a quick sniff test. Clean.

"I didn't mean to snap at you, Wren," she said, rubbing her eyes and leaning back in her rolling chair. The wall of her office was covered with forty-five years' worth of framed thank-you letters and pictures of smiling couples. Mom looked harried. The weight of the world or, more precisely, the weight of every wedding and event, sat on her shoulders.

"Well, I'm here now," I said.

"If one more thing goes wrong tonight, I'm going to jump ship myself. The florist is running late, Chef Hank is complaining about the quality of the salmon, and Marguerite and José called in sick. We're seriously understaffed for this wedding tonight. Any chance Jazz or Madison would want to earn some extra cash?"

"I think they're already out," I said, tightening my messy French knot.

"Then you'd better hustle, sweetie. Cocktail hour starts in less than thirty minutes," she said, standing up and reaching for her suit jacket.

I hurried into the Lancelot to find a dozen or so black-and-white-clad Camelot staff assembling table settings with more silverware than any modern-day person needed. Eben saw me and grinned.

"Hey, 'bout time you showed up."

Twenty-one and working his way through culinary school, Eben Phillips had started at the Camelot around the same time as my sister, Brooke. He was practically part of the family and hands down my favorite work bud.

"Check this out, charitable donations as favors," he said, handing me one of the cards.

In lieu of little glass swans or bars of chocolate with their names on them, the couple had donated money to a charity that distributed mosquito nets to needy families in Africa.

"Cool. That's one I've never heard of," I said. "Need help?"

"I'll be your bestie for life if you take over," he said. "I'm assigned the head table tonight, and they're in Guinevere's Cottage. I have to get over there, like, yesterday, to make sure everything is in order."

"Lucky. Can I be your second in command?" I asked, batting my eyelashes.

Cocktail hour at the Cottage was always fun because it was like being at the epicenter of the party. You caught a glimpse into the lives of the couple and their friends as they rehashed the ceremony and took silly photos. The change of scenery also made the night go faster somehow.

"Aww, baby, maybe if you had your butt here on time. I already picked the new guy," he said, motioning with his chin over to a tall, blond boy who appeared confused as to how to arrange the water goblets.

"New guy? Come on," I said. "But I guess it's not his skills you like."

"Um, don't go there, Baby Caswell. I'm not into jailbait," he said. "You'll just hafta sling those cocktail franks yourself tonight, darlin'." He handed me the box with the rest of the engraved donation cards and summoned Clueless Blond Boy to follow him across the parking lot to the Cottage.

By the time I'd finished setting out the favor cards, there were guests in the lobby waiting for cocktail hour. I closed the curtains on the glass doors to the ballroom so the big reveal would be more dramatic and made my way to the frenzied kitchen to pick up a serving tray for the first round of hors d'oeuvres. I waited and watched as others walked by with platters of mini quiches, fried ravioli, and shrimp-cocktail shooters, getting a sinking feeling about what I'd get stuck serving.

Chef Hank pushed a tray of cocktail franks toward me. I reluctantly grabbed it and made my way to the already bustling ballroom as the opening strains of the wedding band's version of "Fever" echoed through the back room.

Little hot dogs were the bane of my existence. On my first day serving, when a guest asked what they were, I felt like saying, "Duh, are you blind?" but instead came out with "Tiny batter-wrapped kosher frankfurters with dipping sauce" in a formal voice that Eben never let me live down.

"The proper name is *cocktail frank*, but I like your style," he told me, after he composed himself in the back room.

"I was just trying to make them sound . . . I don't know, more impressive."

"Call 'em whatever you want. They're the height of tacky,

but everyone gobbles them up faster than you can say, 'Mustard with that?'"

Since then, whenever a guest asked that idiotic question, Eben and I made up some lavish-sounding name to make the lowly cocktail frank sound classy. The hot-dog name game was more fun when the two of us were working the same room. I was not in the mood.

When I ran the Camelot, they would be banished from the menu.

I put on my cheek-busting service smile and wandered into the crowd, offering the tray to anyone who looked interested. It wasn't long before I ran into the other bane of my existence at work: the group of rowdy guys. They were the ones at a wedding who made obnoxious jokes, drank too much, and flirted with anything that had a pulse.

"The Weenie Girl!" bellowed a ruddy-faced man in a brown suit.

Rowdy guys who gave me a nickname: a special breed. At least I knew they wouldn't ask me what I was serving.

"Not a party till the wieners come out!" someone else said as thick hands emptied the tray, leaving nothing behind but grease stains and crumbs on the paper doily. I went back to the kitchen, hoping to snag more trendy hors d'oeuvres like crab-cake sliders or raspberry Brie bites. Instead I watched helplessly as Chef Hank gave me more of my vile food nemesis.

"You really hate me, don't you?"

He saluted and busied himself with the next server.

Back in the Lancelot, I took my time weaving through the crowd, ducking here and there and trying to avoid the Rowdies.

"Hey, Weenie Girl!"

People actually turned to look at me. I froze, embarrassed from the shouted nickname and the laughter it provoked. My face cramped from smiling. I walked slowly toward them, but all I wanted to do was throw the tray Frisbee-style across the room and let them deal with the fallout.

"Grayson, just the girl you're looking for," said the brown-suit man.

The person in question spun around and flashed a dazzling, white-toothed grin that made me want to fix my French knot. He was younger than the rest of them, with dark, jagged hair that fell into his eyes. I held up the cocktail franks to him, softening my smile and praying he wouldn't ask any questions, since his appearance had completely short-circuited my brain.

"Sweet. Watch this," he said, grabbing at least five dogs.

He tilted back his head, threw one of the hot dogs high in the air, and caught it in his mouth to the applause of the surrounding group. While chewing he kept his eyes on me, maybe wondering why I wasn't cheering along with the rest of them. I should have left, but there was something about the way he oozed confidence while acting so asinine that fascinated me. He was a complete tool, but I bet no one ever accused him of being too quiet.

For his next trick, he threw two weenies in the air at once and successfully caught them in his mouth, to the delight of his rapt audience. This time, when he brought down his chin, he wasn't grinning. The rest of the hot dogs fell from his hand, and he gestured frantically toward his neck.

No one in the group thought he was choking for real. The brown-suit man pounded his fist against a nearby table and chanted, "Gray. Gray. Gray." Gray's face blossomed into a bright shade of red, and drool spilled out of the corner of his mouth. My first thought was that if he would go to those lengths for a joke, he must be a real asshole. I was about to leave when I saw the animal-like panic in his eyes.

I dropped my tray and wrapped my arms around him from behind. The words *fist, thumb in, right above the navel* came out from the recesses of my brain, and I squeezed upward several times to no avail. Someone yelled for help. There was desperate movement around me, but I continued pushing my fist into Gray's abdomen until I felt his body release. Just as the band finished playing "The Girl from Ipanema," a gooey mass tumbled out of his mouth and landed with a splat on the cocktail table in front of him. Someone groaned. Gray gripped the table, head down, and coughed. Sound. A good sign. My arms fell from around his waist, and I stepped back.

His navy-blue jacket stretched taut across his back with

each breath. Brown-suit guy put a glass of water in front of him, but Gray waved it off. He stood up straight and turned toward me, mouth dropped open like he had something to say.

His dark brown eyes held mine for a second. Open. Honest. *Longing*. As if the hot-dog-tossing tool was just some mask he'd put on for the party. A wave of recognition coursed through me. Did I know him? No. I'd never seen him before . . . but . . . I took a step toward him.

He blinked and lurched forward.

"Are you okay?" I asked.

Then he hurled all over my black Reeboks.

REGURGITATING ON SOMEONE'S SHOES IS NOT the best way to make a first impression.

Especially after that someone saved your life.

I wiped my mouth along the sleeve of my suit jacket, eyes zeroing in on her black sneakers and the puddle of upchuck around them. The noise of the room was smothered by the *ba-bum, ba-bum* of my heartbeat in my head—a jagged zigzag of pain. The Weenie Girl was a statue of calm shock, mouth slightly open, brows knit, as her eyes went from the pool of vomit on the floor to my face.

I was breathing, and it was a miracle.

"Grayson?"

Hands were on me. Voices urged me to sit. A chair slid underneath me, and I flopped down onto it. All the while my eyes remained on hers. She brushed some stray hair away from her face, tucking it behind her ear. The distance between us closed, and it was just . . . her. And me. Calm in the chaos. The hair tumbled across her face again. My fingers ached to sweep it away. I wanted to say something, but for once words wouldn't come. Then Pop blocked her from view.

"Grayson, are you all right?"

They all thought I'd been joking. So, okay, pretending to choke would have been some smart-ass spectacle I might have pulled, but I doubt I could have been so convincing.

He clapped his hands in front of my face.

"What, Pop?" I croaked. His weathered brow creased as he tugged me to standing.

"You need some air," he said, gripping my forearm. We knifed through the crowd made up of the extended Barrett family, always ready for a party. I craned my neck, searching over the sea of animated faces for the Weenie Girl, but she was gone.

Pop led me through glass doors into the dark lobby. The doors glided to a close, muffling the band's campy rendition of "I Get a Kick out of You." He took me to a quiet corner, right next to a shiny suit of armor, which was so out of the ordinary, it made the whole episode more surreal. My head throbbed.

"Grayson," he said.

"Pop, I'm fff—" I began, but got distracted by the rise

and fall of party noise as the doors to the ballroom opened again. *Weenie Girl.* But no, it was my stepmother, Tiffany, sauntering over holding a martini glass filled with bright blue liquid.

"What happened?"

"Nothing, I'm fine," I said.

"It's not nothin'," Pop said. "He almost choked to death."

She let out a high-pitched squeak and placed her martini glass on the stone mantelpiece.

"Grayson Matthew, are you okay?" she asked, one hand running through my hair, the other on my cheek, as she gave me a once-over. Tiff liked to use my middle name for emphasis when something significant happened. I'd heard it a lot in anger after I got tossed out of St. Gabe's last spring. This soft version, almost a whisper, was something new, and I felt myself falling into it.

"I'm fantastic," I said, shrugging her off. "Can't we just go back in?"

"Gray, you're loopy. I'd feel better if you got checked out. We can hit the ER and be back before they cut the cake," Pop said.

Tiff ruffled. "Let me get my coat and say some good-byes."

"Tiffany, no. You stay. Mingle," Pop said.

She put her hand to her chest and sighed. "Are you sure?"

"Yep. Gray and I will be filling out paperwork and fannin' our balls at the ER. Nothin' we can't handle."

I stifled a laugh and winced, my throat still raw.

"Really, Blake, do you have to be so crude?" Tiff asked.

"C'mon, you love me," he said, pulling her in for a kiss so intense, I felt like a perv for witnessing. When your father gets more action than you do, it's all sorts of wrong. Like natural selection gone awry.

They were rubbing noses as a woman in a dark suit walked up to us. She tucked a strand of short blond hair behind her ear, folded her arms, and waited uncomfortably until Pop and Tiff broke apart.

"Are you the boy who choked?"

The Boy Who Choked. Pretty much summed up my seventeenth year.

"Yes," I answered.

She turned to Make-Out Master Blake Barrett. "I can call the paramedics if you want. I'm—"

"No, that won't be necessary. We're going to the emergency room," Pop answered, cutting her off. Her eyes widened, and she tucked her hair behind her ear again. There was something vaguely familiar . . .

"You have a daughter," I said.

"Grayson, are you okay?" Pop asked.

"She works here," I continued, ignoring him.

"Yes. Wren. Do you know her?"

"She saved my life." The phrase sounded strange, dramatic as it hung in the air.

"Really? I was downstairs checking on another event. The minute I heard I came up. I'm still not quite sure what happened."

Pop gave her the no-nonsense "he choked on a hot dog, and your daughter did the Heimlich" version, making it sound less epic than it felt. He left out that he'd been at the bar at the time and that my uncles had watched like a panicked Greek chorus while a complete stranger took control of the situation.

A beautiful stranger with a name.

Wren.

"Please, send me the ER bill," Wren's mother said, handing Pop a business card. We were interrupted by a waft of cold air as a vision of white burst through the front door.

"Uncle Blake!"

My cousin Katrina swished across the lobby in her poufy white dress. Pop turned to us and made a short cutting motion with his hand across his throat that I could easily interpret. *Shut your trap. The bride doesn't want to know someone almost died at her wedding.*

"Trini, you're a vision," he said, kissing her cheek.

"The ceremony was so touching," Tiffany chimed in.

I stood back, feeling about as useful as a bobblehead. A brown-haired bridesmaid, who I'd shared some serious eye-fucking with during the wedding vows, waved to me. Two hours ago the adrenaline surge from flirting had made me rethink my foray into monkhood. I hadn't been with anyone since . . . Allegra. A wedding reception where everyone was juiced up and ready to party seemed like a prime moment to get back in the action.

Now hooking up didn't matter. I was more interested in Wren's mother and the waiter she was talking to who'd come in behind Katrina. He put a hand up to his mouth, nodded, and disappeared into the ballroom. I was about to follow, hoping he could lead me to Wren so I could say thanks, or what's up, or whatever was the appropriate thing to say to a person who saved your life, when Pop tugged my sleeve.

"C'mon, Gray." He waved and mouthed something to Tiff as the wedding party rustled into formation, lining up to make their grand entrance. The pretty bridesmaid tapped my shoulder as we brushed past them.

"Dance later?" she asked. Her glossy lips promised sweetness and warmth. A familiar rush, the thrill of being with a new person, made me pause. Then I thought of Wren; her body pressed against my back, soft but strong, and fighting for me. Even though I'd done jack shit to deserve it.

"No, wish I could but I'm heading out," I said, and followed Pop into the brisk autumn evening.

Pop paused at the top of the stairs and fumbled around with a cigarette case and lighter. The business card fell from his pocket. It whirled helicopter-style and landed on the bottom stone step.

"I hate weddings. Here, help me," he said, cigarette dangling from his lower lip. He handed me the lighter and cupped his hands against the breeze coming off the bay. I ran my thumb across the spark wheel until it flickered with a pop. He sucked in, making it look painful. The tip of the cigarette glowed orange. I tossed him the lighter, and he tucked it back into his jacket.

"You should quit, Pop," I said, watching him exhale a long stream of smoke.

"Yeah, yeah, I know. That and eat bran fiber. They're on my list," he said. "C'mon."

At the bottom stair, I picked up the business card.

"Here, you dropped this."

"Don't need it."

"But . . . she was nice," I said, feeling oddly protective.

"Nice?" Pop said. "Gray, she was covering her ass. She doesn't want to get sued. Not that I would do that to the Caswells."

"You know her?"

"No, not her," he answered, shaking his head. He took a hard hit from the cigarette and blew out another deliberate smoke stream. "Jimmy Caswell was first string on St. Gabe's with me. We took 'em to a championship that year."

"You never mentioned him," I said, running my finger across the engraved letters on the card.

Ruth Caswell
Proprietor—Banquet Manager
The Camelot Inn

"Lost touch after high school. He's an attorney with the city now. Thrown a few clients my way, but that's as far as it goes. Why so interested?"

"No reason," I lied, sliding the card into my wallet. "Pop, I don't need to go to the hospital."

"Yes, Grayson, you do." A jet-black Mercedes chirped and lit up as we walked toward it. Pop's leased wheels to impress potential home buyers. "You're acting weird. And your mother will be all over me if I don't take you somewhere to get checked out."

My mother lived with her new family in a galaxy called Connecticut. It had been six years since their amicable split, but Pop still kissed her ass whenever it concerned me, as if one wrong move would send the divorce police swooping in to demand I live with the more responsible parent. Getting kicked out of St. Gabe's had made it worse, like it had been Pop's fault. Sometimes I wanted to shake him and yell, *Stop being a pussy!* and other times, I completely got it. No one did disappointment better than my mother.

"Why do we even have to tell her, Pop? I'm fine."

"She still talks to some of the family, Gray. All I need is for her to hear this from someone else—"

"Pop, who saw? Uncle Pat? The way he's drinking, he probably won't remember anyway. Come on, let's go back in."

He took another drag, then flicked the cigarette to the ground, grinding it out with his foot.

"I can't go back in there. The walls are closing in around me. Weddings are such a farce."

"Says the man on his second marriage," I said.

"That's different. There was none of this bullshit," he said, gesturing toward the Camelot. "Just us. City hall. Garbage pie at Denino's afterward. Remember?"

Getting fresh air had given me a second wind, a desire to go back inside, but I knew Pop would stand his ground. Maybe it was better if I didn't go back. Wren was probably somewhere hosing off my DNA from her shoe. That's not something you get over quickly. There'd be another opportunity to meet her, and if not, I'd invent one.

"You know, garbage pie sounds really good. Probably the same wait time at Denino's as the ER. What do you say, Pop?"

"The Barrett boys on the lam. You sure you feel okay?"

"Never better."

"You drive," Pop said, tossing the keys.

I caught them, focusing on the task at hand instead of the gut feeling that meeting Wren was the start of something important. I shook it off as I slid into the driver's seat.

She's just a girl, Grayson.

A girl who saved my life.

I wanted to sweep the hair away from her face, feel her body against me, without an audience or the threat of my imminent death.

Connecting with her had felt *different*.

Real.

I had to get to know her. At least I had her name. *Wren Caswell*. The rest would be easy.

It was what I was good at.

I STARTLED AWAKE. THE CLOCK ON MRS. FIORE'S wall was ten minutes behind. Every time the second hand reached the number six, it would stick and make a loud clicking noise for a few seconds before continuing its journey around the clock face. With its brown shag carpet and orange vinyl chairs, the dark paneled office made me feel like I'd been transported back to the seventies. The fact that, for a few seconds, time actually *did* stand still didn't help.

As an addendum to the inspiring None of You Are Going to Harvard speech, each junior had "Three sessions of thirty!" to strategize her chosen path. "Three sessions to chart out a map to the future!" the posters in the hallway read, making the future sound like something you could find with a compass and guide dogs.

At least I'd been pulled out of chem lab, my last class on this very sleepy Monday.

Mrs. Fiore returned, the aroma of coffee wafting behind her. Probably announced to the faculty lounge as she was getting her java fix: "That quiet girl, Wren Caswell, is sitting in my office—like *she's* going to get in *anywhere*. How can she be Brooke Caswell's sister? Now, hers was a high school résumé with achievement written all over it." I straightened out of my slouch as she placed the mug of coffee on her blotter. The mug had a picture of one of those saucer-eyed Precious Moments kids on it with the words God Don't Make Junk underneath.

She tapped her keyboard a few times then angled the computer screen so I could see. My name, "Caswell, Wren," was in bold blue lettering at the top of an empty form of some kind.

"So, Wren, where should we begin?" she asked, putting on a tiny pair of half glasses with zebra-print frames.

The truth was, I wanted to like Mrs. Fiore. I wanted to have one of those relationships you see on TV where the guidance counselor is your buddy and you can drop by her office on a whim, just to say hi, and she helps you out of some ridiculous predicament involving laxative-laced bake-sale brownies while the laugh track murmurs in the background. I wanted to be one of those students who had a teacher as a friend, someone who really "got" me, but I clammed up the moment I was around anyone in authority. What was there to talk about except school and the weather? Not exactly the stuff of great bonding.

"I don't have a clue," I finally answered.

"That's pretty exciting. The world is open to you then, isn't it?"

All except Harvard.

"It's overwhelming," I answered.

So overwhelming, it was easier *not* to think about. I thought I wanted to continue with school, but unlike Jazz, who was gunning for Cornell to follow her mom, or Maddie, who was determined to go to Pratt and become the next Frank Lloyd Wright, I never had my sights on anything so specific. Not law, like my father and Brooke. Josh seemed to like Rutgers, but was that a reason to go there? The stark reality of my average grades made me wonder if maybe my path was elsewhere. Did I really need a college degree to run the Camelot? What if I started straight out of school? Would Mom want me to?

"Well, that's why we're having these sessions. You have to reframe that overwhelmed feeling. Take charge. Do you plan on going to college?"

"I . . . um . . . maybe?" I answered. "I've been thinking there might be something different for me."

Her eyes looked bewildered as she peered at me above her zebra frames.

"What do you mean?"

"Well, what about, say . . . Mark Zuckerberg, the creator of Facebook? He dropped out of college and he's a bazillionaire, no degree necessary. Or what if I don't even know what I want to pursue, but I fall into it, like that guy on the insurance commercial . . . the one who made the Vatican out of toothpicks?"

"The Vatican out of toothpicks?" she asked, glancing over her shoulder at the defective clock.

"Yes. Not that I'd do that, I just, well . . ." The words spilled out of my mouth one after the other before I could stop them. I was derailing. A flush crept up my neck. "Well, my family owns a catering hall, the Camelot. I was thinking I could run that someday."

This was something she could grasp on to; the smile returned to her face. "Business, maybe? Or are you more interested in the hospitality part of it?"

"Not sure."

"Well, we can evaluate your interests and test scores and see where that leads. Here's the password to your account," she said, scribbling down a series of letters and numbers on a paper and handing it to me. "Start by taking the personality assessment. We've got incredible capabilities with our new computer programs; you can use some of your study periods to research schools, even schedule visits. We can also see where your application can be ramped up. . . ."

I tried to process all the information, but by the end of the thirty minutes I was more confused than ever. I promised to research at least three schools I'd like to apply to next year and made an appointment for my second visit in February, which felt light-years away.

Jazz waved when I walked back into the chemistry lab with ten minutes to spare. I mimed hanging myself with a noose and let my tongue loll out of my mouth.

"That good, Miss Caswell?" Sister Marie asked.

I truly sucked at the teacher/student-bonding thing.

"So what did you talk about? Does she grill you about your personal life?" Jazz asked as we left school for the day and walked down the long driveway next to the building.

"No, thank God." I imagined Mrs. Fiore's reaction to the cocktail-frank incident at work this past Friday. *"Saving Grayson." What an amazing topic for your personal essay! How did you know what to do? What were you thinking?* The attention of my coworkers was more than I could handle. Even Jazz and Maddie were floored when I told them. As odd as it sounded, I had no clue how I pulled that set of skills out of my ass. I'd learned about the Heimlich maneuver in health class and had passed the poster on the wall in the Camelot more times than I could count, but neither one really prepared me for the reality of having someone's life in my hands.

"Just stuff about school," I continued. "I have to research colleges. Think about how I can possibly shore up the holes in my high school career."

"Since when is going to high school a career?" asked Maddie, panting as she ran to catch up to us.

"Mads, you sound a little breathless there," Jazz said. "You should come with me on my interval runs."

"No, Wren and I are doing the yoga thing. Maybe you should join us?"

"When does that start again?" I asked.

"The Thursday after Thanksgiving."

"I work at my mom's office on Thursdays," Jazz said, "but maybe I could try a class sometime. I'm always so tight after my long runs. Doing both is a great way to cross-train, Mads. Just tossing that out there."

"I can think of better ways to cross-train. Let's toss out something more interesting, like how we're going to spend Thanksgiving break."

"Easy. I'm working," I answered.

"No," they both said.

"Yes."

"What about the Turkey Day game? All those college boys home from school . . ." Mads trailed off as though she were envisioning a stadium full of hot guys.

"C'mon, Wren, it's tradition," Jazz said.

The annual Turkey Day game between St. Gabe's and Bergen Point High was Bayonne's version of the Super Bowl. Everyone went to cheer on the two bitter rivals, the prep boys and the public scrubs. Bergen Point usually wiped the field with St. Gabe's defensive line, and there was always an undercurrent that the game was more a battle of classes than of school teams. Sacred Heart girls were supposed to cheer for our unofficial brother school, but Jazz, Mads, and I went more for the eye candy—prep, scrub, anything in between—didn't matter, we didn't take sides. This year, though, I wanted no chance of seeing Trevor home for the holidays. Huge stadium, small world—it would be just my luck to run into him and do something stupid like dribble hot chocolate down my peacoat. Not. A. Chance.

"Maybe," I lied, offering them some hope as we reached the end of the drive and emptied out into Sacred Heart's thrumming social hub . . . aka the street in front of school.

"Hey, Weenie Girl!"

No. Way.

"Wren, did that guy just call you *Weenie Girl*?" Mads asked, picking up her pace as she realized what was happening. "Omigod, that's Puke Boy, isn't it? You didn't accurately convey how friggin' hot he is!"

Sure enough, two cars away from the driveway stood Grayson, leaning against a crappy beige convertible with a darker tan soft-top. The car was worn and pale, like it had been out in the sun too long, but there was something about it. A car with character. It made him more approachable.

Maddie sauntered up to Grayson, said something to make him laugh, and waved us over.

"Wren, this is so *Pretty in Pink* . . . totally Blaine hacking into Andie's computer and sending his picture," Jazz whispered, taking hold of my elbow.

"Stop," I said, trying to tame my smile, because seeing him here *did* feel as unreal as a movie moment, but I didn't want to be that obvious.

Grayson looked younger than I remembered. His hair was a tousled mess, with those jagged bangs hanging in his eyes, and he wore this retro-style blazer with patches at the elbows that he managed to make look cool. He had an eyebrow piercing by his left eye—something I hadn't noticed at the wedding. And there was that grin again. A dazzling sun drawing me into orbit. The attempt to control my smile was futile.

"Sorry, I couldn't resist yelling that," he said as I reached him. "Besides, we were never formally introduced."

"Wren Caswell," I said, white-knuckling the strap of my messenger bag as if it were a lifeline. God, I wished I'd had the time to pop a piece of gum in my mouth.

"Grayson Barrett."

Jazz poked me.

"Oh, um, this is my friend Jazz, and you already met Maddie," I said, gesturing to her while she scrutinized Gray's car. From the curl of her upper lip I could tell she wasn't impressed—at least not with his ride.

"Jazzzzzzzzz," he said. Jazz loosened her grip on my arm and giggled. "I like it."

"How are you feeling?" I asked.

"I'm breathing, so it's all good."

A girl called out his name, he shrugged one shoulder in greeting, and then it dawned on me. How stupid could I have been? He wasn't there for me. This was just a coincidence.

"Well, I guess I'll, um, see you," I said, backing away.

Gray's brows drew together. "Oh, I . . . I came to see if you felt like getting a coffee or something," he said. "I mean, that's if you, well, can I give you a ride home at least? You too, Jazz, Maddie, if you want."

"Awfully nice of you, Grayson, but we love the party atmosphere of the Boulevard bus—all that BO and rubbing up against perfect strangers," Maddie said, ushering a still-Grayson-struck Jazz toward the crosswalk. "You two kids have fun." Maddie mouthed, *Call me!* waving her cell in the air.

When I turned back to Gray, his eyes gleamed with amusement. I was hyperaware of the mass exodus of Sacred Heart, the urgent rush of girls on their way home and the passing seconds of silence between us. I missed Maddie and her quick quips already. Why was I just standing there? Mute?

Gray's smooth voice broke the silence.

"So, Wren. Do you have to go home?"

Grayson opened the passenger door for me and I slid in, picking up the book on the front seat. Plato's *The Republic*. I fanned through the pages. There were highlights and ink scrawls in the margins of the first half.

"Light reading?" I asked, handing it to him as he got in.

He tucked the book into the front pocket of his backpack then hoisted it to the backseat. "For a class."

"Really? Where?" I asked. Could he possibly be a college guy?

"Saint Gabe's."

Grayson wore faded denim jeans and a well-fitted white Henley tee under his jacket that I caught myself admiring for too long—not the usual St. Gabe's khaki-and-button-down uniform.

"Well, the class is at Saint Gabe's," he continued as the engine grumbled to life. "I go to Bergen Point. They don't offer philosophy."

The car was immaculate—no wrappers or soda cans. He even had a Yankee Candle air freshener, Home Sweet Home, dangling from the rearview mirror. I spun it gently with my index finger.

"Let me guess: Mom?" I asked, smiling.

"Nope. All me. Can't a guy have a good-smelling car?"

"Sure, why not?" I didn't have much experience with guys and cars, but my brother, Josh's, could probably be condemned it was so gross, and Trev's . . . ugh, why was I even thinking of him?

He pulled out of the spot, driving slowly until we hit the first red light about a block away. I'd forgotten to roll my skirt after school and it sat at dweeb length, an inch above my knee. I crossed my legs, hoping to subtly show a little more skin. Grayson noticed.

"So," I said, snagging him mid-peek. "What were you saying—you go to Bergen Point but take a class at Saint Gabe's? I didn't know you could do that."

He flustered, ran a hand through his hair. "Um, oh, philosophy . . . yeah, you can't. I was supposed to take the class this year. Figured I'd just go through it on my own."

"So you *were* at Saint Gabe's?"

"Yep, up until my junior year."

"Maybe you know my brother. Josh Caswell? He graduated last year."

He nodded. "Everyone sort of knows everyone at Saint Gabe's, right?"

"Why'd you leave?" I asked.

The light changed to green, but he hesitated, gripping the wheel, until an insistent beep from behind got his attention.

"They kind of asked me to leave. Listen, why don't we go somewhere? It's not the kind of thing I want to talk about while I'm driving. I can't see your face," he said, giving me a sidelong glance that made me bite my lower lip.

"Okay," I said, trying to calm the hormonal rush that had just surged through my body.

"How about that coffee? We could grab one and hit the park. It's warmish. Any place you like?"

"Starbucks at South Cove?"

He grunted.

"I don't do pretty coffee. I know this hole-in-the-wall deli with the best French roast around. You'll love it."

"Sounds good," I lied. Coffee—pretty, French roast, or otherwise—tasted like battery acid to me, but I didn't feel like mentioning it. Especially after he told me about leaving St. Gabe's. *Awkward.* I wasn't sure if the torqued-up feeling in my gut was attraction or a warning sign. I just knew I didn't want to go home yet.

A tinny-sounding bell announced our entrance as we walked into the deli. The guy behind the counter beamed at Grayson.

"My man, where've you been?"

"Spiro, how's it hanging?" Grayson answered, walking behind the counter to pour our coffees. Spiro clapped Grayson on the back, gave me a once-over, and whispered something to him. They both chuckled. Heat nibbled my earlobes. I waited, expecting some sort of introduction, but Gray handed me the to-go cup.

"Cream and sugar's over there if you need it," he said,

turning back to Spiro. I added enough cream and sugar to my coffee to make it taste like Häagen-Dazs and tried to catch what I could of their hushed convo. . . . *Tough break . . . brinker . . . a friend.* Grayson joined me at the counter to put a lid on his coffee. When I reached into my bag for some cash, he stopped me.

"Wren, please, a coffee for a life. It's the least I can do," he said, pulling out a few bills from his pocket.

"Thanks," I murmured, concentrating on clipping my messenger bag closed. My brain completely fogged over with the way his voice wrapped around my name. I stuffed the feeling down. Whether he was hot or not, I still had no clue what he wanted from me.

"So what should I tell Lenny if he asks for you again?" Spiro asked, handing Grayson the change. Gray shoved it in his pocket and ushered me toward the door. The bell jangled as he held it open for me.

"Tell him I've moved on to other things," he said, the door closing behind us. When our eyes met, Grayson simply said, "Business."

Moved on? Business? What sort of business could he possibly have at a deli?

By the time we reached the park, the sun was already setting, casting an orange glow across the horizon. Gray found a parking spot by the boat pond, and we shuffled through fallen

43

leaves to a vacant bench. Two squirrels quarreled noisily and chased each other up a tree. After their chattering died down, the park was silent except for the occasional footfall of passing joggers.

"So how did you know where to find me?" I asked, determined to keep my thoughts straight.

"I have my ways," he said low, raising his eyebrows a bit. My expression must have showed the ripple of uneasiness I felt, because he laughed.

"That sounded creepy, sorry. Your mom gave us her card. That's how I got your last name. I asked around. Not exactly differential calculus," he said, leaning back and slinging his elbow over the top of the bench so he was partially facing me. I huddled my hands around my coffee cup, letting the steam tickle my nose, wanting to know why he was "asked to leave" St. Gabe's but not sure how to bring it up casually.

"You're too polite. Don't you want to know why I got kicked out of school?" he asked.

"I guess," I said, surprised he'd read my thoughts. "Wasn't sure if it was too personal a question."

"Wren, you've already had your arms around me from behind. I think we're past the 'too personal' stuff."

"Ha, good point," I said, burning up at the thought of how intimately I'd already touched him. I blew on the rim of my cup, avoiding his gaze. "Okay, then why'd you get kicked out?"

He closed one eye, wrestling with the best place to start his story, then took a deep breath and said, "I was a term-paper pimp."

I coughed, nearly choking on the coffee. "Pimp?"

He smirked at my reaction. "No, seriously. I was a middleman. Matched people up with the right guys—I had specialists in chemistry, history, creative writing; some at Saint Gabe's, some elsewhere. Some I did myself. I got sloppy. Someone tipped the principal off. A guy handed in a term paper that was too good. They threatened him with expulsion and nabbed me."

"Didn't anyone else get in trouble?"

"A few of my customers got suspended, but I didn't rat out my suppliers. I wouldn't do that," he said. "That's why they really kicked me out—because I wouldn't rat."

I didn't know what to say. Here I was, afraid to be even one second late for school, and he was so willing to admit—to brag, even—about his total disregard for what anybody with a shred of conscience would know was just . . . wrong. He studied me, waiting for more of a response. He didn't seem embarrassed or regretful at all.

"Didn't you worry you'd get caught?" I asked.

"At the time I didn't really think about it. I had a lot going on."

A lot going on, like what? I wanted to ask, but did I really want to know? Maybe I would have felt differently about our

45

chat if I hadn't been obsessing about my own crappy school record lately. The unfairness of it all bothered me.

"But . . . you knew it was wrong."

"*Wrong* is such a subjective term, don't you think?"

I tried to laugh, but it came out flat. "No. Pretty black-and-white."

"It wasn't the smartest thing to do, but . . . think of it like this—in the real world, people outsource all the time. Some of my customers had jobs on top of their school workload. There was a demand; I filled it. Simple. Econ 101. At least that's how I defended myself. They didn't quite buy it, hence getting the boot."

Grayson's argument was so convincing, I was almost swayed.

"Well, it is different than outsourcing," I said.

"Wren, Saint Gabe's is a wild place. There are guys whose parents make more money than we'll see in our collective lifetimes, and then there are guys on scholarships whose families are barely scraping by. The ones who can't buy their way into college? Good grades are the strongest weapon they have. They needed a business like mine. I felt like I was helping people."

"I guess it's just something I would never do. I've waited until the last minute to write term papers, but no matter how shitty, at least they were mine."

"Wow, you're such a Girl Scout."

He'd turned into the hot-dog-tossing tool again . . . or maybe he always was and his quirky car and inviting smile duped me into dropping my guard. I wasn't that far from home; I could walk. I stood up and tossed my coffee into a nearby trash can.

"Well, um, thanks for the coffee, the ride, but I've got to go."

I began walking away, then realized I'd left my bag in his car. "I need my bag."

Grayson frowned as he poured the rest of his coffee into the dead leaves. He stood up, tossed the cup into the trash, and walked toward the car. I followed behind, taking two steps for every one of his brisk strides. When he reached the car, he opened the passenger side, stooped in for my bag, and held it out for me. My fingertips grazed his as I took it from him.

"Guess you're thinking, Why'd I save this asshole?" he said, leaning against the car.

Our eyes met. The tool was gone. And there it was—that longing—like right after I'd saved him. What did he want from me?

"God, Grayson, no, I'm not thinking that at all," I said, taking a step back from him.

"Then what are you thinking?" he asked, flipping his bangs out of his eyes with a toss of his head. In that second all I was thinking was how charming he looked when he did that. *Wren, get a freakin' grip!*

"You hit a nerve, okay? I'm royally screwing up this semester, and I hate it but not enough to cheat. I totally feel all that bullshit pressure to get good grades. And I'm not. Not like my friends," I said, all the stuff I couldn't admit to Jazz and Maddie came rushing out in one long breath. "Why do we even have to be judged by rank? What does that measure? All my number says about me is that I'm average. And to top it off, I'm supposed to know what I want to do with my life, but I know I won't ever get into Harvard, so hey, at least that's one thing I can cross off the list."

"You're applying to Harvard?" Gray asked.

I huffed. "Just forget it," I said, turning away from him. Leaves rustled beneath my feet, punctuating the rush of my exit. He trotted next to me to gain ground, then stood in my way. I tried to go around him, but he kept dodging in front of me. I stopped, staring up through the canopy of half-barren branches. The sky was a deep shade of dusky blue. It would be dark soon.

"Wren, please," Gray said, putting his face in my line of vision, hands up in surrender.

"I have to go," I said, ducking under his arm. He grabbed my elbow, so I spun back to face him.

"Why did you save me?"

The question stopped me. I wrenched my arm free. "You were choking?"

"I know, I just . . . but why did you step in? If it had been me, and the situation was reversed, I don't think I would have stepped in."

"So . . . you're telling me you wouldn't have saved *me*?"

He ran a hand across his face. "No, that's not what I meant . . . not you, personally, I mean anyone. I wouldn't have known what to do."

"Sure you would have. Simple. Health 101."

"Okay, I guess I deserve that," he said. "I'm just saying I would have panicked. I did panic. I thought I was a goner until you stepped in."

"Someone would have helped you," I said.

"Maybe, maybe not. All I know is you did," he said, putting his hands in his pockets. "I guess what I want to say is thank you for saving my life."

A jogger trotted by. I crushed some leaves under my foot, letting what Grayson said sink in.

"This is weird, isn't it?" I said, stepping away.

"What?" he asked.

"I feel like I know you, but I don't," I began. "It's like we had this intense moment, but . . . it's over, isn't it?"

"It doesn't have to be," he said, "does it?"

I rubbed my hands together, folded my arms across my chest. "I think I'd better get going."

"Sure," he said, taking his keys out of his pocket. "Let me take you home."

"No, that's okay. I don't live too far. But . . ."

"But what?"

Asking for his number crossed my mind, but why would I ever need to see him again? He insulted me. Thanked me. What more did we have to say to each other?

"But maybe I'll see you around," I continued, backing up. "Bye, Grayson."

He called my name, but I kept moving toward the entrance of the park, thankful that I had the green light to cross the street. I jogged, putting as much space as I could between us. The "Wren the Hero" chapter of my life could close now. It was more like an anecdote anyway, something I could tell my college roommates one drunken night.

That is, if I even went to college.

Something nagged at me though. Since the night I saved him, I'd felt a magnetic pull toward Grayson so strong, it scared me. I thought it was some sort of mystical thing, that once you saved someone's life, you always had some connection. But then he'd looked at me, those bangs grazing his eyebrows, the top button of his tee casually undone, and it wasn't only his well-being I thought about.

That was a feeling I wasn't ready to get lost in again. I was supposed to be thinking about what I wanted to do with my life, not who I wanted to do. Or was it *whom*?

ALL WAS QUIET IN CASA DEL BARRETT WHEN I GOT home. There was a note on the island.

> *Grayson,*
> *Your father has a late showing, and I'm off to my monthly sales meeting.*
> *Tilapia in the fridge. Take your shot of acai.*
> *btw—your mother called again. CALL HER. She says it's urgent. Why aren't you answering your cell?*
> *Kiss, Kiss—Tiff*

I dashed off a mental reply.

Hey, Tiff,

Tilapia is too fishy and I need a splash of vodka with my acai, but thanks for thinking of me.

btw . . . I'm avoiding Mom. I DO NOT need reminding that I've completely dropped the college ball once again. They don't let fuckups into Columbia. No matter how many strings her ~~alumnASSmunch~~ alumnus husband can pull.

Gray

I nuked some pizza rolls, grabbed a Coke, and sat down on the sectional in the dark. It was like a reflex. Dinnertime = FOOD. I wasn't hungry or thirsty. I was . . . agitated. Ticked.

Why did I let Wren just walk away?

She was even prettier than I remembered, with her light hair loose around her face. And she'd been anxious, even a little shy at first. The kind of girl I could have eating out of my hand. Instead I'd opened up my mouth and all the old bullshit came tumbling out.

Why? I hadn't intended to confess anything—all I wanted to do was thank her, give her a ride home, and maybe strike up a friendship. Then she mentioned her brother. While I hardly knew Josh Caswell, I'm sure he knew me, or at least *about* me. Hell, the St. Gabe's lunch ladies probably knew the sad, strange tale of my term-paper-pimp demise. Better that the story come from the source . . . but it was more than that too. There was a genuineness about Wren that made me feel like I didn't have to put up a front. Like she really saw *me*. Past the BS, the cool hair, the stupid attempt to draw attention to myself like a silverback gorilla.

I sank deeper into the leather sofa Tiff had picked out to give our great room a more masculine feel. My ass slipped until half my torso was parallel to the floor. The perfect position for how I felt at the moment. Spineless.

Why didn't I have the nerve to ask for her number? I knew I could get it some other way, but I wanted her to give it to me. That would tell me a lot. Just like not giving it to me said something. She didn't trust me. And after today, why would she? Smart girl.

My pocket vibrated. I picked up without even checking. Might as well deal with my mother and her college-application assault.

"Mom."

"Dude, it's about time."

I stiffened.

"Luke," I said, sitting up. "Should have screened."

"Harsh, Grayson. So is it true you almost bought it last Friday?"

"Maybe. How'd you find out?"

"The stepmother mafia. This is huge news down the pike. You choked . . . some cocktail waitress saved you. Sounds like a sexy way to go—was she wearing fishnets and a tight skirt?"

An involuntary smile crossed my lips. It pissed me off that

he could win me over so easily, but I had to admit: I missed my daily dose of Dobson.

"C'mon, Grayee*sun*, you know I'm just jabbin' at ya. Saint Gabe's is so boring without your ugly mug roaming the halls. How are you dealing with the bottom-feeders in Bergen Point?"

"What do you want, Luke?"

"Just wondering why you haven't returned my calls, bro."

There was a time a call from Luke was a call to the hunt. For parties. For girls. For epic nights I knew would be legend in our high school history. My *remember-the-time* friend. Brother from another mother. When I was drop-kicked to the curb last spring, my brother, the one who said he'd have my back, disappeared from my life. It was only about a month ago that he tried to make contact. He didn't even have the decency to apologize.

"No one called me all summer."

"Grayson, what's that, three months? Stop acting like a wounded bitch."

"When I got in trouble, you scattered," I said.

"That's not entirely true," Luke began, as if he were leading a Socratic seminar about the topic of my expulsion. "You agreed it was better if we all lie low for a while. And as for the summer, no one got together. Don't you get it? Seeing you get caught was too close for comfort. But we've regrouped.

54

Operation Amsterdam is on again. Andy, Dev, and Logan are completely on board. This, my friend, is your wake-up call."

"My wake-up call? Why do you think I'd want anything to do with that anymore?"

"Stopped by Spiro's today. He said I just missed you. You were with a preeeeeetty girl," he said, mimicking Spiro's accent.

"I'm not allowed to get a cup of coffee?"

"There are lots of places for coffee. Just thought you might be ready to start up again."

"I'm not," I said, wondering when Spiro had become a gossip hound. Time to find a new coffee joint.

"Don't be stupid, Grayson. We need *you*."

"That's too bad, 'cause Ima-out, my friendah."

"Barrett, come on," he said.

I hated when he patronized me. "Luke, you really have no clue. There are worse things than getting expelled."

All those months of no contact made me realize how lucky we were to *not* get caught. Selling term papers got me a slap on the wrist, but the Operation Amsterdam stuff? I couldn't even go there. Luke was silent, but I could practically hear his wheels spinning, charging up his counterargument.

"Grayson, I know you. Yeah, you got a raw deal, but you'll spin-doctor it up and turn it to your advantage. So, no pressure. We're here when you're ready. Just think about it. Maybe while you're in Welding," he answered.

"Bite me," I said.

"We'll be in touch," he said, hanging up.

I jumped off the couch, grabbed my dish and soda can, and hurled them into the sink. Coke spilled across the white marble countertop, glugging out of the can like a gushing artery. I watched, transfixed; Tiff would have a cow. My mess. Again. I raked my hands into my hair, tugging at my roots and yowling the mother of all curse words up toward the ceiling.

The drums. An hour on the drums would make me feel better. Luke Dobson could kiss my bottom-feeding, public-education ass. Getting away from St. Gabe's was the best thing that ever happened to me. A detour. That's all. Luke, Andy, Dev, and Logan could do whatever they wanted with Operation Amsterdam. I was done.

I stormed downstairs to the haven I'd created for myself over the summer. The white, hot fist of anger in my chest finally began to unfurl. I'd blast some punk, pound the drums like an animal until my muscles ached. Exculpation through sweat and music.

I'd done my time, hadn't I? The course of my life had changed because I wouldn't rat out others like me. There was something noble in that, right?

Ah, and there he was: Grayson, the spin doctor.

What would Wren think if she saw me now? This unhinged?

Would she back away like she did at the park? How strange but sexy it felt arguing with her. It was the first honest interaction I'd had with a girl in . . . well, years. And it felt good. Just listening to her. The rise and fall of her voice as she spoke my name after I asked her if she regretted saving me.

God, Grayson, no, I'm not thinking that at all, she'd said.

The way we met, at this point in my life, had to mean something.

I *needed* to see her again.

FIVE

WREN

THANKSGIVING MORNING I HID FROM THE WORLD, safe in the sweet spot of my mattress where all the lingering worries of school, future plans, and foxy term-paper pimps melted away. Not going to the Turkey Day game with Dad and Josh for the first time in six years felt a bit blasphemous, and when my father yelled up the stairs that the Caswell bus was leaving in ten, I resisted the tiniest urge to yell, *Wait for me!* Instead I rolled over and burrowed deeper under my comforter. Daring to change up tradition. Content to keep the world at bay for at least another hour.

Yeah, right.

The biggest reason I was wimping out was because I didn't want to run into Trevor. And I would have; it was inevitable. I'd overheard Josh on the phone with him finalizing plans to meet up near the concession stand. What if he had a college girl with him? Or worse—what if he didn't and wanted to hook up? I didn't want to stutter out small talk or worry if I had snot running down my face or pretend everything was just fine and that we could be friends for my brother's sake.

It might have been worth the risk though, for the off chance to bump into Grayson. Who did he hang out with? What team would he root for? Did he even go to the game? I tried to put him out of my mind. He was a walking, talking DANGER flag. Cheater. Liar. Secretive. *Hawt.* Ugh. It was maddening. Any time I checked off the reasons to avoid him, I'd picture him in front of school, leaning against his faded car. Hands in pockets, swoon-worthy grin, deep brown eyes full of the promise of amazing. And I felt myself getting sucked in by the desire to wrap my arms around him in a different way than the Heimlich.

The slow creak of my bedroom door pulled me back to the present. I kept my eyes shut, feigning sleep as I heard muted tiptoeing on the carpet. One side of my comforter lifted, and the mattress gave way to the pressure of someone climbing in.

"Wrennie, wake up," my sister cooed, scratching my back.

"Five more minutes," I protested.

"Come on, I haven't seen you in, like, forever. The least you can do is have some cinnamon rolls with me before we become Camelot slaves," she said. Football and freezing were my mother's least favorite things, so her own Turkey Day tradition involved scratch-made cinnamon rolls and the televised Macy's parade before the frenzy of the Camelot buffet. Getting first dibs on breakfast made missing the game even better. Brooke dug more urgently into my sides until I had to give in and giggle.

"Okay, stop, Brooke. I'm up, I'm *up*," I said, batting her ice-cold hands away.

I rolled over to face her. Her cheeks glowed, the tip of her nose red. Cold seemed to emanate off her skin, but her eyes were playful. *Beautiful Brooke.*

"When did you get in?"

"Only about ten minutes ago. Can't you feel it?" she asked, putting her hands under the back of my pajama top by my neck. I squealed and shot up out of the bed; the comforter fell to the floor.

"Nice," I said.

"Had to get you up somehow. Why'd you bail on the game?"

"Do you have to ask?" Brooke had been my breakup guru in the wake of the hump-and-dump. She'd snap me out of crying jags with spontaneous Rollerblading or splurges at Sephora. Telling me over and over again that Trevor, or any guy, was just not worth falling apart over.

"Meh, you should have worn your cutest outfit and shown him how much better off you are being free," she said, leaning back on her elbows.

"I have no cute subdegree clothes," I said, shrugging on my fuzzy blue robe.

"His loss, our gain: The Caswell chicks have the house to themselves," she said, sitting up. "Might not be that way much longer."

Our house, which had always bustled with noise and friends, had been quiet with my sibs away at school. My parents and I had fallen into a predictable daily rhythm of dinner, then heading to our various personal spaces to do whatever. I wasn't complaining, but it was odd being an only child for weeks at a time. Calm. Empty. Lonely. I knew the change was inevitable, could hear it in my father's joking as he talked about downsizing and moving to Key West when he and Mom retired and we were all out of the house, but I held on to these moments when Brooke was home, or Josh was back upstairs pounding around and listening to his music too loud. Even if only for a little while, the house felt full and lived-in again.

"We have a good three hours before Josh and Dad get back," I said, crouching on the floor to see if my slippers were under the bed.

Brooke shimmied her way to the edge of the mattress, toes grazing the floor.

"I'm not talking about the game."

"Is Pete coming over?" I asked, standing up from my fruitless search.

"Not exactly." Her lips curled into a sly grin, eyebrow

cocked in a perfect seductive C curve. Whenever I tried to pull this Brooke face move, I came off like a weathered pirate.

"Why are you acting so weird?"

"You noticed?"

I had no clue why she was being so cryptic and was not in the mood to coax her out of it, especially with the delicious scent of my mother's cinnamon rolls wafting up from the kitchen. I scanned the floor again. Success. My slippers sat askew by my closet. I padded over to get them, and shoved my frozen feet into the warm fleece. Brooke just sat there, the same expression on her face, like she was waiting for me to say more.

"Spill, Brooke."

"I'm pregnant," she said, slow, the words rising and lingering like helium balloons above my head.

"What?"

She put her finger to her lips and motioned with her eyes toward my open door. I clicked the door shut and perched on the bed next to her, keeping my distance, as if her pregnancy were contagious.

"You're the first person I've told—well, besides Pete," she said, letting out a deep breath. "So what do you think?"

Brooke had a plan: living in DC. Law school. Midsize firm. Fighting for the rights of the little people. *Baby* was not supposed to happen until after thirty. And not until she and Peter Hutchins the Third got married in grand style sometime in the fall. Far away from the Camelot. By a lake. With the trees a riot of autumn colors. Me in a champagne-colored, strapless bridesmaid gown. Honeymoon in Bora-Bora in one of those little huts over the water. Yes. "The plan" was *that* detailed.

My hand still covered my mouth in shock. *What did I think?* Holy effing shit! is what I thought, but I wasn't about to tell that to Brooke, who suddenly looked so emotionally naked in front of me, I knew anything other than enthusiasm would knock her down.

"Congrats?" I said.

"You don't sound happy for me," she said, pouting.

"Okay, rewind. . . . That's incredible news! Pete must be over the moon."

Her face brightened at the mention of Pete.

"I know it sounds crazy, but he *is* over the moon. We both are. It's not ideal, I know, but whenever I worry about how things will go, I realize there's this little piece of us growing inside me, and it's just so . . ." She fell back on the bed, golden hair splayed out behind her, and finished with a breathy sigh. ". . . sexy."

"Sexy?" I asked, leaning back on my elbows. "I don't think you should mention that when you break the news."

She traced small circles on her belly with the tips of her fingers. "How do you think Ruth and Jimmy are going to react?"

I wanted to say the magic words my sister longed to hear, but really? How was I supposed to know how our parents would react? Brooke was twenty-one, living with Pete, and almost finished with her first semester at Georgetown Law; my father was thrilled at the thought of another lawyer in the family. Whenever he spoke to anyone about Brooke upholding the tradition, he all but gushed. Knocked up and in her first semester might not be gushworthy, but I think she already knew that.

"Fly off the handle? Shit a two-ton brick? What other cliché can we come up with for a nuclear meltdown? When do you plan on telling them?"

"I don't know. I really don't want to spring this on them with all that's going on with the Camelot, but I'll be showing by Christmas, and I think that would be sort of worse, don't you?"

"What's going on with the Camelot?"

Her eyebrows drew together as she rolled onto her side to face me. "You can't tell me you don't know. Business is down, and that's a prime piece of real estate. Mom has been fielding offers for years, but I think now she might be listening."

I hadn't thought it was possible to be more shocked after my sister's announcement.

"But . . . we're busy."

"Not really, Wrennie. When I worked, there were back-to-back weddings every weekend. Now there's one or two at the most, right? And what about today? One sitting for the buffet. Last year there were three."

"Did Mom tell you this?" I asked.

"No one has to tell me anything. The writing's on the wall. Don't get so upset. Your weekends can be your own again. No more white, starched shirts with grease stains, no more obnoxious guests, no more having to jump in and save people from choking," she said, tugging a strand of my hair.

And just like that, Grayson in all his term-paper-pimp glory exploded back into my thoughts, practically sitting on the edge of my bed behind Brooke, his dark eyes saying, *Tell her about me.* I bit my lip.

"That was pretty amazing, squirt."

I met the guy, Brooke. He's charming and scary and so freakin' hot, I can't stop thinking about him and the sexy way the top button of his Henley tee was undone.

"What can I say? All in a day's work," I answered with a shrug.

"Just think, next Thanksgiving can be normal . . . at home, like in all those holiday songs. Not eating buffet leftovers after serving all day."

"C'mon, it's not that bad, Brooke. I kind of like it. You know, I was even thinking maybe one day . . ." I paused. This would be the first time I said it out loud to a member of my family, and while it seemed like a small announcement compared to bringing a new life into the world, well, it was *mine.* "I could run it. Maybe go to school for business or hospitality or something like that."

Brooke sat up so quickly, I thought she might slide off the bed.

"Oh, God, no. You don't want that."

"Maybe I do," I answered, slightly put off by her quick and emphatic rejection.

She shook her head. "The best thing you could do is get away from here. Sure, go study business, or hospitality, or whatever you want, but *do not* plan on staying to run the Camelot. It's a sinking ship, Wren."

All I'd wanted was a little spark of support. A *Hey, that's not a bad idea, Wren!* Now the thought seemed ridiculous.

"Yeah, because getting away from here has worked so well for you," I said, patting her tummy.

She put her hand over mine, her eyes serious again.

"So you'll support me on this? I just need to know you have my back, in case, well, in case it all goes really bad."

Brooke had never spoken to me quite like this. And I'd never seen her this unsure. I was usually the one going to her for help or just basking in her enchanting Brookeness.

"How is it going to go bad? It's not like they can ground you," I said. "And they love Pete."

"I know, I just . . . their support means a lot. Yours too, squirt," she said, tucking my hair behind my ear. She sniffed, pressed my hand to her belly again.

"So this means you're gonna get fat," I said, pulling my hand away.

"Gee, Wren, thanks!" Her eyes grew round as she gave my arm a pinch. "You know that only means one thing."

"What?"

She got up to leave and reached for the door. "I'm picking the biggest, gooiest cinnamon roll."

I shot up. "Um, no you're not!"

"Catch me," she said, disappearing before I could even make it to the doorway.

The Camelot Thanksgiving buffet ran smoothly. I kept looking for warning signs of Brooke's ominous words that it was *a sinking ship*. All I saw was the Caswell clan working together— well, I was working; Brooke spent a lot of time reconnecting with Eben while Josh, still green from his Thanksgiving Eve bender with his home-from-college buds, tried his best not to puke in the mashed potatoes. Everyone, even my dad, who rolled up his Brooks Brothers sleeves to help plate the sides for the buffet table, was happy, buzzing, joking. No doom and gloom. Nothing out of place to make me think we were in any sort of trouble. Brooke *had* to be wrong.

Being busy made the afternoon go quickly, and soon enough, the five of us were alone and gathered around a table in the empty banquet hall, a little tired but full of the meal Chef Hank had prepared for us.

My mother raised her glass of sauv blanc. "You don't know how happy it makes me to see you all together."

"Aw, shucks, Mom, any time you want me to quit school and be your permanent child, say the word, I'm all over it," Josh said, grinning.

"Please no, I'm finally getting some much-needed peace," my father kidded.

"What, Wrennie doesn't throw any wild parties?"

"Hey, look what the wind blew in," my mother said, raising her glass toward the door.

I turned to see a rather disheveled Pete, as if he'd literally been windblown, walking toward our table. Brooke got up and threw her arms around him. My stomach lurched.

Pete shrugged off his coat and hooked it over a chair at the adjacent table. "Hey, Wren," he said, smoothing down his hair and taking the seat across from me.

With his dark, unruly curls and green eyes, Pete was exceptionally handsome, but he was so goofy once you got to know him that his good looks became less intimidating. I wondered if he knew that I knew he'd knocked up my sister. One thing was for sure: Between Brooke and Pete, this kid was going to be drop-dead gorgeous.

"How was your Thanksgiving? Your parents must have been thrilled you made it home," my mother said, beaming.

Pete chuckled, but it was guarded. He folded his hands and glanced at Brooke. And then the world moved frame by frame.

I could feel the tremor of what was about to happen but

was powerless to act on it. *Please, please, Brooke, not* now.

A waiter came by and dropped off a carafe of coffee for my father. Mom sat in suspended animation, waiting to hear about Pete's Thanksgiving. Josh had nodded off, a shock of dirty blond hair partially hiding his eyes. I pinched his leg, and he jerked awake.

"What?"

"We're pregnant!" Brooke blurted out, grabbing Pete's hand.

Silence shrouded the table. The only sound was the slow trickle of my father pouring coffee into his cup. That cup became the collective focus of the table—as if we knew that, once it was full, something disastrous would happen. My father put down the carafe more firmly than necessary, then turned his attention to Brooke and Pete, waiting for more. Brooke's eyes locked on mine—my cue to have her back.

"Holy shit!" "What awesome news!" Josh and I said at the same time.

My mother was momentarily stunned, mouth open, eyes darting between Brooke and Pete. My father spoke.

"What does this mean?"

Brooke launched into what must have been a rehearsed speech, taking turns with Pete who chimed in as he stroked her hand. My heart cringed a bit, watching them both become so squirmy and awkward. Brooke was holding it together as best as she could. Pete looked like he'd rather be hiding under the table, out of my father's line of vision.

There was a new plan. They were going to get married during winter break. The baby was due in the late spring, so they could both finish their course work. Brooke had already found day care close to campus for the fall. She and Pete would coordinate their classes as much as they could, and while money would be tight, they were sure they could handle it. This was only a blip in their lives. They loved each other, had planned on getting married and having a family anyway. Maybe it wasn't ideal, but that's how life goes.

Halfway through, my father began kneading his forehead. My mother's face was a mask, the giddiness from moments ago evaporated.

"Josh, you and Wren should go," she said, picking at a thread on the tablecloth.

"Mom, we can handle it. It's not like we don't know where babies come from."

Her eyes cut through me. Josh was on his feet, tugging me to get up.

"C'mon, squirt, let's fly."

Once we reached home, Josh retreated to his attic room, and I took solace in a hot shower. I knew I should feel lucky that Mom dismissed us—who would want to be in the middle of *that* conversation? But being sent away made me feel weird, like an outsider.

I dressed in sweats and ventured out to see if anyone had come home. The house was silent, except for strains of Blink-182 coming from Josh's room. I smiled and opened the door a crack. His lights were on, so I made my way up the creaky, carpeted steps into his lair.

He was busy typing away on his computer. I knocked on the newel post so I wouldn't startle him. Next to him, on his desk, was an open bottle of beer. Considering his condition, I thought he'd want to lay off the stuff at least for a night. I raised my eyebrows.

"Hair of the dog, Wrennie, best hangover remedy," he said. "Want one?"

"Drinking . . . here? Don't you think Mom and Dad—"

"Wren, Golden Girl has screwed up. The parental units are officially checked out for the moment. I could be hosting an orgy up here, and no one would know. Come on, live a little, have a brewski with your big bro," he said, reaching into the small fridge by his desk, cracking open a bottle, and offering it to me.

I took the beer and leaned against the edge of his desk. "What do you think is going to happen with Brooke and Pete?"

"I thought you learned all that in health class," he said, leaning back in his chair.

"Duh, I just meant . . . it'll be strange, them being married . . . a baby . . . you'll be an uncle."

He clasped his hands behind his head and stared at the ceiling. "Wow, Josh is not an uncle name. *Aunt Wren*. Sounds like a lady with cankles who bakes great pies."

"Thanks for that mental picture," I said, grabbing his senior yearbook. My heart raced. *Why hadn't I thought of this before? Grayson might be in there.* I plopped myself down on Josh's very unkempt bed. He'd been back for less than twenty-four hours, and his room—littered with dirty clothing, empty cups, and a plate with a half-eaten sandwich—was as though he'd never left. I punched up the pillows and sat back, trying to sound casual. "Do you know a guy named Grayson Barrett? He went to Saint Gabe's?"

He clicked at his keyboard feverishly before answering me.

"Got kicked out . . . that Grayson Barrett? I know who he is, but I don't *know* him. A bit of a douche nozzle around his lax bros, if I remember correctly."

"Don't call him that," I said, grimacing and casually leafing through the yearbook. The end covers were full of signatures and notes to Josh, reminding him to *Stay cool, bro!* and *Party hard!*

"What? Douche nozzle or lax bro? They're interchangeable," he said, pivoting in his computer chair with a smirk on his face.

"Josh, stop."

"Ah, so someone *is* currr-aaaaving a little boo-tay."

"It's not like that!"

"So what's it like, then?" he asked, getting serious.

I ran my finger along a sweat drizzle on my beer label.

"He's the one I saved from choking."

Josh's eyes registered surprise. "Damn, you should have let him choke."

"How can you say that?"

"Wren, I'm not serious. Well, maybe a little," he said, chuckling as he checked his IMs again. "Sorry. I keep forgetting you're quite the hero. Doesn't Barrett, like, owe you his life now or something?"

"Hardly."

"C'mon, why the interest?"

"We hung out the other day. He seemed kinda cool, I guess. What?"

"You don't want to get involved with a guy like that."

"A guy like what? I thought you said you didn't know him. You know, just forget it," I said, leaning back onto his pillows and focusing on the yearbook again. I already had my own opinion of Grayson, and I didn't need Josh reaching into his bag of slang to pull out something more colorful than *douche nozzle*. That was descriptive enough.

"Well, consider yourself warned."

"I'm ignoring you, just in case you haven't noticed."

I thumbed through the yearbook, went directly to the juniors, to the Bs, scanned down the rows of boys, and found . . . nothing. At the end of the junior section, it read . . .

Absent photo day: Grayson Barrett, Liam McNaught, John Skora.

Drat.

I flipped to the sports-and-activities section of the yearbook. Pay dirt.

There was a full-size picture of Grayson, his face ruddy with exertion. He had his lacrosse helmet under one arm and was pouring water into his partially open mouth with the other. His dark eyes were trained on something. He was leaner, sharper, serious. If I had any doubt whether I was still attracted to him or not, my body answered with an instant hormonal rush that left everything buzzing. He was, in a word, smoking hot. Okay. Two words.

I took another sip of beer and sank deeper into Josh's bed. The open book fell flat against my chest as I stared at the ceiling, confused. This was crazy. I couldn't feel this way about someone I'd just met. Especially someone who thought selling term papers was just outsourcing. *Business.* Was that what he'd been talking about at the deli?

I mouthed his name.

Grayson.

Enjoying the way my tongue hit the roof of my mouth on the last syllable.

Would I ever run into him again?

SIX

GRAYSON

"THIS IS GRAYSON, KATE'S SON FROM HER FIRST marriage."

Mr. Motherfucking Home Wrecker introduced me to yet another member of his family, his voice dropping slightly at "first marriage," like what he really wanted to say was, *This is Grayson, worthless knob. I have no genetic ties to him.* It was my first Thanksgiving Easton-style, and I played my role as the good stepson, pumping hands and fielding generic questions about school and life, all the while wishing I could tear the sweater off my back because it was itching like hell.

In the unofficial handshake over "little shit we don't need to get serious about on legal papers," Thanksgiving was my mother's holiday. Pop's one condition was that he had me in the morning to go to the annual St. Gabe's/Bergen Point

Turkey Day game to relive his glory days. Then in the afternoon, he'd ship me out to Connecticut to spend the day with them. For one reason or another, the Thanksgiving bondage with Mom and Mr. MFHW never happened. Until today.

Mr. Motherfucking Home Wrecker's real name was Laird Easton, which can only sound cool if you're a surfer dude and not an ass-clown investment banker. The first time we met was at a company outing at Yankee Stadium before my parents' breakup. I was eleven and caught up in the total awesomeness of being in a luxury box—steak sandwiches, all the soda I could drink, cushy seats. Laird even got me Mo's signature on a game ball. He shook my hand, told me what a valuable asset my mother was to the corporate-credit department. It was only later that I realized what he should have been saying was, *Hey, kid, I'm balling your mom. Here's a game ball for you. Why don't we call it even?*

Later that year, Mom stopped being Katie Barrett from Bayonne, New Jersey, and became Kate Easton from Darien, Connecticut. A few years later, I unloaded that game ball through Spiro. Luke thought I'd been nuts to get rid of it, but I couldn't stand having it in my room.

The Yankees game was the first and last time Laird ever went out of his way to be nice to me. Most of the time it felt like he tolerated me simply because I was "Kate's son from her first marriage." Anytime he said it, it was like a disclaimer to my presence. The only bright points in the Easton union were my half sibs, Ryder and Grier, who both didn't give two shits I'd been kicked out of school and treated me like I was Santa with an armload of toys any time they saw me.

Ryder was five, and his only fault was that he was a mini-Laird, complete with side part and upturned polo collar. I loved how he'd come out with this random stuff like "I don't cry" and "Unown is my favorite kind of Pokémon." He saved me from a college chat with Mom when I first arrived by shoving his Nintendo DS in my face and begging me to help him battle Zoroark.

Grier was three, and all Mom. Brown eyes and light hair, with a ginormous white ribbon perched on the front of her head. She had trouble pronouncing her Rs, which was pretty adorable. We had an ongoing dialogue where she'd try to get me to pronounce her name correctly, but I would pronounce it just the way she said it. . . .

"No, Gwayson, it's Gweewah."

"That's what I'm saying. Gweewah."

"No, no, no . . . Gweewah," she'd say, louder, stomping her foot for emphasis.

"Yes, Gweewah, that's right, isn't it?"

She'd put her hands over her eyes and collapse into a fit of giggles until her face was bright red.

If only it were that easy to talk to Wren.

Insane as it sounded, Wren had become a safe haven. A place my mind gravitated to whenever I didn't feel like dealing with what was in front of me. I replayed that day in the park in my head, how I'd do things differently so she'd give me her number. During calculus. While driving. When I had trouble falling asleep. And now, as I dodged any serious chats during Thanksgiving at Mom's.

"DinnaweddyGwayson," Grier said, in one long breath. She grabbed the tips of my fingers with her tiny hands and yanked. I played along, pretending I needed help off the sofa, then grabbed her, spun her around, and set her down. My reward was another round of giggles and a smile from Mom.

"Grayson, sorry I've been stuck in the kitchen all day," she said, lacing her arm through mine and leading me toward the dining room.

"It's cool, Mom. Smells good."

"We're so happy you're here. Ryder and Grier especially."

"Yep, it's a blast hanging with them." *They don't ask me questions about my future.*

"Laird's off tomorrow. Ryder wants to skate at Rockefeller Center like we did last year. Maybe you could stay the night? Join us?" she asked.

"I sort of have plans, but thanks," I lied.

"Well, if your plans change, please consider meeting us. It would be fun," she said. When we reached the dining room, she went back to playing hostess.

A giant cornucopia with dinner rolls spilling out of it sat in the center of the Thanksgiving table. Each plate had a folded napkin and a clumsily colored turkey-shaped place card that must have been fashioned by either Ryder or Grier. I sat at the end of the table by my mother. On the other side of me was Laird's grandmother, who looked old enough to have been at the first Thanksgiving.

"Dinner is buffet-style, everyone. Food's in the kitchen. Don't be shy," my mother said. I slid the napkin and place card off my plate and followed everyone to the kitchen. I stuck to the basics (turkey, stuffing, mashed potatoes) and kept thinking that, after eating, I'd be that much closer to leaving.

I tried not to scarf down everything too quickly, but it was hard. The food was mouthwatering. Not that I didn't get a home-cooked meal now and then from Pop or Tiff, but it wasn't like this. I was practically humming halfway through my plate. My guard down, I locked eyes with the blond dude sitting diagonally across from me.

"So, Grayson, are you training for the season yet?" he asked, slicing up his turkey and putting a piece in his mouth.

I blanked on his name. Porter? Cooper? Something with an -er at the end. Laird's brother-in-law. What was he asking?

"I'm sorry?" I said, leaning toward him.

"Your mom told us what a great lacrosse player you are. When does the season pick up again?"

The questions were like getting shot in the head. I froze.

"I don't play anymore."

His brows came together in momentary confusion as he

turned to Mom, who straightened up in her chair.

"Injury?" he asked.

"No, the school I go to doesn't have a team," I said, shoving some more turkey in my mouth.

"You're at Saint Gabriel's, no?"

Mom reached for her glass of wine.

"I'm at Bergen Point now," I answered, making it sound like a school he should know.

"I'm surprised you're not here in Darien. Blue—"

"Wave, I know," I said, cutting him off. Darien High School's nationally recognized lacrosse team. That was one of Mom's selling points during her campaign for me to move in with them when I was a freshman. Screw Blue Wave. If it meant having to live with Mr. MFHW, I'd choose no lacrosse, every time.

"Have you found any rec leagues?" Laird asked, from his seat at the head of the table.

"No. I'm fine. Don't miss it," I answered, scraping the last of the mashed potatoes off my plate.

"That sort of thing can open doors, Grayson," he pressed on.

Just. Shut. Up.

"Laird, honey, we're out of the Larkmead down here," my mother said, lifting up the wine bottle. Laird wiped his mouth and excused himself. My mother launched into a report on their fall trip to Napa—it was a banner year for cabernets—ending the awkwardness.

80

I stared at my plate, wishing I hadn't inhaled the food so damn fast so I had something to do with my hands. What did I expect? That my mother and Laird would brag about me getting kicked out of school? Of course no one knew. I reached over for another dinner roll. Granny Easton grabbed my arm.

"Greg, would you get me some more of that sweet-potato soufflé? If I get up, I'm not getting down again," she said.

"Sure." I excused myself and wandered toward the kitchen, pausing in the hallway when I heard Laird's voice. He was talking to his brother-in-law. About me.

"Why no more Saint Gabriel's? I thought Kate mentioned something about college scouts? A possible scholarship?"

"How do I put this?" Laird said, his voice rough as though he were struggling. A soft pop of a wine cork followed. "They asked him to leave."

"Why?"

I wanted to barge in, stop the conversation. I hated the idea of Laird talking about me, but at the same time I was curious to hear his take on it. Would he tell the truth? His voice was low. The *glug, glug* of wine being poured into a glass drowned out the whispers. A vein in my temple throbbed.

"Wow," the brother-in-law said.

"Wow is right. He was damn good, Coop. Could have had a free ride. Smart too. We don't know what he's going to do now though."

"Gwayson!" Grier yelled, jumping in front of me with arms open.

"Hey, Grier," I said, startling slightly. My reaction didn't please her; she pouted and stomped away.

There was a controlled silence in the kitchen. I coughed deliberately and walked in, keeping focused on the task at hand. Laird brought out the wine to the dining room. Coop pressed his lips together and lifted his wineglass to me, then exited. I piled way too much sweet-potato soufflé onto the plate and brought it back into the dining room to find that Granny Easton had left the table. She sat in an easy chair by the fireplace, Grier twirling in front of her.

"Mom, I'm gonna head out," I said, placing the plate on the edge of the table.

"Aw, don't go," she said, standing up with her plate in hand. "I baked a pumpkin pie just for you."

Laird butted in. "Grayson, stay. We've hardly seen you."

I met his stare and bit back the words *As if you care.*

"I have this killer party to go to, lots of people home from school," I said, giving a general wave to everyone, then leaving the room before anything else was said.

I grabbed my coat. The rack wobbled and landed on the hardwood floor with a *crack*. Grier shrieked. I barreled through the front door, punching one fist then the other through my jacket.

"Grayson, wait!" my mother called.

Even in the dark, the Chrysler stood out like a rusty spring on the sedate street of Escalades and Beemers. I kept moving forward, pretending I didn't hear my mother's footsteps. My fingers just about grazed the door handle when I felt her clutch my shoulder.

"Honey, c'mon. Stay. You'll have time to make your party."

"There's no party," I said, spinning toward my mother.

"What?"

"Do you know what a douche I felt like when Cooper asked me about lacrosse?"

My mother bristled momentarily at the word *douche* and wrapped her shawl tighter around her shoulders. She sighed, then peered up at the starry sky.

"Grayson, I'm sorry. We haven't seen Coop in a long time. He doesn't . . . didn't know about your circumstances," she said, leaning against my car. "He's such a competitive ass. Always bragging about his kids' IQs or some exotic place they've all been. You were always our trump card. Smart, athletic, and handsome. His kids have zero physical ability."

Trump card? I chuckled. Hardly the way to describe me now.

We stood in silence, staring back up at her house. It had one of those glass storm doors that gave a perfect view of the foyer. Someone had picked up the coatrack. Ryder and Grier tore across the hallway from one side to the other. Silhouettes of people enjoying the holiday moved behind the illuminated curtains. My awkward departure was forgotten. I felt a momentary pang of loneliness; did anyone even care that I was gone?

"I don't belong here," I said.

"Grayson, yes, you do. We're family."

"No . . . those people in there? That's *your* family," I said, taking out my keys.

"At least consider meeting up with us in the city tomorrow. You can—"

"You know that's not going to happen," I said, shutting down the idea.

Her eyes welled with tears. I knew I should apologize, but I didn't.

"Fine. I wish you'd reconsider."

"I've got to go," I said, opening the car door.

She stopped me, giving me a gentle kiss on the cheek.

"Safe home," she whispered.

I revved the engine while my mother shut the door. She backed away and stood in front of her house, watching, as I pulled out of the spot and tore down the street, leaving a wake of dead leaves swirling behind me.

I drove until I saw an open diner. Slinking out of Mom's was such a wimp-ass thing to do, and now regret was seeping in.

Should I go back? I thought of her face, her tears, as I'd left. I'd made her cry. That was on my shoulders. No one had asked me to leave. Then Laird and his "that kind of thing can open doors" statement popped into my mind, and any guilt I felt for leaving disappeared. *Did he think I didn't* know *that?*

The diner was dotted with people in booths here and there; a few busboys crowded around an overhead TV and watched the Jets/Patriots game. I took a seat on a spinning stool at the end of the empty white counter, my fingers numb from the cold. Coffee. I needed coffee.

I couldn't go back to my mother's . . . to the inevitable looks of pity. No matter how much I kept telling myself that starting over was just what I needed, the fact remained—I pitied myself too. In my lowest moments, I still missed St. Gabe's. I missed the challenge of taking a class like Philosophy and grabbing a coffee with Luke before Lit in the morning. I missed crushing our opponents on the lacrosse field, walking down the halls like fucking rock stars. I missed it so much, sometimes my fingers got blistered from pounding away the memories on my drums. It was easier to deal with the physical pain than think about the future I might have had if I hadn't been caught.

A young waitress came over, order pad at the ready. Early twenties, I guessed. Her brown hair was piled on top of her head in some crazy do.

"Why would anyone come to a diner on Thanksgiving?" she asked, handing me a sizable menu with a picture of a milkshake on the front.

"My family sucks," I answered.

Her eyes lit up and she laughed, deep and raspy.

"Hmm, now *that* I can understand. What can I get you?"

"What have you got?"

"Name it, we got it," she said, leaning on the counter. Her blouse fell open to reveal the lacy trim of her baby-blue bra. She smelled like patchouli, a hint of cigarette smoke around the edges.

"I'd like dessert," I said, holding her gaze.

Just what I needed. A little harmless flirting to make the world go away.

"We've got cheesecake . . . chocolate mousse . . . pie . . . What do you like?"

"Surprise me."

"A challenge? I'll take it. Drink?"

"Coffee, black."

"For real? You *will* be a challenge," she said, grabbing a cup and saucer and putting them in front of me. "So what's your name?" she asked as she poured the coffee.

The familiar buzz of the chase coursed through me.

"Mike," I answered.

"I'm Mia. Mike and Mia, that sounds good, that's . . . oh

crap, what's that called?"

"Alliteration," I said.

"Yes, that's it," she said. "Cute and smart. Bet you're in from college for Thanksgiving."

Compliment and info dig. I was *so* in.

"See, I'm less of a challenge than you think."

"Let me get that dessert. Stay right where you are. You're, like, the most entertaining thing that's happened in this sleepy little dump all day."

Mia kept her eyes on me until she disappeared into the kitchen.

Luke Dobson would be proud. I could almost hear him say, *See how easy it is to get back in the game?*

Is this really what I wanted though? Did I want to wedge my way into a girl's heart to sniff out if she'd be a good hit? Or just a lovely distraction? Mia fit the second bill nicely. She probably lived paycheck to paycheck, so no bank there. But she was as sexy as hell. Killer rear view.

Christ, Grayson, stop lining up her stats.

Mia came back. She placed a large slab of pumpkin pie in front of me, took whipped cream, and, without asking, put a generous spray over the top.

"How'd you know that was my favorite part?"

"Lucky guess," she said, taking her finger and swiping a bit from the top. She put it in her mouth. "I can't believe I just did that! You make me feel a little wicked."

The moment was interrupted by the *ding* of the order-up bell and a loud shout of "Mia!" from the kitchen. She rolled her eyes and huffed. "Be right back, Mike."

The pie sat in front of me. If I took a bite . . .

This wasn't who I was anymore. It felt wrong to be playing Mia for my own amusement. I couldn't go backward. I had to stop feeling sorry for myself about getting kicked out of St. Gabe's, because the truth was—I was the one who screwed it all up. Me. Term-paper pimp. Cheater. No spin-doctoring that. And I needed to figure out how to move forward. I was so damn sick of standing still.

I reached into my inside jacket pocket for my wallet. Right on the top, in front of my license, was Ruth Caswell's card from the Camelot Inn. Wren. I would not mess up this second chance fate had tossed in my path.

"Hey, dontcha like it?" Mia asked.

"Oh, yeah, Mia, but . . . my buddy just called. I have to run. Just the check," I said, getting up. She pouted and scribbled on her order pad.

"Well, if you're bored later, stop by. I get off at midnight."

I took the bill up to the register, ignoring the flirty tone in her voice.

"Here, I think she wants you to have that," the cashier said, handing me back my change along with the check. In bold print it said, *MIKE, U R HOT, CALL ME!* ♥ *Mia* with her number beneath it. I turned to see Mia, behind the counter, helping another customer. I waved the check at her: "got it."

Then I trotted down the steps, crumpled the check, and ignored the bite of guilt I felt as I tossed it in the trash can out front.

A new plan formed as I slid behind the wheel.

And it started with Wren.

"MORNING," I SAID.

My father sat stoically at the kitchen table, reading the *New York Times*. I fixed a bowl of Apple Jacks and sat across from him, wondering if I should bring up what happened last night. He beat me to it.

"Your mother is already at the Inn for that big wedding today. Brooke spent the night at Pete's parents' house. Probably best if things cool down between Brooke and your mother," he said, eyes still on the paper. He reached for his coffee mug.

"So you're okay with it?" I asked.

His piercing blue prosecutor's eyes bored into me over his reading glasses.

"Let's just say this isn't what I envisioned for your sister, but I'm dealing with it."

"It's kind of exciting, don't you think, *Grandpa*?"

My father closed the paper, folded it neatly in front of him, and pushed his reading glasses back into his graying hair. Maybe the Grandpa mention wasn't the best route.

"What?" I asked, wiping a milk dribble from the corner of my mouth.

"You do realize this isn't the best path for her to follow? Or you."

"Oh, God, Dad," I said, blushing. "No, that's not what I meant. It's just—she's an adult. In a relationship with someone she loves. You and Mom—"

"Exactly. Your mother and I have been through it. Student loans. Baby food. Sleep schedules. It's hard enough juggling a new family, but throw in law school? Lots of sacrifices. For both parties. I just hope Brooke can handle it."

"Handle what?" Josh asked, breezing in with a trail of frigid air—a full brown paper bag under one arm, the *Daily News* under the other. He dropped the bag on the island and placed the paper in front of my father. Josh was in the same clothes he'd been wearing last night.

"How industrious. Out early?" Dad asked, suspicious.

"Sure, Dad," Josh answered, winking at me. I knew otherwise, since I'd woken up at 4:00 a.m. in his room, where he'd left me, surrounded by three years' worth of St. Gabe's yearbooks. After my first pic of Grayson, I'd needed more. I'd spent the rest of the night poring over *Grayson Barrett: The*

Earlier Years, piecing together what I could about him from the little info the yearbooks gave. He'd had a major growth spurt between freshman and sophomore year. He was captain of the JV lacrosse team and an alternate on varsity when he was a sophomore. He was also in the Key Club and the chess club. Not that it mattered, since I was never going to see him again.

"Here," Josh said, putting an everything bagel in front of Dad.

"Some example you're setting for your little sister," my father said, slicing his bagel in half.

"Dad, don't be a buzzkill. Had to celebrate Saint Gabe's huge win yesterday," Josh said, flopping down in his seat and grabbing a bagel. "I work hard, party harder . . . your motto, remember?"

I raised my eyebrows at my father as he pushed Josh's hat off his head, revealing his usual dirty-blond mass of unkempt bedhead.

"Don't give away my secrets, Josh. Wrennie's my easy kid. I'd like her to stay like that."

"Great," I said, pushing away my bowl of cereal. "Why don't you just call me boring?"

"I didn't mean it that way," he said. "You remind me of your mother, always something going on behind those eyes of yours. You think before you leap. Quiet is not a bad thing."

"You know what they say: It's the quiet ones you've got to watch out for . . . all those secrets," Josh said, taking a monster bite of his bagel.

"Not my Wren," my father said, giving my hand a squeeze.

Josh mouthed *Grayson* behind Dad's back and put a hand over his heart, batting his eyes in an exaggerated way. I crumpled up my napkin and threw it at him.

"Cut it out!" I said, getting up from the table. "All this bonding over bagels was fun, but now I have to go to work. Are you coming with me today?"

"Um, no. Dad and I have a big day of college football planned. Right, Daddy-O?"

My father sighed, but even he wasn't immune to Josh's charms.

"I'll give you a ride when you're ready, Wren," Dad said, picking up his paper again.

"Can I drive?" I asked. He nodded.

I ran upstairs to shower and change. With my hair still damp, I put it in a loose fish-tail braid. *The easy kid.* There were worse things to be, I guessed. I didn't dazzle like Brooke or light up a room like Josh, but there was something about me . . . wasn't there? Something that made Grayson seek me out at school, for more than just to thank me. I held that thought as I went downstairs and off to work.

When I arrived at the Camelot, I found Mom in her office. She remained silent, going over a contract on her desk, as I walked in.

"Missed you this morning," I said, hanging up my coat.

"I take it your brother chose not to come in with you?" she asked, still focused on her work.

"Right. Wanted to bond with Dad over football, I guess."

"If that's what you want to call it."

"Mom, last night—"

"Wren, I'm not ready to talk about last night. We'll get through this, I know, but right now I need to focus on this wedding. It's deluxe, soup to nuts, so you'd better get to work. By the way, there's a new waiter. We're so strapped, I hired him over the phone this morning. Just, you know, keep an eye on him."

"I'm on it," I said, heading toward the Lancelot.

Eben was busy with the new hire, showing him how to set up the silverware. I tapped on the edge of the table, and they looked up. My jaw dropped.

"Grayson?"

"Hey, what's up?" he responded, reaching for another setup. I tried to mask the surprise on my face. It was unsettling to see him here, on my turf, especially after I'd spent the night before creating a mental dossier about him to entertain myself.

94

Eben spoke. "Are you all right?"

"Um, yeah. I forgot to tell Mom something."

I practically bumped heads with my mother as she walked out of her office.

"I'm walking down to see Hank. Talk to me," she said, moving like a missile toward a target. She pushed the Down button on the service elevator and glanced back at me. "Well?"

"Do you know who that new hire is, Mom?" I asked as we stepped into the elevator and it descended with a shudder.

"What do you mean?"

"He's the guy I saved from choking. Grayson Barrett," I said.

She nodded as the doors slid open with a *clank* and jog-walked off the elevator, me trailing behind. "Yes, we did have a conversation about it. Why?"

I didn't want to get into his past. She didn't need to know he got kicked out of school for being a term-paper pimp. Or that he usually wore a barbell through his eyebrow. She also didn't need to know that being around him made me hyper-aware of every cell in my body. The fact that he'd almost died up in the Lancelot should have been enough for him to never set foot in this place again, right?

"I don't know. I'm just surprised to see him, that's all."

She ran a hand through her hair and scratched the back of her head in thought. Her eyes were sleepy, bloodshot. I felt bad for questioning her about hiring him. It's not like I minded that much. I just needed to process the reality of him being here.

"He seemed nice, polite. Like he needs someone to give him a chance. But I'm so desperate for manpower, I might be blind. Do you think it's a bad decision?"

Hank came up behind her, red-faced and about to explode. He pointed to an elaborate tray table.

"Cupcakes? I'm supposed to arrange five hundred cupcakes on this monstrosity. Idiots. *Sie können mich alle am Arsch lecken!* Excuse me, Wren."

I tried not to lose it.

"What did he say?" my mother asked. I'd taken two years of German at school, but it was Chef Hank who taught me the best slang.

"Something about someone licking his ass."

She put her fingers up to her mouth, stifling a giggle. It was good to see her happy, even for a brief moment.

"What's wrong with cake?" he asked. "Normal, layered wedding cake."

"Cupcakes are *in*, Chef," I told him.

My mother placed a hand on my shoulder. "She's right, Hank. When are you going to get with the program?"

He tried to keep his hard edges but lost them around Mom.

"Fine, but if they fall . . ." Hank said, mumbling the rest in angry-sounding German as he walked away.

"So we're okay about Grayson? Consider today a trial; if he's not pulling his weight, let me know," my mother said, running off after Chef Hank again.

"Yep. Sure," I answered, wondering how I was going to keep an eye on Grayson and keep my composure at the same time.

Half the room was finished with setups by the time I got back. I busied myself with stacking the cold plates for the cocktail buffet. Out of the corner of my eye, I saw Grayson coming toward me.

"Hey, can I talk to you for a minute?" he asked. He had his hands in his pockets, and his usual fringy bangs were subdued, kind of pushed to the side, dark eyes more prominent than ever. I dropped a plate and grimaced, waiting for the crash. Thankfully it bounced off the carpet. He bent down to pick it up and handed it to me.

"Thanks," I said.

"You're surprised to see me," he said.

"Well, yeah, kind of," I answered, putting the dirty plate under the cart. "Are you stalking me or something?"

"Ha . . . Well, I'd rather think of it as strategically putting myself in your path so we can be friends . . . But if you want to call it stalking, okay."

"Okay, but why here?"

"If you don't want me here—"

"No, it's not that. This is probably the last place I expected to see you, that's all."

"I could use some honest work—gas isn't exactly free—and, well, I felt like I might have made the wrong impression the other day in the park. And where else would I get to hang out with you?"

"Hang out? Get ready for a rude awakening," I said, pushing the cart of plates toward him. "You can start by stacking these plates in rows on this table. Then I'll think of something else."

"You're sort of my boss—I dig it," he said, flashing *that* grin.

I pressed my lips together and walked away. That grin was pulling me into the deep end of the pool. The scary part, the part that made me search desperately for some other task I could lose myself in, was that there was a small, insistent voice urging me to dive right in.

I successfully avoided Grayson during the rest of setup. He met me downstairs in the kitchen as we assembled to take the trays of hors d'oeuvres up to the cocktail hour. I got lucky with lobster ravioli. Grayson, on the other hand, was a bit green as the tray of cocktail franks was pushed his way.

"How's that for karma?" he asked, grabbing the tray.

"I'll trade you," I said.

He considered it. "Nah, gotta get back on the horse, right?"

"On the upside they go pretty fast," I said, climbing the stairs to the long corridor leading to the main ballroom.

"So what's the downside?" Gray asked, keeping up with me easily.

"Talk to me in about ten minutes."

"Hmm . . . sounds serious," he said. We walked out the double doors into the cocktail reception. I was tempted to follow him, to see how he would handle it, but I went the opposite way. I only made it halfway around the room before my tray was clean. When I went to the back, Grayson was standing there, just beyond the door, tray empty.

"You must have thought I was a supreme dick at my cousin's wedding," he said, falling into step with me.

"Tough crowd?"

"No, really. I'm sorry," he said, bowing his head slightly, humorous sincerity lacing his voice. "I had no idea what a hassle people can be. I apologize on behalf of my obnoxious uncles."

"No worries. That was a pretty entertaining night. Well, before—"

"I almost choked to death," he finished.

"Definite buzzkill," I agreed, discreetly checking him out before we trotted down the stairs. He held out his hand for me to go first.

"Do you know someone asked me what I was serving?"

"Oh yeah, that happens at least once a party," I said, over

my shoulder. "Eben and I have a running game with it—you make up some wild name that makes pigs in a blanket sound exotic."

"So what's the best name you've come up with?" he asked.

Not that the hot-dog name game was a secret Eben and I swore to take to our graves, but what if Grayson thought I was a complete dork? I faced him as we waited in line for our next round of hors d'oeuvres. He seemed sincere, interested.

"Nitrate-laced mystery meat wrapped in fatty dough," I said, fighting the blush that was creeping across my face. "But I've never said that out loud to a guest. Doesn't exactly roll off the tongue."

"Nice one," he said as we reached the serving station.

A tray of cocktail franks was pushed my way by Chef Hank, an evil glint in his eyes.

"Figures," I said, groaning. Gray snatched the tray before I could.

"I got this one," he said.

"Really?" I grabbed another round of ravioli.

He swiped a hot dog off the tray, tossed it in the air. I held my breath as he executed his trick to perfection, chewing triumphantly.

"Game on," he said. "Stay close."

I followed him upstairs and back into the crowded ballroom. We worked the right side of the room. I kept my distance from him but stayed within earshot. Sure enough, Grayson walked up to a circle of older ladies, and a moment later one of them asked the dreaded, "Ooh, and what are these?" question.

In the smoothest, most serious-sounding voice, he answered, "Micro tube steaks in puff pastry."

I bit my lip to keep from bursting but shook a little and snorted. Eben caught my eye as he passed by both of us and mouthed, *Funny.* Grayson kept a straight face, charming the ladies into cleaning his tray.

We met in the back after my tray was emptied.

"So how'd I do?" he asked.

"Pretty good," I said.

"Pretty good? I thought that was kind of killer."

"Okay, better than pretty good. I nearly lost it," I admitted.

"I know. That was the best part," he said, winking. He was one of those guys who could say things like "I dig it" with a wink and make it seem natural. There was something I still didn't quite trust about it, about him being here, but he was slowly winning me over to Team Grayson. The cocktail hour had never been this fun.

Working at the Camelot had never been this fun. Period. With Grayson there, the night flew by. I found myself making excuses to be near him, all under the guise of helping him out, like showing him the best way to stack dirty dishes to get the most on a tray or the difference between the decaf and the regular pots of coffee—as if any of that took a degree in rocket science. He mastered it all, easily, and more than once

101

I caught the guests flirting with him. I wasn't the only one influenced by his stellar grin.

"So now what?" he asked, coming up behind me after he'd finished taking the last tray of dirty dishes to the kitchen.

"Just waiting until everyone leaves," I said, peering out the windows in the double doors. "Then we can break down the room."

"And then what?" His voice was quiet, low.

I spun to face him, aware of the short distance between us. "And then . . . we—"

Eben joined us, peering out the door. "Are they ever going to leave?"

"I know, right?" I said, dropping Grayson's question without answering.

And then what? My mouth went dry.

"Hey, I'm starving. Want to hit Leaning Tower after this? You can tell me all about Brooke and your Thanksgiving drama," Eben said.

"Yes, that sounds great," I answered, looking back at Gray.

"Why don't you join us?" Eben asked him. My heart froze, waiting for his response.

"If Wren doesn't consider it stalking, sure, I'll go," he said, eyes on mine.

"Yeah, you should come."

"And they're out," Eben said, throwing open the door. The rest of us followed him, a black-and-white wave pulling tablecloths and stuffing them into giant laundry bags. I couldn't finish the last task of the evening quickly enough, the thought of sitting across from Grayson propelling me at record speed. As I yanked the tablecloth off the last table, someone wrapped their very cold hands around my eyes.

I jumped, peeling back frozen fingers. . . .

"Mads!" I dropped the tablecloth at our feet.

"Surprise!"

"What are you doing here?" She was dressed in thigh-high black boots and a black micromini, which would have been obscene if she hadn't been wearing black tights. Her bronze ski jacket gathered at her waist, and her short hair was tousled to pixie perfection. In my Camelot duds, I felt like a prime candidate for an ambush makeover.

"Bringing you a present," she said, motioning toward the front doors of the ballroom. Zach was there, posing in a lewd way next to Sir Gus, while another, taller boy took a picture with his phone. *A present?*

"Mads?"

"Before you say no, he's Zach's cousin from Baltimore, in for the weekend. If you don't like him, you never have to see him again, and hey, if you do, Baltimore is, what, like three or four hours away? Win-win, Wren."

"Hey, you," Eben said, coming up behind Maddie with an armload of tablecloths. "Come on, let me see this ensemble you're rocking."

Mads pivoted gracefully on one foot and curtsied.

"Gorgeous as always," Eben said. "To what do we owe the pleasure?"

"Eben, pretty, pretty, pretty please release Wren from her servitude for some fun!"

Just then Zach entered the ballroom with a howl, lumbering across the dance floor toward us like an escapee from the zoo. For the life of me, I did not understand what Mads saw in him. She was artistic, smart, and cool. He was picking a college based on its Greek life. My "present" trailed behind, his head down, keeping his distance.

"Mads, I sort of have plans," I said, right before Zach engulfed her in a bear hug from behind.

"Oh, Wren, please," Eben said, waving me off. "Go. Have fun. You can—"

"Grayson!" Maddie said, prying Zach's hands off of her.

"Hey, Maddie," Grayson said, plopping a giant laundry bag in the center of our circle.

"Since when are you working here?" Maddie asked, eyes darting between us. Once she and Grayson were talking, I got Eben's attention.

"I really want to go to Leaning Tower," I said low, trying to motion behind me by tilting my head toward Grayson.

Eben squinted a moment until a lightbulb finally came on. "Oh, wow. Wren . . ."

". . . so you see I'm not taking no for an answer . . ." Mads said, tugging on my arm to face a tall boy with chestnut hair. *Whoa.* This guy wasn't one of Zach's soccer dudes. I took a step back, suddenly self-conscious in my work clothes. He smiled, almost apologetically, and chuckled through his nose. His only apparent flaw? He wasn't Grayson.

"Caleb, this is Wren. Wren, Caleb," Zach said. He and Maddie were beaming, as if Caleb and I were getting betrothed in front of them.

"Hey," we said together. Caleb pawed the dance floor with the tip of his Timberland. I turned to Grayson.

"Go. We'll hang another time," he said.

My heart deflated. For real? "Oh, um, okay. Sure you don't mind if I skip out now?"

"Baby, we got this," Eben said, stuffing the rest of the tablecloths into the laundry bag. "Go!"

Maddie linked her arm through mine, and we followed the boys to the lobby, where Zach continued to act like a five-year-old with Sir Gus. I fetched my coat and purse from the office.

"Hey, why don't we ask Grayson to hang out too?" I asked.

Maddie frowned. "Wren," she whispered, "it's a party for four. And it's Zach's *cousin.* Please do this for me?"

I shrugged on my coat and looked into the ballroom. Grayson was still there, giant laundry bag slung over his shoulder. He waved. I waved back, hoping the gesture would communicate . . . what? That I wanted to stay? That I was sorry Maddie showed up unexpectedly with a boy toy for me for the evening? Did he really mean we'd hang out another time?

"Sure," I said, committing to my decision. "But at least let me stop home to get changed first."

"TIMBERLANDS," I SAID. "THE UNIVERSAL SHOE choice of complete tools. Poor Wren."

"Jealous much?" Eben asked, stuffing the last of the tablecloths into the bag.

"Jealous? Of what?" I asked, hoisting the laundry bag over my shoulder. At that moment Wren came into view. She caught me staring. I waved. Me. The village idiot with a nutsack-shaped thirty-pound bag of laundry on his back. Jealous couldn't even describe what I felt when I watched the four of them disappear into the night.

"That was more about Maddie," Eben said. "You do realize that?"

"Whatever." What had I expected by taking this job? Of course she thought I was stalking her. Was I stalking her? No.

Stalking was sinister, like I wanted to scalp her and make a sweater from her hair. I had something more, ah, mutually pleasurable in mind. I thought—well, she felt the same, didn't she? We'd been getting along all night.

I followed Eben to the loading-dock door and slammed the laundry down.

"So we're done?" I asked, wiping my hands off on my pants.

"Still want to go to Leaning Tower?" he asked. "I can see that Wren's leaving has your boxers in a bunch, and I'm as hungry as hell and don't feel like eating alone."

"I could eat," I offered.

"Great, see ya there."

Eben was sitting in a front booth when I arrived. He had a couple of Corona longnecks in a bucket of ice and one opened in his hand. I slid into the cushy, red-booth seat across from him.

"Can I grab one of those?" I asked, taking off my jacket.

"They'll card you," he said, smiling.

"No problem," I answered, taking one and wiping off the excess water with my cuff. The waitress came over. An older chick, probably about Eben's age. Cute.

"I'm going to need some ID."

"Really? C'mon," I said, leaning back. She stiffened. Eben shifted in his seat.

"My manager is over there, and if you want me to open

this for you, you're going to have to prove you can legally drink it."

"Sorry, just messing with you. No one's asked for this since my birthday," I said, reaching into my back pocket and pulling out my wallet. She grabbed my ID and held my gaze a moment before putting it up to the stained-glass lamp that hung over the table. Her light eyes scanned the important information. Satisfied, she handed it back to me.

"Do you want a lime?" she asked, cracking the cap off with a bottle opener.

"Nah," I said. Her fingers grazed mine as she pulled away.

"Don't mess with me, Mike. I'm not in the mood."

I raised the beer to her before taking a sip.

Eben sat bug-eyed across the table. "Mike?"

"It's the name on my ID."

"I get that, but I just witnessed you transform into a completely different person than you were back at the Camelot. It's like the air around you changed," he said, fanning his hand around.

"C'mon," I said.

"So tell me this," he said, leaning across the table. "Why should I be in your corner and not, say, the tool in the Timbos?"

I almost snotted my beer. "What do you mean?"

"Mike. Grayson. Whatever your name is, it's plain to see you're into Wren. You were heartbroken back—"

"Whoa, dude, I don't get heartbroken."

"Well, *dude*, you sure played the part back at the Camelot. And I'm right with you. Maddie means well, has been trying to hook Wren up since her jackwad of a boyfriend dumped her at the beach over the summer—but Wren's not into it."

"Someone dumped Wren . . . at the beach?" I sat up straight, intrigued. "Continue."

"Then today . . . there's something different about her. I didn't put two and two together until the end of the night, after I egged her on to go with Maddie, and she told me she wanted to hang with us. Or more correctly . . . you."

Hope bubbled in my chest. "She said that?"

"Yes, but not so fast—I'm not sure you're worthy of her either."

"Gee, thanks."

"You appear out of nowhere. Mysterious, hair-flinging boy giving all his attention to my pretty little hothouse wallflower. My Spidey sense is up to begin with, and now this . . . *Mike*."

"Hothouse wallflower?"

"Wren is all kinds of awesome; she just doesn't know it. Being dumped really did a number on her pride. So she thinks it's easier to hide out at the Camelot every weekend and call it work instead of putting herself out there. I want to make sure you're not just playing her. Why are you interested?"

A question I'd tossed around myself. Eben seemed like the kind of person who might understand or who would at least listen, and considering my friends were scarce these days, I had nothing to lose.

"You know that saying, 'One door closes, another door opens'?"

"My bullshit meter is off the charts," he said, taking a long sip from his beer.

"Okay, Eben, I'm a total screwup. Got kicked out of school last year; my friends are gone. Any future I thought I had is on hold at the moment, and in walks Wren. . . ."

"And?"

"And I want to know her."

"Know her how?"

Knowing Wren in every sense of the word *had* crossed my mind, but it wasn't the first thing. And that was something I hadn't experienced since, like, never. I dug the way I felt around her. I could be myself, but a new-and-improved version.

"She's . . . sweet. Smart. I feel good around her, like it's okay to be myself. And I think she's the kind of person who is, you know, naturally good. Not because it's right or anything, just because that's who she is, like a moral compass. I want her in my life, and if that's just as friends, well, okay. I'm down for that."

"Well, I was hoping for something sexier than a moral compass, but okay. I like you for her," he said, clinking his beer against mine. "But I smell an iota of bullshit and . . ."

"And I leave the Camelot."

"Glad we understand each other," he said.

The waitress came back with our pizza and set it down on the stand between us. My stomach growled, but something else Eben had said bothered me. He took a plate, doled out a slice, and handed it to me.

"Dude, do I really fling my hair?"

Three beers and four slices later, I left Leaning Tower buzzing with something that felt like good cheer. The Chrysler was safe on a side street for the night, and I walked the ten blocks home, trying to stuff down thoughts of Wren and Caleb. Together. Somewhere warm. *You told her to go, idiot.*

So much for good cheer.

My house was dark, but I made no attempt to walk in quietly. Dad and Tiff were most likely out at some function, playing the part of the power sales couple. I went to the fridge, determined to reignite my buzz, and reached for a can of whatever beer my father chose to stock. I popped the lid, walked over to the great room, and screamed like a second grader when I saw a shadowy figure sitting on the sectional.

"Pop, what the hell?"

His throaty "Gotcha" cackle made me smile in spite of my heart, which was ready to tear out of my chest. "That was a good one."

"Why are you sitting in the dark?"

"Eh, don't know. I've been sitting here awhile. It's peaceful. Tiff's out at a Black Friday blowout sale with her friends. Where've you been?"

"I got a job. At the Camelot," I said.

"Really? Why?" he asked, tipping his nightly glass of Bushmills to his lips. I sat down on the opposite end of the sofa.

"Don't know. Seemed like a good thing to do. A way to keep busy," I answered.

"Guess it's better than pounding those drums."

"Yeah, guess so."

"Your mom called."

I swallowed, hard, the cold beer burning the back of my throat. The taste of grease and cheese snaked its way up, not as good the second time around. Pop and Tiff had been out when I got in the night before and were still sleeping when I'd left in the morning. We hadn't discussed Thanksgiving at all.

"Why did you hightail it out of there before dessert?"

I shrugged. "Watching my figure."

Pop took another sip of Bushmills. "Your mother told me about the lacrosse thing. Grayson, if it bothers you so much, there's got to be some league you could play in."

"Pop, it doesn't bother me," I said, not wanting to get into a conversation about how I missed St. Gabe's, which would just set him off into stories from his glory days. Today had been a good day, a day I'd forgotten about all that other crap.

"Then why'd you leave? You know how much this stuff

upsets your mother. You have to take one for the team now and again."

"What team? I'm definitely not an Easton."

He swirled the whiskey in his glass. "Grayson, you know, if the tables were turned and you agreed to live with her, there'd be no way I'd put up with your bullshit. They are your family. It's about time you came 'round to it."

The day my mother left wasn't monumental. My parents' divorce was sickeningly *amicable*. That's the word I heard them use when talking to friends. I remember looking it up. *Peaceful*. And on the surface, it was true. There were no shouting matches. No glasses thrown across the room. No heated debates over who got what. They simply woke up one day, decided they didn't like the life they were living, and said, "Okay, done with this . . . next." But the one thing they couldn't split down the middle was me.

My mother had wanted me to live in Connecticut with her and Laird. This was before I figured out they'd probably been together before she broke up with Pop. I was in sixth grade and didn't want to leave my friends. That was natural, she'd said, but I'd make new friends. Have better opportunities. A whole new world. And a dog.

I'd been groomed by Pop to go to St. Gabe's. The silver and crimson Crusaders. Sat and froze my butt off during every Turkey Day game with him telling me, "That'll be you some-day, kid." And even though I had no interest in football, the way he took such pride in it, the way he talked about the good old days, made St. Gabe's sound like the only place for me.

But the dog . . . the dog was a tipping point. My mother had given me an out clause: If I completely hated it, I could come back and live with Pop. I would have weekends and holidays in Bayonne and summer vacations wherever he chose to take me. It would all work out great, she assured me. And I had decided as much. It was after school, on a Friday at dusk, when I'd padded down the stairs to tell him I'd give the Connecticut thing a try.

He'd stood with his back to me by our sliding doors to the deck. We had this thing about scaring each other, and I was stoked, because damn, this was a good one. He'd been so deep in thought, he hadn't even heard me walk across the living room floor. I was about parallel to him, ready to pounce, when I noticed he was crying. Not sobs, just quiet, wet streams on his face. He was holding his glass of Bushmills, swirling the ice in the glass. And in that instant, even at eleven, I knew that if I left, this was what his life would become. When he saw me, he staggered back and dropped the glass of whiskey. The moment became about mops and blotting and vacuuming the shards, and it all took a good ten minutes to clean up.

We'd had a frozen Red Baron pepperoni pizza that night, and I'd told him I wanted to stay with him.

My mother already had Mr. Motherfucking Home Wrecker and a wedding date and a house in Connecticut. Pop had me,

Bushmills, and frozen pizza. Maybe it all would have gone down the same if I chose to live with my mother. Maybe Pop would have found Tiff, and his real-estate business would still have boomed. But maybe it wouldn't have.

"Screw them," I said, standing up. Sick of the darkness, the beer, and the depressing direction this conversation had taken, I clicked on the lamp and squinted in pain. My father put his hand over his eyes.

"Hey, don't talk that way about your mother," he said.

"Why? If she cared so much about keeping the family together, why'd she go create a new one?"

My father made an attempt to stand up, but he kept sliding down, losing his footing. He slammed down his drink on the end table; a splash of whiskey came up over the side.

"I hate this effing couch; my ass keeps slipping!" he yelled. A beat passed where neither of us said anything, just stared until we both cracked up. I reached out, gave him a hand, and pulled him to standing. He squeezed my shoulder.

"They are your family, Grayson. Even Laird."

"Whatever."

"Don't whatever me. I won't be here forever."

"That's the whiskey talking. Stop."

"Maybe. But promise you'll make an effort at Christmas."

"Yeah, sure," I lied.

NINE

WREN

"SO TELL ME AGAIN, WHAT WAS WRONG WITH Caleb?" Maddie asked, handing me another piece of tape.

In an attempt to build some community-service hours, I'd joined the Sacred Heart Spirit Club. The club must have been a holdover from the century when most Sacred Heart students got married right after graduation. The bylaws were an old-fashioned decree about learning how to beautify the world at large, beginning at home. I was pretty sure that hanging glitter stars and snowflake garlands along the hallways after school wouldn't impact the world at large, but if it counted as community service, then I was determined to beautify. Mads was along for moral support.

"Let's see, he licked my neck—and not in a sexy way, in a Great Dane kind of way. Sloppy," I said, securing part of the garland and shimmying across the step stool to drape the rest of it. I reached out for more tape.

"That's it? One flaw was enough to make you blow us off for the rest of the weekend?" she asked. She pulled the tape away as I reached for it, forcing me to turn to her.

"What?" I asked, grabbing it.

"There's more to this, Wren. I know it. Caleb was hot, funny, and here for two nights. In a word, perfect."

"Then why didn't you offer Jazz that perfection?" I asked, taping the last bit of garland to the crease where the wall met the ceiling.

"I did. She wanted to rest up for her long run on Sunday, so she said. I think she's just afraid that no one will live up to her movie-romance ideals," she said, giving me a hand down. "Besides, Caleb was really into *you*."

"What do you think?" I asked, stepping back to admire my work.

"I think you're above decorating the hallway," Maddie said. "Wren, why did you join this lame club? You know it's like—"

"NHS lite, I know. It's not all about decorating the hallway. They do some cool community-service projects too. I just want to do something, Mads, not sit back and wait until I'm worthy enough for the NHS."

"What about yearbook? You'll be up for editor next year."

I loved yearbook. Of course, it helped that both Jazz and Mads were on the committee. The solitude of working on copy or figuring out the puzzle of an interesting layout was perfect for me, but I wanted to do something different too.

"Yearbook's great, but it's not exactly social, is it? I need to get myself out there. Prove being quiet doesn't mean I don't want to be a part of anything. So Spirit Club it is. I think that garland looks exceptional, don't you?"

"It's crooked," said a voice from behind us.

We parted to see Ava Taylor, vice president of the Spirit Club and all-around annoying suck-up. For some reason Ava liked to pretend that she wasn't once the third corner of the Maddie/Wren/Ava triangle of St. Vincent de Paul grammar school. During the summer between eighth grade and freshman year, she got her first kiss from a high school guy and dumped us as if we were some Barbie-playing ten-year-olds. At freshman orientation she already had a circle of friends and made it clear we weren't welcome by completely ignoring us. Soon after we stopped analyzing why and went on with our own social lives. We met Jazz, and she more than filled the void Ava had left.

But, still.

Our disbanded friendship was the big pink elephant in a tutu pirouetting in the hallway. Part of me believed that if I stared into Ava's eyes long enough, the girl who could write in cursive backward and touch the tip of her nose with her tongue would still be in there. The same girl who insisted we build a tent of blankets in her room to sleep under, but who later laid out such a whomping fart, we had to vacate and sleep in her den.

These days it looked like Ava farted pixie dust, if she farted at all. Her cool, green eyes surveyed my work. The corner of her mouth downturned slightly. She got up on the stepladder and moved the end of the garland two inches to the left.

"Perfect," she said, stepping down.

"Big difference," Maddie said under her breath.

Ava folded up the stepladder, put it against the wall, and clapped her hands together as if she were trying to get dust off of them.

"That's all for today. Be here fifteen minutes before the first bell tomorrow. That should be enough time to finish up."

"Why can't we finish up now?" I asked.

"I have dance-team practice. Competition season is coming up. Don't worry about being late to your first class. Spirit Club is always excused."

"Great," I answered, not thrilled with the prospect of having to wake up earlier all for the sake of hanging decorations.

"You know, I've been dying to talk to you, Wren," Ava said, coiling her arm around mine. My body stiffened. Maddie's eyes nearly popped out of her skull. My expression had to be the same.

"About what?"

"Darby Greene told me Grayson Barrett picked you up after school last week? Is that true?" She asked the question slowly as we strolled down the hallway, keeping her eyes forward until the last word.

"Yes."

She snickered. "Oh my God, I didn't believe her. How do you know him?"

My skin prickled.

"She saved his life," Maddie said, stopping in front of us. I'd been about to give a less informative answer.

Ava unhooked her arm from mine and her hand went up to her mouth. She puzzled a moment until her eyes charged with understanding. "Wait, so *you're* the cocktail waitress?"

"Cocktail waitress?" I said. How could she possibly know any of this?

"That's right. You work at your parents' catering place; Gray was at his cousin's wedding. Now it makes sense, sort of. Still, why did he pick you up after school?"

"I don't know why he picked me up. He just did. Why do you care?" I asked, my eyes narrowing.

She stepped back, her full ponytail swaying with the movement. "I don't. Just wondering how you know him. You don't exactly hang out with the same people, do you?"

"Where do you get off—" Maddie began, but I put my hand up to stop her and then glared at Ava.

"We work together. At the Camelot. We're pretty tight," I said, fabricating.

"Seriously? Grayson works with you?"

I spun away from her, done with the conversation, angry with myself for giving her one shred of information. Why didn't I just keep quiet? Maddie caught up to me, her mouth a thin line.

"Why did you stop me? I wanted to let her have it," she said.

"I can fight my own battles," I snapped, galloping down the stairs ahead of her to the locker dungeon.

"Wren, why are you mad at me?" she asked, calling after me.

I growled and stomped off to my locker. I took out my frustrations by shoving books into my messenger bag. I wasn't even sure what I needed. I flung a scarf around my neck, grabbed my coat, and slammed the locker shut, turning the dial in a violent twist. Maddie was waiting at the top of the stairs in the vestibule.

"Sorry for losing my shit," I said.

"I know, but hey, that's what friends are for," she answered, leaning against the wall.

"How did Ava even know what happened?"

"She must know him. It's sort of big news, Wren. He wouldn't be breathing if it weren't for you."

I pushed open the door and squinted in the sunlight.

"But did you hear her? That tone in her voice? Is it so unbelievable that Grayson would pick me up after school?" I asked.

Maddie stopped midstep. "Omigod, you like him! I'm so stupid."

"No, it's not like that."

Maddie studied my face. "Oh, yeah it is soooooooo like that. It's the way you say his name. That's why you weren't into Caleb. That's why Queen Bitch got to you. I thought you said you thought he was a bit of a jerk after he gave you a ride home. Why didn't you just say you changed your mind?"

"I don't know what I'm feeling, okay?" I answered. This budding friendship with Grayson, his explosive entrance into my life—it was mine and mine alone. Something apart from school, my family, Jazz and Maddie, the Trevor hump-and-dump. I didn't feel like analyzing it; I was enjoying just letting it happen.

Maddie swayed into me as we continued to walk the tree-lined driveway toward the street.

"Hey, he has a shitty ride, but otherwise you have my blessing, Wren."

"Mads, is that stuff so important?" I asked.

"Not when a guy is that scorching," she said.

I exhaled deliberately, lowering my gaze to the ground. "I don't know if he's just being friendly or if there's more to it. We only—"

"Well, you'd better figure it out fast, because he's right there," she said.

Grayson was perched on the rear bumper of his car, reading *The Republic*. Pretty much the sexiest model of literacy awareness I'd ever seen. I smiled as a jolt of recognition pulsed through my body. He was there for *me*.

"Bet you wouldn't mind if *he* licked you like a Great Dane," Maddie whispered.

"Mads!" I shrieked. Grayson grinned as we walked up to him. I slowed my pace, trying to calm my heart rate, which was racing for reasons that had nothing to do with exertion.

"Hey," I said. Maddie waved and continued to walk past.

"Maddie, want a ride?" Grayson asked, over his shoulder.

She walked backward in the crosswalk for a moment. "No, thanks," she called, mischief in her tone. "I think Wren wants you all to herself."

I bit my tongue and held my breath as I watched her walk toward the bus stop.

"Still reading Plato . . . any good?"

"Kind of heavy. Some of it I can get behind, but I'm too much of a hedonist to relate to most of it," he answered with a wink.

I nodded, pretending to understand.

His smile faded a bit as he waved to someone behind me. I peered over my shoulder to see Ava in sweats and a tee, opening the gymnasium door. She stood stock-still, eyebrows practically up to her hairline. This was fun. I waved too.

"See you bright and early tomorrow!"

Ava said nothing, her ponytail swaying behind her as she walked back inside.

"So how do you know Ava?" I asked.

"She kind of stalked me last year," he said, wrinkling his nose. "She had this on-again, off-again thing with a friend of mine. She's, um, a bit much."

"When you say she 'stalked' you, you mean she was strategically putting herself in your path to be friends?" I asked, touching the tip of his sneaker with the tip of my ballet flat.

He laughed this infectious belly laugh that made the unpleasant events after school evaporate. *I* made him laugh. God, it felt great.

"Well, when the attention is unwanted, it crosses the stalking line," he said, shoving the book in his jacket pocket and bouncing on his toes. "I hope I'm not crossing that line."

I chewed my lip. By answering that question, I'd be admitting that I liked having him around. Which I did. A lot.

"No, no line crossed."

"Good. Feel like getting a coffee?"

"Why didn't you tell me you hate coffee?"

It was too cold for our usual (could you claim a usual spot if you only visited it once?) boat pond/coffee outing, so we ended up at the Starlight Diner. A place whose claim to fame was the World's Best Pies, which were displayed in a six-foot glass case with shelves that rotated slowly to make sure each dessert had its moment in the spotlight.

"I don't know, you seemed so passionate about it . . . *I don't do pretty coffee* and all that," I teased, taking a sip of my hot chocolate. He laughed.

"Don't remind me what an asshat I was that day."

"You weren't," I said, tucking some loose hair behind my ear. He leaned forward, eyes on mine, lips parted like he had something to say. My mind went blank. *Breathe, Wren.* There was no discomfort, no squirmy feeling, no wanting to fill the silence. I could have sat that way, looking at him, for hours.

"Here you go." A redheaded waitress placed Grayson's second slab of Boston cream pie in front of him. I finally looked away, smiled at her.

"Thanks," I said.

Grayson grabbed his fork and tucked in. "That day in the park . . . what did you mean you were screwing up your semester?" he asked, before shoveling the pie into his mouth.

"You remember that?"

He chewed quickly, wiped his mouth with a napkin. "I remember everything."

Now *that* made me squirmy. "I suck at math. It's just not my thing, you know. I study, or at least I think I do, but then I just freeze on the tests."

"You're in luck. Math *is* my thing."

"And that would help me . . . how?"

"I can tutor you."

"Yeah, I'm not sure that would work," I said, seriously

doubting I could focus on anything with him so close.

"Totally legit," he said, raising his hands. "I used to tutor at an after-school program once a week. I'm good."

Oh, God, of course he is.

I cleared my throat. "And you could tutor me in algebra and trig?"

He was about to take a sip of his coffee, but he paused, the side of his mouth curling up, eyebrows arcing slightly. The gleam in his eyes made me blush.

"I could tutor you in anything you want," he answered, voice low.

Holy crap, I walked right into that one.

"I might be interested. I'll think about it," I said. "But why the offer? Aren't you busy with your own stuff? College applications and everything?"

He took his fork and played with the whipped cream left on his plate, making four little rows, then crisscrossing again. "The sort of schools that were on my wish list frown upon academic fraud."

"Like where?"

He pressed his lips together, smiling slightly. "Harvard."

I put down my cup and covered my eyes with my hands. "Oh, wow."

He laughed. "It was a reach, but I figured why not? Penn was my top. NYU. Columbia . . ."

"But would they even find out?"

"Technically no, but the transfer after three years might make them wonder. And I'm too embarrassed to ask my old teachers for letters of rec. Besides, *I* would know. At one point that didn't bother me, but now . . . it does. I'm thinking of going somewhere local, get a strong year in, figure stuff out, then transfer. I'm not even sure I want to go into finance anymore."

"You still have more of a plan than I do."

"I want to help you. That day in the park . . . what you said . . . I've been thinking about it ever since."

I puzzled for a moment, trying to remember what else I could have said that made an impression.

"About being a number. What bullshit it is. You're right. And I used to be so into that. Christ, I built my whole term-paper business around it."

"But it is important," I said. "It's what they look at, isn't it? I should take it more seriously. At least I'm trying to. In the meantime I'm ramping up my extracurriculars just in case my average number doesn't measure up."

He put his hand over mine, sending a charge through my body that made it hard to sit still. "You're one of the most genuine people I've met. You're not average, Wren. Not even close."

I moved my thumb out from underneath his fingers and ran it across the top of his hand, forcing myself to lock eyes with him.

"Okay, tutor me," I said.

He breathed out, squeezed my hand. He was about to say something when his phone went off, "Flight of the Bumble-bee" sounding furiously from his pocket. He rolled his eyes and pulled his hand away.

"Sorry, I've got to take this. Hey, Tiff," Grayson answered, eyes still on mine. I turned away to give him privacy. "I don't understand. What?"

The waitress placed the check on the table. Grayson put his hand over it before I could grab it. I was about to protest but stopped. His eyes were dark, his face serious. Something was wrong.

"Yeah. okay. I'll be there as fast as I can. Bye."

"What's the matter?" I asked.

"My father was rushed to the hospital."

TEN

GRAYSON

"MY FATHER WAS RUSHED TO THE HOSPITAL."

The words came out of my mouth, but they felt foreign. I slid out of the booth and stood up, hoping it would help me make more sense of the conversation.

Wren sat bolt-upright, shock in her eyes. "What happened?"

I rubbed my face, stumbling through my thoughts, trying to remember what Tiff told me.

"They think he had a heart attack. He's at Bergen Point Memorial. I need to get there," I said, raking my hand through my hair. *The check, I need to pay the check.* I moved toward the cashier. Front of the diner. One foot in front of the other. Wren came up behind me and grabbed the check out of my hand.

"Just go. I'll take care of this," she said, waving her hand toward the door.

A blast of icy wind greeted me as I rushed out the door into the parking lot. I jammed my hands into my front pockets for warmth.

Pop was in the hospital.

Heart attack.

Why hadn't I answered the phone earlier? It wasn't like Tiff called after school every day. I tortured myself, milling around the parking lot, blind to where I'd parked my car. My teeth chattered as I searched the lot and finally located the mud-brown soft-top of the Chrysler. I fumbled for my keys and realized I'd left my jacket inside. I turned back toward the diner to see Wren coming down the stairs, my jacket draped over her arm. Her hair fanned away from her face as she trotted toward me.

"You forgot this," she said, handing me the jacket.

Thank you, I thought, though the words never quite made it to my lips. I shivered as I pushed my arms through the sleeves. Wren dropped her bag by her feet and unwound the blue knit scarf from her neck.

"Here," she said, her breath disappearing in a puff of white. She reached up, on tiptoe, and tossed the scarf over my shoulders, winding it around my neck twice. The wool was still warm from her body.

My teeth chattered as I stuffed the fringy ends of the scarf inside my jacket.

"You'll be okay?" she asked.

Mute, I nodded.

"I can walk from here," she said, staring down the expanse of Broadway.

"I c-c-can give you a ride," I stuttered. When did it get so cold?

"No, you need to get to your dad," she answered, slinging her bag over her shoulder. I nodded again and watched her walk away, the word *good-bye* forming a lump in my throat. She was right, I needed to get to the hospital, but my feet wouldn't move.

Wren came back.

"I'll drive," she said, eyes sweeping the parking lot.

"What?"

"I don't think it's a good idea for you to be behind the wheel right now. Hand over the keys."

No one had ever driven the Chrysler but me and Pop. It wasn't a sweet ride, but it was mine. The guys had always given me shit about how neat I kept it. How I practically made them take their shoes off before they set foot in it. Without protest I dropped the keys into her open palm.

Getting into the passenger side was alien. Wren tossed her messenger bag into the back and slid into the driver's side. Her plaid skirt hiked up to reveal another two inches of milky white thigh that I couldn't tear my eyes from. The sight of her bare skin sent a current of desire through me.

Grayson Matthew, you filthy horndog. My conscience took

on Tiff's voice. *Your father could be dying, and you're thinking with your prick.*

Wren put the car into Drive. We lurched forward out of the spot as she lead-footed the brake to let another car back up out of a space directly across from us. The near miss wiped my brain of pervy thoughts.

"Sorry, I'm used to driving my dad's car," she explained, tucking a few strands of static-charged hair behind her ear. I cranked up the heat, then reached across her to switch on the headlights.

"It's dusk. You'll need those," I said, leaning back into the passenger seat.

Gripping the wheel in the perfect ten and two o'clock position, Wren maneuvered out of the spot as if the car were the size of a boat. In the time it took her to get out of the parking lot, I could have been to Bergen Point Memorial and back.

Once we hit Broadway, she visibly relaxed. She kept doing all those things new drivers do—checking the side mirror and rearview, slowing down as the light changed to yellow. Conscientious. Adorable, even. But fucking three-toed-sloth slow. My knee bounced up and down with pent-up energy. I chewed on my thumbnail as we stopped for our third red light in what seemed like two minutes.

"This is a bit of a shock?" she asked, her voice unsure as she stepped on the gas again.

"Yes," I answered quickly, but then thought about it. "No,

133

I guess not really. Pop doesn't take care of himself. Tiff's been trying to get him to eat better for years. And he smokes. Maybe not as much as he used to, but probably more than he lets us know. So not a total shock. But. I didn't really think this is how I'd be spending my day."

"You call your mother 'Tiff'?" she asked, clicking on the directional. A few cars sped by before she could make the left turn onto the same block as the hospital.

"Tiff's my stepmom. Five years. My mom lives in Connecticut. I don't see her that much. There's a spot," I said, almost ready to jump on her lap and take over the wheel.

I was out the door before she killed the ignition. She caught up to me halfway down the street. Then I felt the warmth of her hand wrapping around mine. Surprised, I glanced at her. She gave my hand a gentle squeeze. I held on, and she took the lead.

We barreled through the sliding doors at the entrance and tore across the lobby. A stout security guy who must have lived for moments like this sat at a podium in front of the archway that led to the rest of the hospital. He held up his hand, and we skidded short across the marble floor in front of him.

"Visiting hours are—"

"My dad's in the emergency room."

"Your best bet would be to go back outside—"

"Can't we get in through here?" I asked, cutting him off again and gesturing toward a sign that said ER with an arrow pointing down another hallway.

He soured as his eyes shifted to Wren. "Are you family?"

I glared at him, ready to verbally tear him a new one, but Wren intervened.

"Sir, he's a mess. I want to make sure he gets where he needs to be, then I'll leave, I promise," she said, voice calm, working some sort of spell on him with her eyes. With a jerk of his head he gave us a quick, "Go." We race-walked down a hallway and through so many doors, it would have been funny if I wasn't so panicked. By the time we got to the last one, I half expected to be outside again.

We emptied into the grubby, basic white waiting room of the ER. A woman cradled a crying infant in front of a small reception window that slid open and closed. The old woman behind it either didn't hear or didn't care. Her name tag read Myrtle. I knocked, and she peered at me through rimless glasses.

"My father was brought in about an hour ago," I said, fingers twitching to reach for the magic door she had to buzz me through.

She picked up a clipboard, sliding a pen into the top clip, and paused to cough into her shoulder.

"Name," she said, placing the clipboard between us.

"No, I'm not here for me. I'm here for my father," I said, pushing it back toward her.

"You have to sign in, son," she said. I grabbed the pen and

scrawled something in one of the sign-in spots.

"Ma'am, he had a heart attack. I'd really like to see him," I said, handing her the clipboard. She glared at me and pushed the magic button.

I pulled Wren through with me, ignoring Myrtle's outcry of "Family only!" We hurried toward the back of the large room, which was completely devoid of ER-type activity. Tiff stood at the end of a row of curtained-off spaces. Her arms were folded across her chest, her hand up to her mouth. My heart dropped to my feet then shot up into my throat. I wanted to go back to the diner, the car, my fantasy starring Wren's thigh, anything to escape facing what was behind the curtain.

"Grayson," Tiffany said, opening her arms. I released Wren's hand from my vise grip and gave Tiff a quick hug.

"How is he?" I asked, going past her.

"See for yourself," she answered. I walked into the curtained makeshift room to see Pop sitting up straight, arms folded across his chest, IV drip next to him. A rush of breath escaped my lips. He was alive.

"Pop, you okay?" I asked, gripping the rail on the side of the gurney.

"Tiff, I told you not to worry him," he said, looking past me at Tiffany and then noticing Wren. The gleam in his eye told me that, for the moment, things were okay.

"I thought you were on your deathbed," I said.

"Tiff thought so too. Doc said I just have angina," he said, patting his chest.

"Yes, he needs to take care of it. It's like a warning sign of things to come—*if* you let it get out of hand. Which I won't let you do." I noticed for the first time that Tiff wasn't her usual put-together self. Her hair was in a ponytail, and she had on the fuzzy black tracksuit she wore on her self-proclaimed schlep days.

"What are you gonna do, Tiff? None of us gets out of here alive."

"Blake."

"Pop, come on."

"Are you going to introduce your friend, Grayson?" he asked, tilting his chin toward Wren. Now that things had calmed down, both he and Tiffany gave Wren their full attention. She stood at the foot of the gurney, chewing her bottom lip, hands in pockets, eyes shifting from Tiffany to Pop to me.

I'd never brought a girl home to meet them. There was prom, and special occasions where they'd catch a glimpse of my social life, but not like this. Not this personal. This was new territory for me too.

"Hi, I'm Wren. Wren Caswell," she said, reaching out to shake my father's extended hand. "Hope you're feeling better, Mr. Barrett."

"Caswell?" Pop asked. "She's the girl who—"

"—saved my life," I said, finishing his sentence. "Yep."

He grabbed her hand with both of his.

Wren flushed bright pink as she accepted Pop's gushing thank-you. Tiffany moved toward Wren and pulled her in for a hug. Wren gave Tiff a quick squeeze. She bowed her head, professing it was "nothing, really, anyone would have done it," as she stepped from one foot to the other, obviously uncomfortable with the attention.

"I played football with your dad in high school," Pop said.

"You were a Crusader?" Wren asked.

"Yep, running back. Your father was defensive tackle. No one could get by him. Tell him I was asking about him."

"I will," she said.

"When all of this drama calms down, Wren, you'll have to come over for dinner," Tiff said.

"That's all I'm worth, a dinner?" I asked, joking. Tiff frowned and clipped me playfully on the arm. I scowled, exaggerating how much it hurt. Wren laughed.

"I'd like that," Wren said to Tiffany.

We stood there grinning for a moment, until Wren finally spoke. "I'd better get going."

"Okay, I'll walk you out," I said.

Wren waved good-bye to Pop and Tiff. When she turned her back on them, they both gave me faces of approval. I shook my head. *It's not what you think.*

But what was it?

We walked out of the ER entrance, back into the cold. It was dark now, the sounds of rush hour echoing through the streets. Wren zipped her coat up to her chin. I burrowed deeper into the scarf she'd wrapped around my neck. The chivalrous thing would have been to give it back, but I couldn't. Her scent, something citrus and tropical, surrounded me, making me think of summer.

"I forgot my bag," she said, digging in her pocket.

"Why don't you just take the car? I can swing by and pick it up later," I said.

She held out the keys.

"No, really, I insist," I said, touching her hand lightly and pushing the keys back toward her. She flipped them around her fingers.

"No, really. I can't," she said.

I took the keys from her. "C'mon, I'll get your bag."

We walked side by side to the car. I wanted to hold her hand again. Like at the diner. Or like before, when we ran into the hospital. Now, without a reason . . . would she let me? I opened the car and grabbed her messenger bag from the backseat.

"You sure you don't want the car? Really, I trust you with it," I said, trying another angle.

"Gray, thanks for the offer, but . . ."

"I know, I know," I answered. "You don't want to be seen driving it."

"No, no, that's not it at all," she said. "I can't drive."

"What?"

"I mean I can, my dad's taken me out a few times, but I'm supposed to be supervised by a legal adult. I didn't want to get into it back at the diner because I thought you might say no if you knew and I didn't want you to drive here by yourself and I—"

Without thinking I brought my mouth down to hers and swallowed up whatever else she was going to say. She was stiff with surprise at first, but then her lips softened under mine, parting, kissing me back. My hand found her face, my thumb caressing her cheek. Her tongue was warm and tasted like chocolate. It wasn't my sexiest effort, but it felt right for the moment. Wren pulled away first. Had I just blown it?

She looked down, her face hidden behind her hair. Then she tipped back her head and laughed. God, her smile nearly knocked me over. I reached for her hand and brought it to my mouth. She got quiet.

"So you broke the law for me," I said, my lips slowly grazing her knuckles.

"Um . . . yeah . . . I guess you could say that, but it was for a good cause."

"Then at least let me give you a ride home," I said. She gently pulled her hand away then gripped the strap of her messenger bag.

"No. After all that rushing and breaking the law? You

should go back to your father. But wait," she said, opening the flap of her bag and rummaging through the main compartment until she pulled out her phone.

"What's your number?" she asked. I rattled off the digits. My phone rang. I grabbed it out of my pocket and answered.

"Hey, 'sup," I joked.

She added the number to her contacts. "Call me later. Let me know how your dad is doing. Crazy that our fathers knew each other in high school, huh?"

"Yeah, really," I said.

We lingered a moment longer before Wren came closer, put her hand on my shoulder, and brushed her lips softly across mine.

"I had fun breaking the law with you," she whispered. "Bye."

I watched her disappear up the block, her plaid skirt swaying. When she was out of sight, I landed with a thud and walked back to the reality of the ER. I pulled Wren's scarf up to my nose, inhaling her scent and getting dizzy all over again. I was happy to have my face covered—no one walks into the hospital with a grin that wide unless he's heading to the psych ward. But I couldn't help it.

She kissed me.

ELEVEN

WREN

Oh the weather outside is frightful

So come inside and get good and schnockered

Andy's house

Dec 4—8:00 p.m. till whenevs

Be there, or don't

So, no work tomorrow—wanna go? G.

I stared at the text invite, silent, like any false move would make my phone explode. We were in a mandatory yearbook meeting, and although it was technically after school, and checking my text messages wouldn't garner me detention, I knew Mr. Fuller, our new yearbook company liaison, might freak at me squealing out loud.

I slipped my phone to Jazz, who was sitting next to me and paying way too much attention to a recap of how we were supposed to upload text and pictures to the yearbook for our midyear deadline. She mouthed the word *schnockered*, then passed the phone on to Maddie. To my horror Mads texted something back to Grayson.

I waggled my hand for her to give it back.

"Are you getting this?" Mr. Fuller asked, zeroing in on the three of us.

"Yes, Mr. Fuller. We need to minimize the photos before the initial upload," I answered.

Satisfied, he continued with the presentation. Maddie's eyes lit up at an incoming text and at lightning speed texted something back before handing me the phone. When I checked the message log I nearly fainted.

"Mads, I would never say 'fuckin' A' in response, are you crazy?" I said, once we were outside heading toward the bus. I tried to sound mad, but I couldn't. The thought of Grayson's reaction was too funny.

"Sorry! When he said 'hells yeah' after I asked him if Mads and Jazz could come, well, I got caught up in the moment."

"Who said I want to get good and schnockered this weekend?" Jazz asked. "And who's Andy? We don't even know these people."

Maddie jumped in front of both of us, hand up, like an elfin traffic cop with her woolen newsboy cap slightly askew and her blond, spiky tufts sticking out. "Would the two of you get over yourselves?"

Jazz opened her mouth, but Maddie interrupted again.

"Look, I applaud your decision to do a half marathon, but missing one training run to go to what sounds like a helluva party isn't going to ruin your finish time. And you?" she continued, focusing on me. "You keep debating whether Grayson likes you as more than a friend—well, get a clue—he just invited you to a party! Probably with plans to continue where he left off the other day. Hells bells, chicas, we need this."

"Mads, stop," I said, reddening at the thought of Grayson's ambush kiss. It had been stunning and warm and incredible. And scary . . . I'd never felt such an immediate rush with anyone. If I hadn't pulled away, I might have still been there. But anytime I thought of continuing where we left off, it completely consumed me.

"I never said I wouldn't go," Jazz said, her eyes wary. "Just wanted to think about it."

"What's to think about? I don't know Andy either, but he uses the word *schnockered*, and I kind of love that in a person. And your potential new boyfriend just earned major friend points by being enthusiastic about our presence at said party. It's a win-win sitch."

"Fine then, I'm in, but I'm not getting schnockered," Jazz said.

"Yay, she's agreed to go," Maddie said, linking her arm through Jazz's. "We'll work on the schnockered bit. Wren, make sure you get the deetz. Could this really be happening? Could the three of us have plans *together* for the weekend?"

After dinner I called Grayson for the deetz.

"'Fuckin' A,' Wren, really?" he asked, laughing.

"So you know that wasn't me?"

"Maddie got a hold of your phone?"

"How'd you guess?"

"So you *don't* want to go?"

"I do, yeah. Want to go. It's okay for you to go? With your dad and everything?"

"Tiff's got everything covered. He just needs to take it easy and, well, yeah, when Andy sent me the text, I didn't think twice. This is just what we need. Don't you think?"

We. Oh, how I loved the way that sounded. "Definitely."

"Cool, but you guys need to meet me there. I kind of have to help set up," he said.

That stopped me cold. "Um, sounds formal?"

"No, not like that. I'm part of the entertainment."

"Get out."

"Yeah, Andy and I have a band. Haven't played together in a while though."

"So you're in a *band* band?"

"Yes. A *band* band. You know, we play *music*."

"So what are you? Lead singer?" I asked, trying to envision Grayson behind a mike.

"Ah, you see me as a front man? Nice . . . but no."

"Then what? Guitar, bass, tambourine?" I asked.

"You'll have to come to the party if you want to find out."

"Grayson, please."

"Nope. You have to promise me you'll be there."

"Fine, yes. We'll be there."

On the night of Andy's party, Mads came down with a stomach bug—which must have been really, really, *really* awful, for her to bail on our night out—but she mustered up enough strength for a pre-party fashion confab via Skype.

"So which one would he be in *The Breakfast Club*?" Jazz asked.

"What?" I asked, holding up a black miniskirt and Brooke's True Religion skinny jeans that I had on loan during her pregnancy for Mads to see.

Mads coughed, her pale face filling my laptop screen. "Oh, God, Wren, no jeans and TOMS tonight—please sex it up! What does this have to do with *The Breakfast Club*?"

"Fine," I said, tossing the jeans onto my bed.

"You know, I think it might help to know what kind of guy he is . . . brain, athlete, criminal . . . so you can tailor your outfit," Jazz said, rocking in my computer chair. Mads had talked her into wearing dark skinny jeans tucked into five-inch knee-high boots, which made her incredibly toned legs look like they went on forever.

"Jazzy, have you seen Grayson? Who cares about his personality type? Lemme see that purple sweater, the one with the deconstructed neckline, and that, um, black top with the shirred waist, the one that ties on the sides."

"He's kind of all three," I answered, grabbing the tops from my closet and showing them to her.

"Purple, with the matching tank. Your boobs look awesome in that shirt," Mads said, "and the common denominator for brain, athlete, and criminal is the boobies."

"Do you have to be so juvenile?" Jazz asked. "What do you mean he's all three?"

"He's just . . . I don't know . . . a little bit of each," I answered, from behind my closet door while pulling on my tights and shimmying into my outfit.

Mads laughed, her voice hoarse. "Yum. A hybrid. That's hot. So he's kind of a . . . brainathiminal."

Jazz clapped her hands. "Omigod, that's perfect!"

I chuckled, climbing into my riding boots.

"I guess. So what do you think?" I asked, twirling in front of the computer. I caught a glimpse of myself in my full-length mirror. Mads was right; the shirt did hug me in all the right places. A bold choice. I smiled. What would Grayson think?

"Wren Caswell, I would do you," Mads said.

"Thanks, I think."

"Me too," Jazz said.

"Guys, stop."

"Okay, my work is done."

"What are we going to do without you?" Jazz asked, getting up from my chair. The two of us stood in front of the computer, waiting for words of wisdom. It would feel strange without Mads there. She brought up her fist to her mouth, cleared her throat, and sat up straight.

"Ladies—go forth. Flirt enough for all three of us and, for fuck's sake, have *fun*! I expect a full debrief après party. This is a dare-to-be-great situation."

"*Dare-to-be-great situation?* Mads, you just quoted *Say Anything*!" Jazz said.

"Do you think that was by accident? See, I pay more attention than you think. Maybe you'll find your Lloyd Dobler tonight, Jazz. And I hope you and your *brainathiminal* need a fire hose to break it up, my smoking-hot girl wonder. Now excuse me, I have a date with a *Supernatural* marathon and my trash can."

"Are you sure this is it?" Jazz asked.

"Yep, five twenty-three Oak," I said, staring up at the brick town house. No sounds of a band. No lights on inside. The street itself was a dead end, lonely and dark. Only a small, lit evergreen tree on Andy's stoop suggested the season. I knew

Grayson wouldn't have tricked me, but maybe I'd remembered the numbers wrong. I pulled off my glove with my teeth to check my phone again.

"It's freezing, and my feet are killing me," Jazz said, stomping. I shivered as I scrolled through the messages.

"Nope, right address," I said, staring up at the town house again. "I guess I could call him."

Just when I was about to dial Grayson, a guy carrying a case of Stella Artois appeared out of nowhere.

"Here to see Sticky Wicket?"

On closer inspection he was probably too young to be carrying the beer, but he definitely looked like he knew where to find the party. Grayson had never told me the band's name, but I figured I'd give it a shot.

"Yeah, Andy's house?" I asked.

"Yep, follow me. Name's Logan."

As Logan led us, Jazz showed me her pepper-spray key chain. I rolled my eyes. We followed him down a narrow alleyway along the side of the town house. My eyes adjusted to the dark, but there wasn't much to see. Just when I was thinking the pepper spray wasn't such a bad idea, we finally reached a door. Logan fumbled with the doorknob. I grabbed it for him.

"Thanks, angel," he said. *Angel?* Seriously? Who was this guy? I gestured for Jazz to follow him before I went in.

Strains of music surrounded us as we tromped down

wooden stairs to a laundry room. Logan put his beer on top of the dryer, shrugged off his leather jacket, and covered the case of Stella with it.

"Here, let me," he said, helping Jazz, then me, with our coats and slinging them over a peg on the wall that was already piled high with cold-weather gear.

"How do you know Andy?" he asked, giving each of us a not-so-subtle once-over.

"Oh, I don't. We're here with Grayson Ba—"

"Gray, should have known. He's always with the prettiest girls," Logan said, looking from me to Jazz before I could finish my sentence.

Jazz beamed with the compliment. My mind was stuck on the *always* part. What did *that* mean?

"C'mon." Logan pulled open a white door to a crowded room. We wedged ourselves into a wall of people and got absorbed whole, squeezing our way to an open pocket. Sticky Wicket was doing a cover of "Howlin' for You," and the whole room seemed to sway along to the beat. It felt like we'd wandered into a secret underground club, which in a way I suppose we had.

The room was huge, with exposed brick walls and dim lighting. The cartoon version of *How the Grinch Stole Christmas* played on a huge flat-screen TV in the corner, for show apparently, since no one could possibly hear it over the music. There were couches and chairs and one couple going at it so hot and heavy on a giant beanbag chair, I felt like a voyeur. I stood on tiptoe and caught a glimpse of the shaggy-haired lead guitarist/singer, but couldn't spot Grayson. That's when the crowd parted slightly, and I saw him.

The drummer.

He was completely lost in the song, his eyes closed. He moved his head with the beat, hair flipping in and out of his face. The crowd swelled and blocked my view again. I moved to get a better look, leaning against a pillar and craning my neck. Grayson's eyes were open. He and the guitar player nodded to each other in mutual approval.

"Maddie's right," Jazz whisper-shouted into my ear.

I cupped my hand around her ear. "What?"

"You're a fiending lust puppy around him," she said, tilting her chin toward Grayson.

I covered my mouth, reeling from her observation. Crap, was I drooling?

I watched Grayson, his arms lean and muscled, as he banged out the beat. His taut gray CBGB shirt moved with his body; his mouth puckered slightly, skin flushed. I couldn't tear my eyes away from him. He finally spotted me in the crowd. My legs went weak. I ran a hand through my hair and smiled, watching him retreat into his drummer bliss once again. Then it was over with a thrash of the drums and the singer's loud voice promising, "Be right back!"

"Hey, there's a new game of king's cup forming, want to join in?" Logan asked, forcing his way through the crowd back to us.

Jazz and I stood frozen, his invitation hanging in the air.

"She'd love to," I said, nudging Jazz. She turned to me, eyes wide.

"Dare-to-be-great situation," I whispered.

"Hardly," she said.

"For Maddie then."

"For Maddie. And you'd better need a fire hose."

I laughed. "Fine. Gross, but fine."

We hooked pinkies in solidarity. "For Maddie."

"Sounds great!" Jazz said, turning toward Logan. He took her elbow and pulled her through the horde. I looked back to the band.

Grayson shielded his eyes with his hand, with exaggerated movements pretending to search for someone over the sea of heads until he caught my eye. He pointed toward the bar. I wove through the thick crowd, stealing glances at him as I made my way over.

Grayson was already pouring something from what looked like a wine bottle into a drink shaker when I broke through the crowd. He added vodka and put on the top.

"You made it," he said, shaking it vigorously over his shoulder.

152

That mouth.

Had been.

On mine.

"Yeah, pretty crazy."

"Andy's house always is," he said, placing the shaker on the bar and leaning below. He pulled out a few shot glasses and poured the purple liquid from the shaker. He pushed one of the glasses toward me. It had a picture of the Three Stooges on it. I brought it up to my face and sniffed, which Grayson found funny.

"What is it?" I asked.

"Absolut and acai berry."

"You lost me at Absolut."

"Tiff sells this stuff by the case. Acai-berry juice. Supposed to be like megavitamins, boosts your immune system. So half of this shot is good for you, and the other half not so good. Kind of like us," he said, raising his glass.

Us.

The shot was smooth and sweet. Warmth spread through my chest as it went down. I ran my tongue along my bottom lip, trying not to react to the tart berry flavor. Grayson leaned in closer, resting his chin on his hand.

"So. What did you think?" he asked.

"Of what? The drink?" I teased, pushing the shot glass toward him.

He rolled his eyes. "Of the band. Of me."

The first thought that came to mind was *I think everything about you is amazing, Grayson Barrett,* but I wasn't about to share it with him. Instead I leaned back and shrugged.

"Damn, Wren. Nothing?" he asked, reaching into the fridge and pulling out an orange Gatorade and some water. He cracked open the cap on the bottle of water and handed it to me.

"I thought we were pretty good, considering we haven't practiced in months," he said, taking a gulp of Gatorade.

"Do you want to know what I really think?" I asked, feeling brave from Maddie's pep talk.

He leaned on the bar again, curious. "Um, yeah."

What was I doing? My thoughts raced. The word *brainathiminal* popped into my head, and I laughed. Grayson waited. I picked at the label on my water bottle. "I think you're so . . . well . . . you're smart, you play the drums, you play lacrosse. Seriously, what don't you do?"

A slow smile crept across his face. "I never told you I played lacrosse."

Snagged.

"Well, so, I did some info digging. Same way you found me, right?"

"If you want to know anything about me, just ask."

There was so much I didn't know about him. Where to start? Logan's comment about Gray always being with the prettiest girls? God, no. What made him kiss me the other day? Did he want to kiss me now? Were we just friends?

"This," I said, touching his piercing lightly. He seemed vulnerable there. "Did it hurt?"

"That was sort of the point," he said, closing his eyes, leaning into my hand. My fingers took on a life of their own, moving through his hair. I didn't care that I didn't know much about him. All that mattered was this. Now. Giving into the overwhelming urge to press my lips against his again.

As if he read my mind, he opened his eyes, closed the space between us . . .

"Barrett, where've you been?"

We snapped out of our trance, brought back to Andy's house by a tall boy who stood a few inches away. Grayson stood up, arms straight, hands firmly on the bar.

"Luke. What's up?"

My eyes were drawn to the boy's mouth. His upper lip was slightly fuller than the bottom, giving the impression that he was frowning. Deep-set hazel eyes held mine more intimately than was called for, but it somehow felt impolite to look away.

"Grayson, aren't you going to introduce me to your girl?" he asked, leaning on his elbow against the bar.

"This is Wren," Grayson said. "And she's not my girl. Just a friend."

My breath locked up. How quickly he said it. I tried not

to flinch but felt hot with shame. Hadn't we just been connecting? Or was it my imagination? Not that a shot and me running my fingers through his hair meant I was his girl, but it meant we were . . . *something*, didn't it?

The corner of Luke's mouth upturned, eyes still on mine. Chin-length golden-brown hair framed what should have been a pleasant face. All the right parts were there, but there was something unnerving and charged about him.

"Luke Dobson," he said, nodding slightly.

"We went to Saint Gabe's together," Grayson added.

"Bro, we went to Saint Gabe's together?" Luke said, turning toward Gray. His shoulder brushed against mine, sending a shiver through me. He bowed his head like he was about to tell me a juicy secret.

"Wren, don't let him fool you. We were besties with testes. C'mon, fix me up with one of those, Grayson," he said, tilting his chin toward the drink shaker. Grayson pressed his lips together as if he didn't want to laugh, but he chuckled anyway. He freshened up the batch of Absolut and acai while Luke and I watched him.

He poured three shots and pushed two toward us. I reached for mine. I didn't even want it, but I had the feeling not taking it would mean something.

Luke held out his glass. "In vino veritas."

We clinked our glasses together. Luke downed his before I even had the shot to my lips. I could feel his eyes on me as the

Absolut and acai slipped down my throat. The same warmth filled my chest, but the mood was different. I placed the glass back on the bar and met his penetrating gaze, feeling self-conscious but not wanting to show it.

"So do you always get so close to your friends?" he asked.

"What?"

"You and Grayson seemed pretty chummy a moment ago. I was just wondering if that's how you are with all of your friends?"

"Luke, get out of her face," Grayson said, clapping a hand on his shoulder.

He looked at Gray's hand, then at me. "Dude, just talking. Maybe I want to be Wren's friend too," he said, eyes moving from my mouth back to my eyes.

"Ava's trying to get your attention," Grayson said, pointing. My eyes swept across the room to my favorite Sacred Heart schoolmate, Ava. She wore an oversize, metallic flower in her hair, which she pulled off as chic. Her face lit up when she spotted Grayson and Luke, but the moment she saw me between them, she frowned. The expression on her face read, *OMG, WTF are you doing with them?* If it weren't for the weird encounter that had just taken place, I might have enjoyed her reaction more. She gestured for Luke to come over.

"Ah, she can't let me out of her sight for long," Luke said to me. "Dude. I need to talk to you later." He pushed off the bar and pointed at Grayson, then snaked his way through the crowd. The whole scene left me feeling confused. Grayson put a hand on my shoulder.

"What was that about?" I asked.

"That," he answered, "was about Luke."

I wanted to ask him to elaborate when Jazz sidled up to me. Grayson offered her a shot, but she shook her head vigorously.

"We need to get out of here. Now," she whispered in my ear.

"Why? Did something happen with Logan?" I asked.

"No. I just . . . can't do this . . . I have to leave," she stated again.

Arguments filled my brain. *We just got here! Grayson and I came this close to kissing again! One more set!* But what did it matter? Truth was, I didn't feel comfortable at all. Not with Luke. Or Ava. Or even Grayson. The way he'd thrown out the "friend" remark so quickly. And as I recognized others from school—girls who might ask for notes in class but would snub you in the hallway—I wanted to leave too.

"If you want to stay with Grayson, I understand, but I'm outie," Jazz said. "I can pick up my stuff from your house tomorrow. I just had to sit through Darby Greene describing what she did to a guy in the bathroom. And by the way, if you stay, don't use the bathroom."

"No, let me just say good-bye to Grayson. We'll go."

"I'll wait for you by the coats," she said, heading toward the side door as quickly as the crowd allowed her.

Grayson was just finishing up a conversation with the guitar player. Unlike Luke, the guitar guy was an open book, loose and relaxed and holding out his knuckles to give me a fist bump.

"I'm Andy, little Caswell. *Mi casa es su casa*," he said. A moment ago this would have been charming; now it felt forced. I knocked my knuckles against his before he walked away.

"Grayson, I have to go," I said.

"What? Why? You just got here."

"Jazz feels sick. I want to make sure she gets home okay."

"Can you come back?" he asked, leaning on the counter like before.

"No," I said, ignoring the tingle of regret I felt as his eyes darkened.

"Let me walk you out." And before I could protest, he was behind me, his hand on the small of my back as he guided us toward the door. Jazz was in the laundry room, my coat in her hand, chatting with Logan. Grayson acknowledged him with a tilt of his chin. The lie I'd told about Jazz feeling sick was obvious. Grayson's eyes told me he knew it too.

"Feel okay?" he asked her.

Jazz handed me my coat. "Oh . . . no, I feel a migraine coming on. If I don't get out of here now, I'm going to be doubled over in pain." Score one for friend telepathy.

"I keep telling her a beer will fix that right up," Logan

said, raising his bottle. His remark was met with tense silence. Logan nodded to Jazz, then skulked back to the party.

I put on my coat, and we climbed up the stairs.

"Grayson, the band was great," Jazz said, leading the way down the dark alley.

"Glad you could enjoy it before the migraine hit."

We emptied out onto the street. A light dusting of snow was already on the ground, and flakes seemed to be falling sideways on us.

"Jazz, would you mind if I talked to Wren for a moment? Alone?" he asked. She prodded me toward him.

"No problem. I'll wait by the corner," she said to me. "Bye, Grayson."

We watched her walk toward the streetlamp. Finally Grayson spoke.

"If Jazz has a migraine, then I have dengue fever," he said, shrugging his shoulders against the cold. "Did I do something?"

"No, Grayson."

"Then what is it? I thought we were having a good time," he said.

"We were, I guess, then . . ." I trailed off, not knowing what to say. The truth made me sound pathetic.

"Come on, come back."

"Gray, I suck at parties, okay? I thought I could deal, but it's just not me."

"Wren, it's a party, not a pop quiz. What's to deal with?"

How could he understand? He *was* the party.

"I don't know half the people in there, and the people I do know I can't stand."

"And what half do I fit into?"

I toed the snow collecting at our feet. "Jazz wants to leave, and you'll be playing another set soon, and then what would I do? Call me later if you want. Or I'll just see you next week, at work," I said, backing away from him.

"You're sure we're okay? You can get home all right?" he asked, stepping from one foot to the other.

"Yep. No worries." I gave him an awkward wave and caught up to Jazz. What was I doing? Why was I walking away from him?

"Are you sure you want to leave? I'm fine leaving solo," Jazz said, linking her arm through mine as we braced against the cold.

She's not my girl. Just a friend.

"Yeah, totally."

TWELVE

GRAYSON

WAS I DESTINED TO WATCH WREN WALK AWAY?

Why couldn't it always be like earlier tonight, when I saw her in the crowd? That smile. *Pow*, like an electric jolt from across the room. I'd had to concentrate on not losing my sticks, focus on the song, play for her. That smile made me feel like Keith fucking Moon.

The snow fell faster. I closed my eyes and let the flakes hit my face. Part of me held out hope she'd change her mind and come back.

The other part of me was cold.

I walked back to Andy's, trying to shake the feeling that I'd done some douchebag thing to screw this up.

Things had been good . . . hadn't they? Why didn't I kiss her again? She was right there, in front of me. I could taste the sweetness of her breath, would have licked the acai from her bottom lip.

Until Luke and his *besties with testes* and in-your-face sociopathic stare conveniently got in the way. What was he up to?

I didn't realize how cold I really was until I walked back inside. My face and hands were numb. I stomped the snow off my Vans. I'd need another acai shot just to warm up; otherwise I wouldn't be able to hold my sticks. Then I realized the fire I'd felt about playing earlier had more to do with Wren being there than hanging out with my so-called friends.

"You so want to nail that girl."

Luke was at the foot of the stairs, holding on to the railing.

"What are you talking about?" I asked, not in the mood for a Dobson mindfuck.

"Grayson, come on. I know the Barrett work over when I see it. She seems a little pure for you, don't you think?"

Before I knew what was happening, I was down the stairs, my hands on Luke's chest, shoving him across the small walk space between the stairs and the door, until he hit the back wall. Shock flashed in his eyes when I put my forearm across his neck, pinning him. He turned his face sideways. I leaned into him with all my weight, got right in his face.

"Stay outta this, Dobson," I said through clenched teeth. I held him against the wall, panting harder than if I'd just run a full field clear.

"Are you done?" he asked.

I held him there, fighting every urge to crush his windpipe, until my breathing returned to normal. I backed off.

He grabbed my wrist, twisted my arm back behind me until a jagged pain shot through my biceps to my shoulder. My cheek met the wall, hard.

"What's happened to you, Barrett? You're as flabby as a chick," Luke breathed into my ear.

"Screw you."

He gave my arm another twist, just to the edge of pain, and let go.

"Dude, 'besties with testes,' really?" I asked, shaking the pain out of my arm.

Luke leaned back on the stairwell, grinning.

"You didn't like it? Thought it was catchy, myself. So what's up with the quiet chick if she's not a thrill or kill?"

Thrill or kill. This was Luke code—*kill* meaning a great hit, *thrill* meaning a great lay. Hearing him saying it, especially in reference to Wren, made me ashamed I'd ever thought it was funny. I wanted to deck him.

"Why can't you believe I'd be friends with a girl?"

Luke walked over to the dryer and pushed aside a leather jacket.

"Ah, Logan and his Stellas. Don't think he'll mind if we grabbed a few," he said, pulling two bottles out of the case. Logan preferred his beer from the bottle and would notoriously hoard his own secret stash during parties. It was something we kidded him about, but whenever the keg was tapped out he became the most popular guy in the room. After three years, we knew all of his hiding places.

Luke used the edge of the stairwell to pry off the caps, then handed me one of the bottles.

"Drop the friends bit. You were about to taste her tonsils before I broke it up."

"Fine. Why *did* you do that?" I asked, tipping the bottle to my mouth.

He swigged his beer. "Because Wren seems like the kind of girl to get serious with. And I need you *not* to be serious."

"Really?"

"Grayson, come on, why are you here? You're not that good a drummer. Are you forgetting the summer of debauchery? The five of us crossing Europe, big finish in Amsterdam?"

"Not interested."

Luke's eyes sharpened. "*Rosse buurt* was your idea. Beer, coffee shops with legal weed, chicks behind glass ready to do anything you want. And you're giving it up just because you got in trouble for the term-paper thing?"

"That 'term-paper thing'? You make it sound like all I got was detention."

"I know you've been through some heavy shit the past few months, but that's all the more reason to—"

"I'm out."

He stared at me, searching my face for some hint that I was messing with him.

"You can't back out. My old man changed his mind about financing my airfare—he set up an internship for me at the stock exchange next summer. Wants to brainwash me; thinks liberal arts is for pussies. So I have to get serious about this again."

"Hey, here's an idea . . . why don't you just get a job?"

"Yeah, keep up a four-point-eight GPA, get us to another championship, and hold down a real job. Even I can't do all that. C'mon, Grayson, you're the one who got the best hits. Andy, Dev, and Logan suck at that part. You can't tell me you're satisfied with the minimum wage you get from being a . . . wow, I can't even say it . . . wa . . . wa . . . wa . . . waiter. The hunt used to get you high."

He was right. It did get me high. Rarely a thought that what we were doing was wrong, that anyone would get hurt or caught. All a game.

"Just bang this chick if that's what you want. Get it out of your system."

I shoved him away from me.

"So that's what's stopping you, isn't it, this girl? The one who saved you."

"How did—"

"Ava's all nuclear about it. Gave me a friggin' earful when

166

I went over there. She doesn't think Wren is good enough for you. But that has more to do with the thing she still has for you than anything else."

My lip curled thinking of the *thing* Ava had for me. About a year ago, at another Andy Foley party, I'd been hammered to the point of stupidity. So gone, I'd checked out upstairs on the couch, wishing like hell my head would just stop spinning. It was pitch-dark, and someone snuggled up next to me.

"Grayson," a girl whispered, and then lips were on mine.

As sick as it sounded, this wasn't out of the ordinary at Foley's house. I'd been talking to so many chicks that night and just went with it. Then the lights clicked on. Luke stood across the room, fists clenched.

Ava. She'd been coming on to me for months, but I'd never given her any reason to think I was interested. Besides, Luke was into her, so even if I'd been remotely attracted, I would have made it a point to stay away.

The moment I realized what was happening, I sprung away with such force that I nearly knocked myself out on the corner of the coffee table. Without a beat Ava gasped and looked at Luke.

"Omigod, baby, you told me to meet you up here! I thought he was you."

Luke and I were the same height and build, so it wasn't completely off the wall, except for one thing. She'd said my name.

That night he either bought it or was too blitzed to care. Luke may have joked about Ava liking me, but I knew somewhere in the recesses of his twisted brain it had to bother him.

"How do you stand that?"

"What? Being her second choice? Easy. She's a warm body, no strings. What's not to like? We've got our whole lives to be serious. You used to understand that."

The door opened. Andy popped his head out.

"Dude, the girls are threatening to put on Gaga. We have to go back on."

"Yeah, be right there."

Andy came out to the laundry room, shutting the door behind him.

"So are you with us again?" he asked me, sliding his hands in his pockets. Then it hit me—being here wasn't about the drums or hanging out with my friends. They wanted me back, but not really me. They wanted Grayson the playah.

"He's undecided," Luke said, stepping back. "But I think we can convince him."

Andy clapped his hand on my shoulder. A small plastic Baggie filled with something dark fell from his pocket and landed with a *thwap* at his feet. I picked it up.

"Dude, really, do you have to travel with that?" I asked, handing it back to him.

"Gray, come on, you have to go to Amsterdam. Just keep

168

thinking . . . legal weed," he said, shaking the Baggie in front of my face like he'd just won a carnival fish. "Fucking Mardi Gras and Christmas all wrapped up into one, man."

"Yeah, yeah, I'm thinking about it."

"Cool, come on. Let's go."

"Give us a minute," Luke said. Andy grabbed a Stella and went back to the party.

"Here's the truth," Luke said, pointing at me with the neck of his beer bottle. "Ava's got it wrong. Wren Caswell is too good for you. Imagine how she'd react if she ever found out about all the chicks you've been with? She has no clue what you're really like, does she?"

"Stay away from her," I said. "She's got nothing to do with this."

"Well, she's screwing with your head. And I need you. You know I wouldn't mind having that conversation with her. Or maybe I could get Ava to do it. She sees her. Every day. You know how chicks can be so catty."

"Why are you doing this?"

"I need my wingman, Grayson. All there is to it."

"I'll think about it," I said, knowing this was the only thing that would get him to drop it for now.

"Don't take too long," he said, finishing the rest of his beer. "We need to get our cash flow going again. And Christ, Grayson, lighten up. It's a party. I can name about ten girls in there who would wrap themselves around you and make you forget all about Wren."

"Shut up," I said, heading back into the party with Luke close behind.

I tore across the room to the drums, practically shoving people out of my way. Andy had scribbled a set list. Only one song I wasn't familiar with, one song I'd have to think about. I smashed the drums, refueling myself from the conversation with Luke. Everything fell away, and I got lost in the sound. Picking up my head now and then. Wishing I could see Wren there.

Instead I saw Ava with that stupid silver flower in her hair. Draped across Luke, but eye-fucking me just the same. I kept my head down after that.

When we finished the set, I was soaking wet and ready to bolt. I found Andy.

"Dude, hey, I gotta cut out, not feeling so well," I said, putting a hand over my stomach.

"Ya sure, Gray? You can go upstairs and crash for a while if you want. It's only twelve thirty, my man. Early."

"Nah, I'll pick up my kit tomorrow, 'kay?"

I grabbed my jacket from behind the bar.

"Hey, how about one of those acai shots for me?"

Ava stood in my way, Luke right next to her.

"Luke knows how to make them," I said, maneuvering around them.

"Dude, where you off to?"

I shrugged him off as I darted through the crowd to the door. I took the stairs two at a time and burst out the side door. The cold air hitting my face felt good for about two seconds. Then it went right through me, practically turning my sweat to ice. What was wrong with me? I'd wanted to come. Parties used to be my thing. Now I couldn't get away fast enough. Luke's threat had pissed me off, but without Wren . . . the room felt full of strangers. How could I have ever thought this was a good idea?

After brushing the snow off the Chrysler, I drove away, even though I knew I should have footed it home. The adrenaline from the last set counteracted most of my buzz, and I drove extra slow, one destination in mind. Wren's house. She *had* said to call her, right? I knew where she lived, but this was the first time I'd gone there.

It was a large stone house, decorated with icicle lights for Christmas. A place I'd imagine Wren living. With the snow falling, it looked like a Christmas card. I wondered which window was hers. Was she awake? Sleeping? Thinking of me? I did feel like a stalker. I took out my phone to text her, then paused.

Was Luke right? Was Wren something I had to get out of my system?

No.

I'd never felt like this before.

Something had made her leave though, and if it wasn't a

sick friend then it was me. I'd had such hopes for this night: to kiss her again, to move past friendship . . . wait. She had to know I wanted more, that my intro to Luke was just . . . *Grayson, you effing moron.*

I drove off, heading for home.

Being with Wren meant something to me. I wanted to be serious. Whatever serious meant. Was this what it felt like to fall in love with someone? Was it too soon to know? And after all I'd done—could we ever have a normal relationship?

But when she'd run her hand through my hair, touched me, asked me, *Did it hurt?* . . . it was like everything else in the room had faded to black. Except her. And me.

And that was too important not to fight for.

THIRTEEN

"WREN, YOU SHOULD HAVE STAYED," JAZZ SAID, bringing her mug to her lips.

Our hot party personas had quickly returned to their former state—the two of us in flannel jammies sipping hot chocolate with a half-eaten package of double-chocolate Milanos between us on my bedroom floor.

"In my movie Grayson would be outside right now, throwing a snowball at this window to get my attention," I said, peeking out my bedroom curtain at the sound of a car passing. Two red taillights pierced the falling snow as they disappeared down the street. I let the curtain drop.

"And you'd race downstairs . . ." Jazz continued.

". . . and throw my arms around him, and he'd take my face in his hands, and we'd have one of those movie kisses that make you shift in your seat just imagining what it would feel like," I said, thunking back down on the floor next to her.

"'Since the invention of the kiss, there have only been five kisses that were rated the most passionate, the most pure. This one left them all behind,'" Jazz said, tilting back her head, eyes closed, smiling. "*The Princess Bride.* I bet your kiss with Grayson would be more epic than that."

I sighed. "Yeah, well. I got nothing, not exactly the après-party debrief Mads was hoping for."

We sat silent, the party ghosts of what might have been dancing around us. The night had started with such . . . possibility.

"We'll call her tomorrow," I said. "Maybe the Darby details will be enough."

"How I wish I could unhear that," Jazz said.

"You really can't tell me?"

"Nope. What I don't get is why she told me. Maybe because she was drunk . . . no, wait, *schnockered* . . . off her ass and wanted to shock the science geek. But it's the way she said it, like she could have been telling me how she ordered her sandwich at Subway."

"Sandwich?" Maybe some things were better left to my imagination.

"How could she be so casual? Is that what guys want?"

"I don't think so," I answered, wrestling a Milano out of the bag. "Maybe some do, I guess." With my track record, I had no business offering advice.

"In a way I envy Darby and her ability to be so matter-of-fact about it. I don't think I could ever be that way, Wren," she said, leaning on the edge of my bed, her long, dark hair fanning out against the flowered comforter. "And then the whole king's cup thing . . . I didn't get it. They called me out for not drinking when I didn't even know I was supposed to be having one. Logan took the drink for me."

"Well, that sounds kind of sweet."

"You'd think after watching all these romance movies I'd have some clue how to talk to a cute guy, but I was completely dumb about it. I couldn't think of one thing to say, and even if I had it was so freakin' loud. How could anyone hear anything? I wanted to make Maddie proud of me tonight. *Dare to be great . . .*"

"Jazz, it's a stupid drinking game."

"I know, but . . . Logan was cute. Nice. And I was so . . . pathetic around him."

"Pathetic? There's no way anyone would use that word about you. Jazz, you have such a clear vision of what you want out of life, and you're running a freakin' half marathon, which is about the furthest thing from pathetic I could think of. You blow me away. As corny as it sounds, some guy, someday, will appreciate that. And it won't involve king's cup."

"Well, you're my friend. You have to say that . . . thanks. But before that elusive perfect boy arrives, I'll be dateless for prom."

"You and me both," I said.

"What are you talking about? You have Grayson," she said, jabbing me in the shoulder.

"*Have?* Yeah, right."

"Wren, seriously, Grayson is into you. Why can't you see that?"

"He introduced me to someone as his friend—more specifically 'not my girl, just a friend.' What does that sound like to you?"

"Really?" she asked, sitting up straight. "That's . . . weird. He does *not* act like he wants to be just friends."

"Well, that's what he said. Maybe it was the party. One-on-one we're great, but being around all those people like Ava . . . it just didn't feel right."

"You'd better watch out for her," Jazz said.

"Why?"

"She was next to me during the king's cup game and kept grilling me about what we were doing there and if you and Grayson had a *thing*. Her words, not mine. She's morbidly curious about you guys. Seriously, sort of creepy."

"That's what I mean—like even though everyone is there having a good time, getting along to each other's faces—all this other unspoken stuff is going on," I said, thinking about the way Luke Dobson had acted around me.

Jazz stood up and tightened the drawstring on her pj bottoms. "If I don't stop eating these cookies, I'll be dragging my ass on my long run," she said, before leaving to go to the bathroom.

I got up and peeked out the window again. Steady snowfall covered the street in a blanket of white. Was Grayson still at the party? I didn't want to imagine him there, playing the drums, smiling at someone else. Maybe one little text to let him know I was thinking of him wouldn't hurt.

I grabbed my cell off my nightstand, punched in a text, and pressed Send before I could change my mind.

The text had been simple.

Hey. Sorry I had to leave.

A friendly gesture to make sure Gray and I were "okay," as he'd said.

I waited.

And waited.

And waited some more.

Complete. Radio. Silence.

Not that I expected him to drive over to my house to profess his . . . intense like and shower me with a dozen roses. But I expected . . . *something*.

And the expecting something sucked more than the party itself, because Grayson Barrett was the most unexpected something to come along in my semester of discontent. It was never about looking for him, it just . . . was. So I hated the feeling of twisted anticipation. I kept checking my phone and searching for him after school, hoping to see him leaning on the Chrysler like he had been for the last few weeks.

Nothing.

Both Jazz and Maddie knew enough not to bring it up anymore. We'd exhausted all the party talk by Tuesday. So by Wednesday, at least outwardly, life was back to normal. I thought of texting Grayson again, but I couldn't think of anything to say. There was a huge wedding booked at the Camelot for Friday, so I knew he'd be working, and I supposed it wouldn't be out of line to send a "Hey, are you working Friday?" text. So I did.

Crickets.

Which was worse. I tried to reason it away. Maybe he'd lost his phone. Maybe the battery was dead . . . for four days. Maybe he was busy with his dad, or school, or his life in general. But there was no reason for him not to text me. And while I went through the school day, absorbing most of what was taught, having lunch with Mads and Jazz and not bringing up the G-word at all, there was still that niggling little part of my brain analyzing the details to death.

The very last person I expected to discuss Grayson with was Ava.

Ava strolled up to me in Lit, a thick haze of flowery perfume following her. She wore her green blazer with the sleeves pushed to three-quarters, her cuffs peeking out the bottoms, making the Sacred Heart uniform as trendy as anything you'd see in a *Teen Vogue* fashion spread. She perched on the desk adjacent to mine playing with the silver heart that hung from her necklace as she spoke.

"Could you meet in Mrs. Fiore's office for lunch, Wren? We have to talk about the Spirit Club Christmas project."

I stared at her through my too-long bangs, chin in hand, and wondered why she was talking to me about Spirit Club, which I'd completely blown off after she'd dissed me about knowing Grayson.

"Hey, I know I was a complete bitch the other day, but we really need the numbers for this project. And, well, I was just surprised you and Grayson knew each other. Can you blame me?"

Again with the subtle dis. I remained a blank. She sat down, mouth curled in a conspiratorial grin.

"I was wrong, okay? I apologize. You two were so completely into each other at Andy's party. It was like no one else was there. He left a little while after you did, which is really saying a lot for him. Did you two hook up after the party?"

Suddenly I didn't care if she was Medusa come to life . . . she'd seen me with Gray. A witness. I caved just a little. Could she possibly be sincere? Jazz's warning to watch out for her remained in the back of my mind.

"Um, no."

"But you are together, right?"

How could I answer that?

Sister Katherine clapped her hands to bring the class to order.

"So, lunch? Meet me in Fiore's office, okay? C'mon, we work with the Saint Gabe's Key Club for the Christmas project. *Boys*," Ava said, before standing up and heading to her desk.

Boys. Didn't entice me. Especially since the boy I craved didn't go to St. Gabe's anymore. But out of sheer curiosity, at lunchtime I texted Maddie my change of plans, grabbed my brown bag and went to Fiore's office, expecting to find the Spirit Club assembled. Only Ava was present. Shoes kicked off, legs curled under her, Ava ate her salad seated in one of Mrs. Fiore's funky orange chairs.

"Hi, Wren, have a seat," Mrs. Fiore said. I placed my books on the floor, sat down, and rustled open my paper bag to pull out my turkey sandwich.

"So what are we doing for the Christmas project?" I asked.

"We're going to host Saint Lucy's annual Christmas party. It's a retirement home in Jersey City. It's so cute, all those adorable old people."

"Let's call them senior citizens," Mrs. Fiore said, gazing over her glasses at Ava. "As co-coordinators, you'll be acting as the liaisons with the home. I know I'm Spirit Club adviser, but I'd like to give you both as much responsibility as possible."

"Co-coordinators?" I asked Ava. Judging from her bright-eyed glow, this was supposed to be good news.

"Don't let the title scare you," Mrs. Fiore continued. "This event pretty much runs itself. Your job is to make sure we have enough volunteers and step in where you're needed so that the party runs smoothly. Everyone is required to meet here at school, and we'll head over together in the bus. We'll be back here by one o'clock, so it's not an all-day thing."

Ava pulled out a blue folder and handed me a list of names of Sacred Heart girls who had signed up for the event. I felt like reminding her that I wasn't one of them. That this event I was co-coordinator for was about the last way I wanted to spend a random Saturday morning. Instead I smiled and nodded, emptying the last of my juice box with a rattle.

"Let me know if you need help with anything. I'll also contact the local paper, so wear something pretty. You never know, if it's a slow news week, they might show up," Mrs. Fiore said, bringing her Precious Moments mug to her lips. I peeked at her ten-minutes-behind, time-warp clock and calculated how much was left of lunch period. Only five minutes. Ava gathered her things. I followed her lead.

"So have either of you given any thought to your top three college choices? February is right around the corner."

Ava rattled off not just three but five colleges, giving reasons why each made her list. I busied myself collecting my things, making sure my books were stacked in ascending size order, doing something, *anything*, so I wouldn't have to speak.

"And you, Wren? Had the chance to do any research?"

I threw out my trash and clapped my hands together.

"Well, I like Rutgers," I answered, picking up my neat stack of books from the chair, "but other than that I hadn't given much thought to anything. Well, except maybe to Harvard. Good school and all, but you know, I hear Boston winters pretty much suck, and I hate the Patriots, so not sure if it's going to make my list."

Mrs. Fiore's face contorted in mild confusion but then her chin drew up, eyebrows raised.

"I'll make these phone calls, pronto. This project sounds like such fun," I said, before turning on my heels. "See ya!"

My stomach knotted, but I felt an odd rise of triumph. I'd never dissed a teacher like that. I couldn't believe I'd gotten away unscathed, when I felt a hand on my shoulder.

"Omigod, I can't believe you just said that," Ava said.

"Was she pissed?" I asked.

"No, I don't think she got that you were talking about her little speech. She was too caught up with the fact that you said the word *suck* to her."

"So *you* know what I was talking about then," I said as we walked down the empty hall to our respective classes. The bell hadn't sounded yet.

"Yep. Fiore's given that 'You're not going to Harvard speech' for a few years now. It's her way of 'gettin' real,' as she says," Ava answered, her green eyes rolling upward. "She's cool though. I've gotten to know her through Spirit Club. Not a bad friend to have around here, you know?"

It figures Ava would consider Mrs. Fiore a friend.

"I just don't like being told what I can't do," I said.

"And that's why you're just the kind of person we need for Spirit Club. I hope you don't mind that I picked you as co-coordinator. I think it'll be fun hanging out again."

I kept waiting for the subtle put-down. She was being too nice to me.

"Besides," she said, leaning into me, "if you're dating Gray, we'll probably hang out more often too. Luke is Grayson's best friend."

"Luke, right," I answered, deciding to do a little digging of my own. "So you two are together?"

Her face scrunched in thought. "We haven't labeled it or anything, but we gravitate toward each other if we're in the same place, know what I mean? He's so freakin' hot, it's like I can't resist him. That mouth. Mmmm," she said, her voice becoming gravelly. "He really knows what to do with it."

I squeezed my eyes shut, willing my mind to stop creating mental pictures of Luke's mouth and what he could do with it. *T to the M to the fucking I, Ava.*

"How about you and Grayson?" she asked, wiggling her eyebrows suggestively.

"Excuse me?" I asked.

"C'mon. He's pretty hot."

My mind blanked. What was I supposed to say? He sure as

hell gave off the vibe of someone who knew what to do with his mouth, his hands . . . everything. But touching his eyebrow, running my fingers through his hair, a kiss that I was beginning to think I imagined? That didn't qualify as anything that could be described as . . . well . . . mmmmmmm. At least not to anyone but me.

"We have fun," I answered, which encompassed the whole of our relationship at the moment. The bell rang. The patron saint of getting out of embarrassing conversations interceded and I didn't need to elaborate as we were caught up in the rush of everyone getting to their next period. Ava waved and trotted off to class, leaving me unsettled. As if the last thirty minutes had been all a show. But for who, I wasn't sure.

Before class I reached into my bag and checked my messages.

One reply from Maddie that made me chuckle.

WTF? Ava doesn't even EAT.

But still nothing from Grayson.
Nothing.

WREN CASWELL IS TOO GOOD FOR YOU.

Luke Dobson's words were a time bomb. I hadn't given it a second thought when he'd said it, knew he was just trying to get in my head. But as I was about to answer Wren's text, which had been adorably vague and shy . . .

Hey. Sorry I had to leave.

Badaboom.

The truth hurts.

She *was* too good for me, and I'd known it since the day she saved my sorry ass from choking. I'd hypnotized myself into believing I deserved her. She was right to leave Andy's party and better off getting far, far away from me. The inconvenient thing was . . .

I was pretty sure I was falling in love with her.

Luke's threat to speak to Wren gnawed at me. She didn't need to fall victim to the Dobson mindfuck, and if I didn't do something, I knew he would get to her one way or another. The best way to avoid that was for me to stay away. For now. Or forever.

So I lay on my bed on a Thursday afternoon, pondering what route out of Wren's life I should take and deciding whether to answer her second timid but logical "Hey, are you working Friday?" text, because yes, in fact, I was working on Friday, but if I took the *Gray the total douchebag* route, I'd just exit stage left. Never text or call again. End of story.

And the conclusion I came to as I stared at my popcorn ceiling (which was really more like an acne-vulgaris ceiling, because it sure as shit didn't resemble any popcorn I would eat) was that I couldn't do that. I wanted to see her again. I kept thinking of her eyes, the depths of them, the way she looked right into me, and I wasn't afraid of what she'd find. Even though I should have been, because if Wren knew all the shit I'd pulled . . . the way she looked at me would change forever.

And that was instant freakin' karma.

"Grayson? You home?"

My rumination was interrupted by Pop's voice. I grunted something that hopefully sounded like "Come in" and continued my staring match with the ceiling.

"When did you get in? I didn't hear you."

I propped myself up on my elbows.

"About fifteen minutes ago," I lied. I'd been home for about two hours, skipped out on Physics. Ditching at Bergen Point was easy. They didn't hunt you down and publicly flog you like at St. Gabe's. I'd get a slap on the wrist and a computer-generated phone call telling Pop and Tiff I'd missed fourth block, which I could easily intercept, and no one would be the wiser. Call it a mental-health break.

He inhaled and made a face.

"Smells like a sewer in here."

Pop swung my door back and forth to get the airflow going, then gave two clicks to the ceiling fan. Satisfied, he pulled out my desk chair and sat down, gathering his plaid robe around his bare legs.

"I'm about to crawl the effing walls," he said, leaning back and swiveling toward me. Pop was usually hair-gelled, suited-up, real-estate-mogul perfection. His eyes looked rested, but his hair stuck up every which way, like he'd been trying to pull it out of his head. Tiffany had made Pop go cold turkey— no smokes, no Bushmills, no trans fats. Sugar was next on the roster. He was not a happy camper.

"Feeling better?" I asked.

"Yeah, like a cool mil," he said.

"What's up?"

These father-son powwows had been routine in the weeks following my expulsion from St. Gabe's. At first it had been all anger. *You're smart, effing brilliant,* he had yelled. How could I do this to myself? To him? To Tiff? To my mother, *who always deserved better?* On nights he'd been mellowed with Bushmills, there were high school confessions. Things he'd screwed up royally himself, admitting that if he'd been smart enough to pull off what I did, he probably would have done it too. That if I needed money, why hadn't I just come to him? And more anger with the brow piercing . . . *You come home with a tat and I'll kill you, Grayson.*

But things had changed when school began. I spent less time staring at my ceiling and more time trying to pick up the pieces of my life. Our one-on-ones became few and far between. Something was up.

"I've been talking to your mother," he said.

I rubbed my eyes. *Oh, what, now?*

"Grayson, this is a wake-up call for me," he said, patting his chest. "Life's too short. You need to have a relationship with your mother and her family."

"Thanks, Dr. Phil. I do have a relationship with them. It's just not a good one."

"I mean a more solid one. Once you had a car, you were supposed to visit more. What's it going to take?"

A rewiring of my frontal lobe.

"She's having a tree-trimming party—" he began.

"Oh, no fucking way, Pop."

"Hey, cool it," he said. He wasn't enough of a hypocrite to

188

really mind my dropping an F-bomb with him, but he had to pretend. "Tiffany found a box of ornaments up in the attic— belongs to your mother, some antique hand-blown glass she thought she lost. Your mom would like you to bring them and stay for the party."

"You're kidding."

"You could bring Wren. Have some fun, Grayson. You're allowed, you know."

Hearing Wren's name made me smile. I could practically hear Grier saying, *When and Gwayson.*

"I'll think about it."

"It's nice to see you getting serious about a girl, Grayson."

"Serious? Pop—"

"I know, I know . . . you don't want to talk about this with your old man, but even in the ER I could see the way you were around each other. She seems like a nice girl, Gray," he said, rising from the chair with a creak. "I always liked those Sacred Heart girls. Thought those plaid skirts were cute."

Guess the horndog doesn't fall far from the tree.

"Dinner's at six, when Tiff gets home. Will you be around?"

"I guess," I said. My butt vibrated.

I made a deal with myself. If it was Wren, I'd answer. I could explain away two texts, but ignoring three would just be plain cruel. I stared at the screen.

Fuknuts, cum pick up ur drums @ Andys. L

Andy's house had been the hub of my St. Gabe's extracurricular life. And it was one constant after-party. After school. After lacrosse practice. After games. As a freshman, I had my first beer in Andy's basement. It was also where I got my V-card stamped by some girl who was friends with Andy's older brother. The Foleys were loaded and spent a good portion of their time working for it, overcompensating for their absence with a rec room that was pretty much a wet dream. Plasma TV. Killer sound system. Every video-game console as soon as it came out. The bar was always fully stocked with premium liquor, although I wasn't sure how much of that was their doing and how much was Andy's and his brother's.

Andy's basement was also where Operation Amsterdam was conceived.

The name was a goof, but it stuck, because it was better than saying "selling stolen goods to finance our post-graduation trip to Europe." We all liked the sound of backpacking across Europe, but Amsterdam, an eighteen-year-old's version of Disneyland, was our goal. Our reward for four years of breaking our balls at St. Gabe's.

And the whole thing had been started so innocently . . . by yours truly.

I'd met Caitlyn just over a year ago in the fall at a lacrosse tourney in West Orange. She was there watching her best friend's brother play. I'd told her she looked bored, and she answered, "Not anymore." We hung out on the sidelines, and by the end of the game I had her digits. We spent a week or so exchanging racy texts, then set a date to meet. This was pre-Chrysler, so our hookups were limited to whenever I could catch a ride from Andy's brother, who was seeing someone from the same town.

Our relationship was no-strings-attached, purely physical. The first night we hooked up, we did it in her pool house.

This pool house made Andy's basement look about as tricked out as a grass hut, and I wasted no time bragging about it to Luke. When Caitlyn texted me that she was going to Cabo with her family for winter break and she'd have to cancel our plans, I joked with Luke that we should go to her house anyway. He talked Andy and his brother into going too, because we had nothing better to do, so the four of us headed over.

We didn't intend to take anything that first time, just hang out. I'd seen Caitlyn punch in the door combination for the pool house, and I tried it—making sure my hand was in the sleeve of my jacket so I didn't leave fingerprints. Once inside we weren't that careful. We drank the six-pack we'd brought with us and watched a Vin Diesel flick while the guys pushed for details of my hookups with Caitlyn. All in all a pretty boring night, and at some point, it felt *wrong*. We were about to leave when Luke suggested we make the visit worth our while by swiping some stuff.

Andy and his brother were stoked by the idea, which I

didn't get, because they already owned half the stuff anyway. We ended up taking a small flat-screen TV. The whole time I felt detached, not really participating but not stopping them either. We left without the headlights on and tore down the street, pumped up with adrenaline from doing something so stupid. We stopped at a White Castle on the way home and didn't talk about it again.

Until Caitlyn got back from break and wanted to show me her tan lines.

"Dude, you have to see her again. Show her you're not afraid of going there—you're not guilty of anything," Luke said, almost making me believe it was true.

My nerves were on edge when I saw Caitlyn, but it was same old, same old. We hung out in the pool house. The TV we'd taken had been replaced by a bigger model. There was no mention of anything that had happened while she'd been away. I left that night, promising to call her, but I knew I wouldn't. I changed my number the next day. And I never saw her again.

That was when the seed was planted. Hadn't it worked out great? We didn't even need to break in, Luke said. If we could do this . . . find a way to get in without being obvious, get to know the lay of the land, find out when a family would be there and when they wouldn't . . . It was too perfect. I told him I thought we'd just been lucky. He said he was going to prove me wrong.

And he did. Swiping a gold necklace that he sold for the equivalent of five of my term papers. Our Amsterdam fund was born, but if we were really going to make a go of it, Luke said, we needed to get smarter.

We didn't use our real names or personal cell phones, just in case there was a slipup. Logan and Dev, our lacrosse teammates, each wanted in, so then we were six. At first we took turns finding hits, but soon enough our talents sorted us out. Luke and I were best at finding the right mark. Andy, Dev, and Logan swiped the stuff. Andy's brother unloaded it.

The selling part was a bit trickier. Andy's brother dealt with the electronic stuff, the ones with serial numbers, the stuff that could be traced. Gold was a cinch to sell—Luke found a guy through Spiro willing to take our stuff, no questions asked. Deep down I knew what we were doing was wrong, but since I wasn't physically stealing anything and was directly involved with only two or three hits, I could kid myself that I wasn't a thief. I was only doing my part for the team. And with each successful job, we became more confident. Cocky. We were gods, on and off the lacrosse field.

Occasionally someone's conscience would bubble up, but Luke was fantastic at talking anyone down from the ledge of *I want out*. We weren't robbing people blind. Just lifting stuff here and there. GPS systems, iPods, jewelry people probably didn't even wear anymore. Extra stuff, easily replaceable.

And we ate it up, all of us, the feeling of being . . . invincible.

So walking into Andy's on that Thursday afternoon felt a bit like stepping back in time. Andy's brother had moved on to Seton Hall, but the rest were assembled as always. Logan and Dev were planted on the futon playing *Black Ops* on the wide-screen. Andy had headphones on, strumming his guitar. Luke was sitting behind the bar, to-go cup of coffee in one hand, *The Life of Pi* in the other. I could picture myself there too, walking in with a sack of burritos from Taco Bell, setting up my laptop, writing my term papers, running my business. All separate parts of a whole. Would it be that easy to fall into it again?

Then I saw my drums. Or, more specifically, my bass drum, with a huge tear. Andy pulled off his headphones when he saw me.

"Grayson, sorry about the drum, man. Things got out of hand. Some chick put her heel through it. Accident."

"Accident," I repeated as I knelt down to assess the damage.

"Yeah, wouldn't have happened if you'd stayed at the party," Luke said. I stood up and turned to him; he was still reading. He used a drink stirrer to mark the page, closed the book, and placed it on the bar next to his coffee.

"Nah, probably would have happened anyways. Things were pretty outta control when I left," I said, breaking down my kit.

"Grayson, why the rush? Hang out awhile, man," Andy said.

"Yeah, hang out," Luke said, hands in pockets.

Logan and Dev came up behind me. I stood up with the feeling I was about to get jumped . . . mentally, at least.

"What?" I asked.

They all just stared at me. Finally Logan spoke.

"Gray, you gotta come back. It hasn't been the same without you around."

"We're sorry about, you know, not calling—" Dev began.

"But really, dude, if the great Grayson Barrett could get caught, what chance did we have?" Andy finished.

"Like it or not, you're the proverbial glue that holds us together, Grayson," Luke said.

If I'd heard this speech six months ago, I would have fallen into step again. Now it seemed contrived. Getting kicked out of school for selling term papers was humiliating enough, but I was picking up the pieces, working my way through it. Getting caught for the Operation Amsterdam stuff would be damaging beyond anything these idiots would be prepared for. I may have missed St. Gabe's, but I was not willing to go back to the way things were. I'd broken free of the cave and the shadows on the wall. Maybe I wasn't too much of a hedonist for *The Republic* to sink in after all.

"You're doing fine without me," I said.

"Maybe we are," Luke said, "but we're expanding a bit."

"Yeah, my brother's got a lock on apartments at school, an easy hit," Andy said.

"And none of us can score the best hits like you, Gray," Logan said.

"Well, except maybe for me, but I'm just one. Strength in numbers," Luke said, putting a hand on my shoulder.

I returned to breaking down my kit, silent, but their questions and pleas swirled in the air around me.

"I'm rusty," I said. It was all Luke needed to hear.

"Dude, please. It's like riding a bike. Easy. Remember that hit you were working on, the chick from Hollister in Staten Island? Pick up with that again. You'll be back in the swing of it in no time."

Allegra.

"No, don't think so," I said.

Luke smirked and pulled out his phone. My stomach sank as he scrolled through his contacts and lifted the phone to his ear.

"What are you doing?"

His eyes were planted on mine.

"Hi, can I speak to Wren, please?"

I charged toward him, reaching for the phone, but he spun his back to me, moving away. Logan and Dev grabbed my arms. I squirmed against their hold, but four months without so much as lifting a five-pound barbell and I was no match for them. Only Andy appeared shocked at what was happening.

"Luke. Don't," I begged.

He turned to me then, still on the phone.

"Oh, she's at yoga? No, no message, I'll just call back later. She'll be in after seven? Okay, thanks, Mrs. Caswell," he said, pressing End. He slid the phone back in his pocket. Logan and Dev let go.

"You're fucking crazy."

"No, I think *you* are," he said, getting in my face. "I think getting tossed from school did a number on you. And since I'm your best friend, it's my job to shock you out of it. We've been working on this since last winter. Don't quit now. Wren is inconsequential."

My jaw clenched. "Wren is not inconsequential."

"Tell you what, just go see the Hollister chick—sniff it out—then you can do whatever you're doing with Wren, take her to freakin' prom for all I care. My theory being that once you get a taste again, you won't want to stop."

"And after I do this, you'll just let me walk away?"

He folded his arms across his chest. "Sure, you can walk away and have polite, monogamous sex with your uptight, little, quiet chick. Although, yoga, hmm, she must be very bendy."

"Fine, then," I said. "Just stay away from Wren."

He held out his hand. Andy chanted my name, quietly at first, "Gray-son, Gray-son," until Logan and Dev joined in. I shook Luke's hand. He grinned.

"Enough of this girlie-man shit. Let's have a beer," he said.

MY MOTHER STOOD IN MY BEDROOM DOORWAY, waving two dresses at me.

I took out my earbuds. "What?" I asked, propping myself up on an elbow.

After school I'd told her I needed a quick nap, but the truth was the thought of going to work and facing Grayson made my stomach churn. It was a pathetic, annoying feeling, and I wanted it to go away. He hadn't texted me all week, but there'd been a strange phone call to the house yesterday. *A boy*, my mother had said, prodding me to elaborate. The caller ID read Unknown.

I hoped it was Grayson, but I didn't need anyone to know that.

"The black one or the burgundy one?" my mother asked, annoyance edging her voice.

"The black one."

"Right, it's slimming."

She disappeared in a rush, the dresses fluttering on their hangers in her wake. I put my iPhone on my bedside table and followed her to her room. She was already putting her arms through the sleeves of the black dress.

"Could you zip me?" she said, standing with her back to me. I pulled up the zipper, which stopped at the middle of her back—leaving a good three inches of zipper just gaping, like a taunting, sharp-toothed mouth saying, *Fatty!*

"Um, Mom," I said.

"Is it stuck?" she asked.

I tried bringing the two sides closer together, but even with all the breathing in and the tight, binding underwear that promised to take off ten pounds, there was still a good inch between both sides of the zipper. She muttered something under her breath, grabbed the burgundy dress from her bed, and disappeared through the bathroom into her walk-in closet.

"Why all the fuss?" I asked, following.

"I didn't tell you?" she asked, walking out of her closet in the burgundy dress and standing in front of her bathroom mirror. The size tag stuck out at the nape of her neck. I walked over and tucked it in.

"Tell me what?" I asked.

"We're meeting Brooke and Pete for dinner. Pete's parents will be there. This is the first time we're all meeting since . . ." She hesitated a moment, squeezing out some beige liquid makeup from a tube onto the back of her hand, then smoothing it onto her face with her fingers. "Well, since the announcement."

"Oh," I answered. My mother hadn't brought up Brooke's pregnancy with me, but I knew it was something she thought about . . . a lot. I'd seen her sneaking her mini pretzels and Nutella—her go-to comfort and stress foods—more and more over the past few weeks.

"I'm heading over to the Camelot just to make sure everything's in place. Eben will be maître d' for the wedding tonight."

"Eben's maître d'? He must be stoked!" I said.

"He's earned it." She dipped a brush into light cosmetic powder and twirled it onto her face until her skin was matte perfection. "I just wish we had more to offer him."

"What do you mean?" I asked, leaning against the counter.

She placed the brush back in a cup on the vanity, then fished through her makeup bag, pulling out a compact of different shadows. She fumbled with it for a minute.

"Here, let me," I said, taking it out of her hand. Her eyelids twitched as I smoothed on champagne-colored shadow with a brush.

"Business is down from last year, even after the renovations," she said. I picked out a contour brush and ran it across a shade called Fawn to put in the crease of her eyelids.

"But we've been busy," I said, using the tip of my finger to smudge the color to her outer lids. My mother blinked fast a few times, then glanced at her reflection in the mirror. She turned her face from side to side with approval.

"Brooke told me about what you said on Thanksgiving—"

"What?"

"About how you thought you could run the Camelot someday. Wren, I had no idea."

"Mom, that was random," I answered, grabbing an amber eye pencil. "Close 'em."

She obeyed, and I gently pulled her lid taut to draw a line as close to her lashes as possible.

"We have an offer on the land. A builder. They want to put condos—"

"Don't talk, unless you want crazy Cleopatra eyes. Almost done," I said. My heart sank. The tug of sadness I felt surprised me. Tears clouded my vision as I finished up. I stepped back to admire my work.

Her eyes met mine and softened. "Wren."

"Close one more time. I just have to smudge the line—"

She took my hands in hers.

"Mom, I don't know why I'm crying. It's fine, really."

"Believe me, I thought long and hard about this, but the

Camelot isn't the place it once was—people want exotic locations."

"And cupcakes," I said, pulling my hands away and swiping a tear.

"Did you really want to run it someday?" she asked, leaning against the vanity counter, arms folded.

Having the question asked point-blank made me realize that my answer was a resounding *no*. The Camelot had only been a "just in case," because it felt so comfortable. Safe. The news still made me feel ungrounded. The Camelot had defined so much of our lives. My life. Everything kept changing so fast; I wondered if I'd ever catch up.

"No," I answered, reaching over to finally smudge the liner. Satisfied, I stepped away. "It was just an idea, that's all. I change my mind a hundred times a day."

"I would never want any of you to be forced into taking over the business. I fell into it myself. The Camelot was my grandfather's baby, but he would have known when to get out."

"Does the staff know?"

She spoke as she put on a coat of mascara. "No, I haven't said anything. I've got mixed feelings about closing. We've tried so hard, and I hate the idea of knocking the place down, but in the end we're just not making our nut. And it's an excellent offer. This influx of cash will help with so many things, but it's still not an easy decision. Some of the staff are like family. It's why I've been so tense. Well, part of the reason. I'm not even sure I should have told you," she said, putting the lash wand back into the mascara tube. "I think I just wanted to hear how it sounded."

"Mom, don't shut me out of something this important. You can talk to me," I said. "About Brooke's situation too. I can handle it."

She squeezed my shoulder. "Wren, I'm not shutting you out. Not purposely anyway. You don't need to worry about any of this. You've got enough on your plate with school. I'm not sure I'm handling it that well, myself. It's a lot to wrap my mind around. I didn't think I'd be a grandmother this soon."

"You'll be a young grandma," I said, nudging her. "A hot, young grandma."

"I'm glad you see it that way," she said, putting her makeup bag into the vanity drawer. "Hey, better get a move on. We're leaving in fifteen."

"Do I have time for a shower?" I asked, panicked.

"A really quick one," she said, eyeballing her clock. "Go, go."

The Camelot was as frenzied as usual. Eben pushed through the doors of the Lancelot ballroom, looking more like a groom than a maître d'. I felt that tug of sadness again. It was hard to believe this place would be leveled for condos. Did he have a clue? I would miss seeing him on the weekends.

He beamed when he saw my mother.

"Ruthie, I won't let you down," he said, "but it would help if your daughter was on time."

"It's my fault completely," I volunteered, taking off my coat.

"Here, I'll take this," Mom said, grabbing my purse.

Eben led me by my elbow into the banquet room.

"Wren, I do *not* want to screw this up. This is huge for me. I know we usually pal around, make jokes, but I can't be that person tonight. So in case I snap at you or something, just know I'm in management mode, nothing personal."

"Eb, you'll be awesome. My mom totally believes in you. So do I," I said. "No worries. I won't give you anything to snap at me for. By the way, am I allowed to say you're quite, um, dashing in your tux?"

"Thank you, luv. Calvin Klein. Damn well better make me look dashing," he said. "And Miss Wren, as my last official duty as your pal this evening—you and your favorite dark-haired new hire are working the head table. So scoot over to Guinevere's Cottage. They're setting up now."

I gave Eben a quick kiss on the cheek and hurried off across the parking lot to the cottage. My stomach became a jangle of nerves again at the thought of seeing Grayson. *Just be casual, Wren.* Even though the first thing I wanted to blurt out was, *Why haven't you texted me all week?* I had to come off like I didn't care.

Grayson was taking champagne glasses out of a storage

crate and lining them up on the bar. The cottage was a reno-
vated home from the 1800s, and the ceilings were low. This
particular feature gave the cottage its cozy feel, but anyone
who was over six feet had trouble navigating the space. The
top of Gray's head was only about three inches away from
grazing the ceiling, which made him look gargantuan. He
smiled when he saw me, but it wasn't the smile of reuniting
with someone you hadn't seen in a week. More like an *Oh,
you're here* kind of smile.

"Hey, what's up?" I asked, attempting to be casual, even
though my heart was about to jump out of my mouth.

Before he could answer, Lisa, a Camelot seasonal employee,
came bounding out of the kitchen with a pitcher of ice. She
stowed it behind the bar, her dark, angular haircut swaying
with her every movement.

"Hey, Wren, how's it going?" she asked. "We have to tell
Tall-Drink-of-Water here to be careful." She elbowed Grayson in a way that made my stomach tighten.

"Well, Leese, guess you have to remind me to duck when
I'm going through a doorway," he said, pushing his hair aside
to show a red mark. I covered my mouth to keep from laughing in spite of the jab of jealousy I felt when Gray called her
Leese. How long had they been out here?

"Come on, Wren, help me cut up the garnish," she said,
grabbing my hand. I ducked as we walked into the small
kitchen.

"Wow, the help has gotten decidedly foxier since I've been away at school," she whispered, handing me a lime. I reached for the paring knife and cutting board, doing my best to disregard her apparent attraction to Grayson.

"Mmm, hmm," I mumbled, cutting the lime lengthwise so I could make fresh wedges.

"Dave's going to be tending bar for cocktail hour in here. Damn, I haven't seen him since September. Think maybe he'll let me sneak a little sip of something? I've got a raging hangover from last night. I'm so relieved my exams are over. I'm surprised Joshie isn't here. His exams must be over too, no?"

I shrugged, finishing up the lime. "Not sure."

"Hey, um . . ." She stopped midsentence and motioned with her head out toward the parlor, mouthing, *What's his name?*

"Grayson," I whispered.

"Um, Grayson, can you bring us that white compartment thingie that holds the fruit on top of the bar?" she asked, collecting the lemon wedges she'd sliced up.

"Sure," he called back.

One plus about working with Lisa was that she held up the conversation all on her own. Perfect sometimes but not quite what I envisioned when I heard I'd be working with Grayson. He walked to the doorjamb and made an exaggerated motion to avoid it by ducking. Lisa batted her eyelashes and grabbed the condiment holder from his hands.

"Thanks, babe," she said. "Here, can you open these?"

Grayson took the jar of maraschino cherries from Lisa and twisted off the top.

"Honey, I'm home!" Dave-the-bartender called from the front door.

Lisa wiped her hands quickly on a bar towel and ran out of the kitchen, squealing.

"Crazy Davy!" she said, before disappearing down the hallway to greet him.

Grayson leaned toward me and whispered, "Does she ever shut up?"

I giggled, taking the jar from him. "Not really."

He leaned on the counter next to me as I placed the cut-up fruit garnish into the various compartments. I handed him a jar of olives, my thoughts racing.

"Could you?" I asked, avoiding his eyes and trying to think of an appropriate way to ask him why he hadn't answered my texts.

"My pleasure," he said, inflecting a formal tone to his voice, then gritting his teeth when the jar top didn't budge as easily as the last one. He took the bar towel, wiped the lid, then tried again, finally opening it with a pop.

He handed me the jar. "Do people normally order the kind of drinks that need to be garnished?"

"Well, you've got to be prepared," I answered, feeling so

damn foolish that we were discussing fruit. "And besides, it makes it pretty. I didn't hear from you all week."

My last sentence just hung there as the olives thunked into their compartment.

"Yeah, sorry. It's been a crazy week, and my phone's been acting all wonky. I didn't get your texts until this morning. It does that sometimes. Weird. But since I figured I'd see you, I didn't answer them."

I stared at him until he looked away. *That* was his excuse?

"I'll take these out there," he said, grabbing the tray.

"Wonky," I said to myself as I wiped up the counter. When I turned around, Chef Hank came into the kitchen, arms full of containers of hors d'oeuvres that needed to be heated. He placed them on the counter.

"No worries, Wrennie. No tiny hot dogs today," he said, clicking on the oven.

A no-cocktail-weenies party usually meant a great night, but not this time. The bride was one of those divas who wanted everything yesterday, and no matter how quickly it was delivered, it wasn't quickly enough. Bridal-party glasses were to be full at all times, all bridal-party dinners delivered first. I half expected them to ask us to cut their food and accompany them to the bathroom. We worked like dogs through most of dinner, so much so that Grayson said in passing, "Christ, I feel like I'm getting bitch slapped every time I go out there." It felt nice to have some common ground with him.

After every dinner had been served, and every glass filled yet again, I found my way to the break room. Lisa was regaling the rest of the staff with stories from the cocktail hour. I wanted to find some place quieter. The darkened vestibule adjacent to the swinging doors of the ballroom was just the ticket. The band was on break, and dinner music played. Frank Sinatra. I closed my eyes and drifted off with "Summer Wind." Moments later I felt someone in front of me and opened my eyes. Grayson.

He twirled a pink daisy between his fingers. Without saying a word, he tucked the flower into my hair, behind my ear. I felt the warmth of his hand next to my cheek as he untangled his fingers from the tendrils that had escaped my French braid. He stepped back to admire his work.

"That fell out of Bridezilla's bouquet. It made me think of you."

I blushed. "Crazy night, huh? I had to take a moment to myself."

"Yeah, loud in the break room," he said. "I was just going to grab a soda before we have to become slaves again. Want one?"

"That sounds great, thanks."

"Be right back," he said.

I leaned against the wall, giddy from the upturn of my evening.

Moments after Grayson left, Eben came through the

swinging doors, throwing up his hands, his face contorting into a silent scream.

"Rough night?" I asked, wincing.

"Rough night? This wedding is the bridal equivalent of a Tarantino film. I almost wish I smoked," he said, running a hand over his face. "At least it's half over."

"That's very glass-half-full of you," I answered. He inspected my hair.

"That's not from Bridezilla's bouquet, is it?" he asked.

"Oh, it fell out. Grayson gave it to me," I said, touching the flower.

Eben snapped his fingers in front of his face to reboot. "Okay, I've got about five until I have to be ringmaster again . . . so, spill."

"Spill what?"

"I don't see any other girls with daisies in their hair, so . . . What's going on with you and Grayson?"

"Um, nothing."

Eben rolled his eyes. "Nothing? Get a clue already, Wren. He likes you."

"Well, he's acting . . . weird."

"And you aren't?"

"No, I'm not," I answered, glancing over my shoulder to see if Grayson was coming back yet.

Eben put his hand on my shoulder. "What do you want?"

"What do you mean?"

210

"I mean when you think about Tall, Dark, and Mysterious, what do you want?"

What did I want? I wanted to see him more than once or twice a week at work. I wanted to hear the way his voice lowered when he spoke my name. I wanted to run my tongue across his bottom lip to see if it made him shiver. I clapped my hand across my eyes.

"Exactly. What are you waiting for?"

"But when? How?"

"I can't maître d' your tryst, Wren, but I'll tell you what," he said, reaching into his pocket to pull out his key ring. He fingered through the keys until he came to a shiny silver one and loosened it. He gestured for me to take it.

"What's this?"

"The key to the love shack," he answered.

"And what am I supposed to do with it?"

He stepped back, his brows bunched up in confusion. "You mean Josh or Brooke never put you wise to Saint Gwen, the Patron Saint of Clandestine Work Hookups?"

"Um, no, Eben."

"Well, let's just say, Guinevere's Cottage is a lovely place to be alone."

"Are you kidding me? Have you ever?"

"That's for you to speculate and me to never tell. Wren, I'm not saying go ravish him; it's just a place with no distractions, quiet, dark," he said, lowering his voice at the word *dark*.

"Yeah, right," I said, feeling slightly queasy. "How would I even get him over there?"

"Use your imagination. Tell him you lost something from before or that I need you to get something or just tell him, *Hey, I've got the key to this place where we can be alone.* I bet he'd be there faster than you can say . . . Grayson, hey. Good job tonight."

I turned to see Grayson holding two glasses of soda. He handed me one, then took the straw out of his and chugged. His neck stretched, his Adam's apple moving slightly as he drank. For some reason it made me think of his lacrosse picture. I bit my lip.

"Some night," he said, putting the empty glass down on the table next to us.

"Well, get ready for part two. Cake, garter, bouquet, chicken dance, and *out of here.* . . ." Eben said, clapping him on the back as he walked by. "Going to rally the troops." I watched him walk into the break room, could feel Grayson's eyes on me. I shoved the key into my pants pocket. *Now or never, Wren.*

"Hey, think you could give me a ride home after work?" I asked, nibbling on my straw.

He hesitated. The moment felt agonizingly long, but he finally answered.

"Yeah, sure."

"The Mercedes-Benz of corkscrews?" Grayson asked as we walked up to the cottage.

I grimaced at my stupidity; I was happy my back was to him. Trying to find Dave-the-bartender's made-in-France, Laguiole corkscrew was the best excuse I could come up with. Why couldn't I have thought of something without the word *screw* in it?

"Yeah, he has a carrier for it and everything. Is completely obsessive about it, which is why he's freaking out," I answered, jiggling the key in the lock. The door squeaked open. Eben's last words of wisdom were to keep the lights out so no one would investigate. How we were supposed to be in here searching for something without lights was beyond me, but I was making it up as I went along. And Grayson, being the above-average guy he was, immediately realized we needed some light.

"No," I said, sort of batting his hand away from the switch. "We need to check the kitchen first."

"I'd like to get to the kitchen."

"We can't have lights on in two rooms at the same time. It'll blow a fuse," I answered.

"Um, okay."

The cottage was dark, but streetlights from the parking lot cast a greenish tint so we could see outlines of furniture. I felt my way along the wall, edging around the doorjamb and into the kitchen, thinking of my next move as seductress.

Thwap.

"Oh, fuck," Gray spluttered behind me. He was hunched forward, hand on his forehead. I went over and snaked my arm through his.

"Are you okay?" I whispered.

"No. I think I'm seeing stars. I forgot to duck. . . . Maybe if the lights were on . . ." he kind of growl-spoke through gritted teeth.

"I'm so sorry," I said. I opened the freezer and pulled out a handful of ice. A spare bar towel hung over the sink and I grabbed it, even though it had a slightly sour smell, and wrapped the ice in it, handing it to Grayson. He waved it off.

"I'm okay," he said, rubbing his forehead.

Just then the front door opened with a loud creak. Without thinking I dropped the towel and reached for Grayson's free hand.

"Wren?!"

"Shhh . . ."

I dragged him over to the pantry door.

"Duck," I whispered, pulling him into the tiny space. We faced each other, him hunching over me a little as I shut the door, plunging us into darkness.

"Hello? Anyone here?" a deep male voice called.

"That's the band guy," Grayson said.

"Shh," I whispered so violently, I spat. *Attractive.*

"Wren, what's—" He stopped when I put my finger up to

his mouth. I let it linger, feeling the warmth of his lips, until I was sure he wouldn't speak.

There was shuffling and movement and a few heavy thuds. The band guys must have been stowing their equipment. They did that occasionally, when they knew the main building wouldn't be open before they needed their stuff again. My muscles began to ache from being still. How long would this take?

"Wren, why can't we just go out there?" Gray whispered.

"No one knows we're here."

"But—"

"Grayson, please."

"Did you hear that? I swear this place is haunted," the band guy said. Grayson's body rocked with laughter.

"Don't," I whispered, leaning into him to stop myself from cracking up too. The darkness cocooned us, heightening my senses. Gray's breathing returned to normal, but his heart pounded. Or was it mine? A strong, insistent beat. He curled into me, his earthy-scented hair tickling my forehead. One tilt of my head and my lips would be on his neck. The thought made me swoon.

A door slammed.

"I think they're gone," Grayson whispered, a warm rush against my ear.

Just kiss him, Wren.

Grayson broke away, opening the pantry door and stepping into the kitchen. I emerged, squinting—even the dim light from the parking lot hurt after being in the dark for so long. I stood there, adjusting to the light and space.

"We're not here for a corkscrew, are we?" Grayson asked.

"No, not really."

"Then what?"

In the shabby light of the kitchen, all my thoughts in the dark seemed ridiculous. Wind rattled the window, and a draft seeped through the ancient sills. I hunched my shoulders up for warmth.

"Nothing, let's go," I said, walking out of the kitchen and smack into the band equipment. "Great," I muttered, turning. Now Grayson stood in my way.

"Wren, talk to me. Please. Why are we here?"

"I wanted to . . ." I began, rocking back on my heels, avoiding Grayson's eyes.

He leaned against the wall, waiting, his face half in shadow.

Soon this place would be leveled. St. Gwen, the Patron Saint of Clandestine Work Hookups would have no love shack to watch over. Grayson would no longer be my coworker. There would be no other casual way to see him. Unless I told him how I felt. But what if he . . . Why was I so afraid of things changing? I had nothing to lose.

"Gray, I wanted to be alone with you," I said.

"Alone," he echoed, trying on the word for size.

"I felt bad leaving the party last week, and when you didn't text or call—"

"Wren, I'm sorry about that, I told you—"

"I know. I get it, really. It's okay if you just want to be friends."

He squinted and shook his head. "Where would you get that idea?"

"When you introduced me to Luke," I said.

"That's why you left, isn't it? I introduced you to Luke as a friend because you're none of his business. I didn't mean . . ." He trailed off.

I waited for more of an explanation.

"Wren," he said softly, shaking his head. I stepped toward him, putting my hands on his chest again. He wouldn't look at me.

"Our timing sucks," he said.

"Why?"

"It's . . . I . . . hard to explain. I'd just rather be with you when my life is less . . . complicated."

"Then you want to be friends," I said, letting my hands fall. I knew I should be okay with it, but my heart felt like it was free-falling down to my feet. *Complicated* . . . Damn, what a cliché.

His fingers trembled as he swept loose strands of my hair away from my face, tucking them behind my ear with his index finger, tracing my earlobe. He breathed out hard.

"Oh, screw it."

He pulled me against him. Our mouths touched, lips

217

parted, my breath disappearing into his. My body sparked to life again, the disappointment from moments earlier replaced by a warm, liquid whoosh that filled me up. His hands were on my face, in my hair, snapping off the elastic that held my braid together.

I fumbled with the zipper of my coat. Grayson's fingers covered mine and unzipped it fiercely, pushing the coat off my shoulders in one swift motion. Eyes on mine, he tugged at his pullover. His hair fell across his face as he brought it forward. I peeled the pullover from his arms and dropped it to the floor as he moved toward me. He shook his hair off his face, practically growling as he reached for me again.

Our lips couldn't meet fast enough.

I closed my eyes, ran my fingertips across his jaw, into his hair. Firm hands caressed my back, untangled my braid. We swayed backward, mouths still touching, toward the sofa, where only hours before Bridezilla and her friends had toasted her marriage. I reached behind me to soften our downward plunge onto the cushions. We fell diagonally, feet hanging off the edge.

Part of me was aware that things were getting wildly out of hand. That the Wren and Grayson who existed before this moment—the harmless flirtation—was over. There would be no going back to friends or coworkers. This changed everything.

Grayson burst out laughing.

He rested his forehead on my shoulder, his body convulsing with each new round.

"What?"

He grinned. "Wren, *help me look for a corkscrew*? That's the best you could come up with?"

I clapped my hand to my forehead, spreading my fingers to cover my eyes.

"Oh, God, I know . . . I know. It's ridiculous." He coaxed my fingers away from my face.

"Nah, I love it," he said, pausing to kiss the tip of my nose. "You're so adorable, it kills me."

I maneuvered my body so we faced each other, side by side. He reached for my hand, entwining our fingers.

"So if I had said, *I've got a key to the cottage; we can be alone,* you would have said, *Sure, let's go*?"

"Are you nuts? I would have said, *No way, I'm out of here,*" he answered, pretending to get up.

"Stop."

His eyes got serious again, and he gently nudged me to my back so he was on top of me, the pressure of his body making me weak and warm at the same time. He kissed me lightly on the cheek, nuzzled my neck.

"I'd go anywhere for you, Wren," he whispered.

And then he kissed me.

SIXTEEN

GRAYSON

WREN.

Wren. Wren. Wren. Wren.

I couldn't stop thinking.

About.

Her.

But I had to. In order to do what I needed to do, I had to put her out of my thoughts, at least for the morning.

It was so hard. The night before had been so . . . *sweet.*

Yes, sweet. Me. Grayson Barrett, former male slut, kissing, *just kissing.* Well, and getting a preview of Wren's curves with my hands. I fought back a grin. Pop noticed.

"What's up with you?" he asked. We sat around the breakfast table, him with a bowl of cereal that resembled something you might find in a horse's feed bag, me with two well-done

English muffins dripping with butter. Tiffany put three shots of her acai-berry wonder juice on the table and then sat down, cup of Greek yogurt in one hand, *Ladies' Home Journal* in the other.

My father picked up his shot. *"Salut,"* he said, tossing it back and wincing.

I did the same.

Wren.

"So have you given any more thought to what we talked about yesterday?" he asked.

Wren. Wren. Wren. Wren.

"Um, what?" I asked, taking a bite of one of the muffins, butter dripping down my chin.

"Going to your mother's next week," he said, then looked at Tiff for backup.

"Oh, that," I said, catching the butter drip with my thumb. "Um, yeah, maybe."

"Maybe?" Tiffany asked.

"I do think I'll ask Wren though. Have some fun like you said, Pop."

Saying Wren's name out loud, tossing it into casual conversation, felt good.

"Wren," Tiff said. "Maybe that's why you're in such a good mood this morning?"

I put my coffee mug to my lips and shrugged. I hadn't planned on last night being a good one. As a matter of fact,

I'd wanted to put off hooking up with Wren until I'd finished up my business with Luke. When I went into work last night, I tried to play it cool, but I could see how much it bothered her. I hadn't planned on our hour-long gropefest. And while I initially resisted, the thought of touching her, of her *wanting* me to touch her . . . Well, damn, I just wasn't strong enough to abstain from that.

But I still had to find a way to separate the two: my life with Wren and my life with Luke.

And I had no clue how I was going to pull it off.

"Of course that's why he's in such a good mood. You think he got that job because he likes to wait tables?"

"Pop."

"I told you, even from my deathbed I could see you two were diggin' each other."

"Cool it with the deathbed," Tiffany said. "Gray, it's just nice to finally see you getting serious about a girl. You've been running around for so long."

"Running around?" I asked, laughing. "Why would you think that?"

"Well, you must have been doing something. You're too much of a catch to spend your Saturday nights alone."

"He and Luke were racking 'em up and forgetting names, like his old man back in the day."

Tiff leaned over and gave Pop a pinch on the arm.

He chuckled. "Honey."

"We're going out together later," I said.

"A date?"

"They don't label it anymore, Tiff. Don't you know that?" Pop said, laying out the paper beside his cereal bowl.

"No, it's a date," I said, trying to tame my lame-ass grin. "I'm taking her ice-skating."

"Skating? How retro," she said.

"Not retro. Perfect. Movies are a gamble. Dinner breaks the bank. When you skate you can hold hands without looking like you want more. And, well, if she falls, you can help her up, be the hero."

Tiffany smiled. "That sounds like classic Blake Barrett."

"You must like this girl," Pop said casually, flipping over the paper.

Ice-skating had been his advice when I'd asked where I should take my twelve-year-old crush, Bethany Frazier, on our first (and only) date. It worked like a charm—and we shared our first kiss by the snack bar as we waited for hot pretzels. When I'd asked Pop later how he knew it would work, he told me it was one of the first dates he'd had with my mom.

"Maybe, we'll see." I scarfed the rest of my remaining English muffin and got up from the table.

"Well, Grayson Matthew, I think it's great," Tiffany said, beaming.

If she only knew how much running around I'd done. Being with Wren was something else entirely, and it was something I wanted so bad, it scared me. So bad, I was willing to hold back, to take things at a snail's pace, to jump this final hurdle with Luke so it would be smooth sailing ahead. And I almost believed it would all work out as I climbed up the stairs to shower, before boxing up all these innocent feelings so I could find my inner deviant.

The soulless freak known as Mike Pearson.

Mike had a date with the Hollister chick.

For the record, I *loathe* Hollister.

It's a pretentious, overpriced, assault-of-the-senses nightclub of a store for middle schoolers who think this is what you need to dress cool.

I also happen to loathe the mall on Saturdays, but to Mike . . . hell, it was like spring break. At 11:00 a.m., parking was a bitch. I found a spot about a half-mile away from the entrance. The walk helped me get back into a Mike Pearson frame of mind.

The Hollister chick's name was Allegra. We met at a billiard hall on Staten Island. Me, Andy, and Luke had heard from a couple of St. Gabe's guys that Jake's Bankshot, just a quick ride over the Bayonne Bridge, was a decent place to shoot pool, scope out chicks, and throw back a few without too much ID scrutiny. Staten Island was a little too close to home for a hit, so I figured we were taking it easy, just going out to chill, something we hadn't done in a while.

It wasn't until Luke introduced himself as Brinker Hadley to a girl who'd come up to talk to us that I realized we were "on." Brinker was Luke's alter, picked from the book *A Separate Peace.* Whenever I brought up the fact that someday, someone might call him on that, he dismissed it, saying that the first girl who recognized the name Brinker Hadley was someone he'd fall madly in love with and take to Amsterdam.

Allegra didn't give us the time of day at first, maybe because we were staring at her with our tongues hanging out. She was about half my height with this perfect, little body that she didn't mind showing off. She wore a denim jacket over a top that looked more like underwear, which she filled with juicy C-cup perfection. Judging by the noise from across the room, she knew how to shoot a decent game—although they could have been cheering about the view every time she bent low to take a shot, too.

She wasn't the queen bee of her group; that was the obnoxious girl who latched herself on to Luke/Brinker. Andy hooked up with some blond chick and they each teamed up and played a game of doubles for a while. I was content with just taking in the scene. I didn't want to be Mike Pearson that night. The lying was a constant mental strain, and with my term-paper business booming and the lacrosse team undefeated, I just wanted to be *Gray.*

Then I felt someone tug on my shirtsleeve.

"Hey," I said. She was a knockout even close-up.

"Hey, yourself," she said, touching my chest with a manicured finger. "A few of us are getting out of here. Party at my place. Wanna come?"

"They don't seem too happy over there," I said, motioning to the group of juicehead guys she'd been playing pool with.

"Screw them. *Carpe scrotum*, right?"

"What?" I didn't think I heard her right.

"You know, seize life by the balls, live a little," she said, grabbing my hand. She spun herself around, her dark hair swaying behind her. "C'mon. You won't regret it."

Hot and funny. Just. Wow.

"Sounds good, um . . ."

"Allegra."

We followed Allegra and her bright yellow Miata through the winding Staten Island roads to a two-story brick house with a U-shaped driveway.

"Score," Luke said as Andy pulled in front of Allegra.

"You're designated driver, *Mike*," Andy said, tossing me the keys. Our unspoken rule was that whoever was hooking up with the hit stayed sober. Tired as I was, I was glad to be our DD. A few beers, and I was sure I'd be sloppy with the details.

The backyard was sunken, with one of those pools that looked like you'd wandered into a private oasis. A rock waterfall emptied into the deep end. The patio was spacious, with heaters and lounges and a built-in fire pit that Allegra ignited with a flick of a switch. A house this bank had to have a security system the likes of which we'd never dealt with, and Luke had an instant hard-on about the challenge.

I'd been lounging in a chaise, enjoying my fly-on-the-wall status. Both Andy and Luke were in the hot tub with their hookups. Everyone else who'd wandered in from the billiard place seemed to know one another and took no interest in me. I felt myself drifting off when someone straddled me on the chair. I opened my eyes to Allegra. Her denim jacket was off; just the little black top and a lot of tanned skin poured into white shorts. She had a belly ring with a crystal dangling from the end of it. I put my hands on her smooth hips, ran my thumb across that jewel, and she shivered.

"Are you always this quiet, Mike?" she asked.

"No, had a rough week, that's all."

"The hot tub is great for that."

"Uh-uh. Don't need a staph infection."

"Ick, you're not one of those freaks who washes his hands like a million times, are you?"

I shook my head and moved my hands to her waist.

"What do you want to do then?"

You, is what Mike would have said, but I didn't. Maybe my conscience had already begun its ascent from the underworld that was my brain. Or maybe I knew this chick . . . girl . . . was the kind of person I could see myself with . . . for real. My silence didn't seem to faze her.

"C'mon, you didn't come here to go to sleep," she said,

tugging the collar of my shirt.

"Big house. Are we all alone?"

"Yep, house-sitting for Daddy while he's in Vegas with wifey *número tres*."

"And he lets you party?"

"Are you kidding? If he were here, he'd be in the hot tub with us. *Mucho* guilt for missing years of dance recitals and soccer games. I get to use the place whenever I want."

"Ah, so you're a daddy's girl," I said.

She straightened up and swung her leg around, so she was sitting at the foot of the chaise.

"Don't call me that. I make my own way."

"Hey." I nudged her with my foot. She flinched, then crossed her arms.

"Allegra, I was just teasing," I said. "My parents are divorced. My stepfather is such a friggin' tool. I get it, really, I do. And I don't even get the benefit of a pimped-out swimming pool."

She faced me, still frowning.

"Sorry?" I reached toward her.

A gleam returned to her eyes, and she pulled me to standing.

"Fine. I've got a way you can make it up to me," she said, leading me into the house.

I woke up then.

After we did it, she snuggled up against my chest.

She fit so perfectly, one leg draped over mine. For a moment I felt a stab of regret that I wasn't just Grayson. That I wasn't just a guy meeting a girl. A girl I could be myself with; someone who would trust me enough to open up to. And as I lay there, stroking Allegra's hair, I allowed myself to imagine that this was the start of something. Even if it wasn't.

"Well, that was phenom," she said, pushing herself up.

"Can I see you again?" I asked.

"I'm counting on it."

I left that night with her digits, work schedule, and the feeling that I was the ruler of the free world. A week later my term-paper business blew up in my face. In private the guys rallied around me. In public I was the plague. I was cut from lacrosse and kicked out of St. Gabe's. And soon, one by one, my phone calls went unanswered. I couldn't even bring myself to go to Andy's house.

Months later, as I wandered through the mall, listening to Johnny Mathis sing about a marshmallow world, the conscience that had grown since I'd stopped being Mike Pearson was screaming in my head: *You don't have to do this.*

At the same time, there was an insistent competitive sliver that wanted . . . no, needed . . . to prove to Luke that I wasn't pussying out. That he couldn't intimidate me. That Wren was worth fighting for. I tried to fan that spark to a flame as I walked toward Hollister. The dim lights and pounding beat in the store helped me get my inner swagger back. I ran a hand through my hair, checked out the register. Allegra was there, wearing far more clothing than she'd had on when we first met. I sauntered up to the counter, by the end, and leaned on my elbows. Waiting. Until she saw me.

She did a double take—good sign. Then she smiled. Even better. She said something to her coworker on the register and wandered over to me, hips swaying deliberately.

"Hey, I know you, don't I?" she said, leaning toward me.

"I know you," I answered.

"Where've you been?"

"Around."

"And why should I even talk to you?"

"Because you want to," I said, leaning closer.

She pursed her lips to one side. "Yeah, maybe I do, but I don't know why. It's been months."

"Too long, Allegra," I said.

"So I get a break in about fifteen. Want to get some lunch?" she asked, running a finger along my forearm. "It's the least you can do after blowing me off."

"Sounds good," I answered, playing with a strand of her hair, not really knowing where I was going to take it after this. I hadn't thought past just making contact. *Stupid.* Playing it as I went along.

She turned to someone who stood about a foot away from us.

Putting on her Hollister-girl perky voice, she said, "Hey, want to try those on? Great! Let me just get the keys." She raised her eyebrows at me before she left.

I stood up, pondering my next move as I checked out the chick waiting for Allegra to come back with the keys. Figured I could share some of the Mike Pearson charm, because that's just how Mike rolls.

The world stopped.

Tilted.

"Hey," I said. A stupid, meaningless little word, but it was the only one I could come up with as she stood there.

I'd done a lot of stupid shit over the past few years. Hurt so many people. But I never had to look them in the eyes, never had to think about it.

And I never felt worse, ever, even in the blackest moment of the blackest day since I was kicked out of school than I did at that precise moment, not knowing what I could possibly say to make it all go away. Make it better for her.

Wren.

SEVENTEEN

WREN

THE MUSIC WAS SO LOUD, A THUDDING, OVERPOW-
ering bass with which my pulse seemed to keep time.

Grayson's mouth moved, but I didn't hear what he said.
The only thing I was aware of was the feeling that my face
was slowly dripping downward, like melting wax. I felt dizzy
and off-kilter, like I'd wandered into a dream, and any minute
I'd pull out my teeth, or Chace Crawford would appear from
behind the hoodies and offer to take me to prom.

I hadn't recognized Gray at first. He wore a black leather
jacket and dark jeans. His look was calculated . . . *slick*. The
way he'd leaned into that girl behind the counter, playing with
her hair, acting like they were together. The desire on her face
as she spoke with him . . . that stabbed me right through my
heart, a true physical sensation that almost made me gasp.

And yet there I stood. Silent. Shocked. Holding three shirts on hangers and not wanting to say a word, because I might embarrass Grayson or the Hollister girl.

And so I followed her to the dressing room.

Her in her flip-flops.

And fucking *jeggings*.

And close-fitting blue hoodie

And shiny, dark hair that fell straight and perfect and gleamed in the dim light.

She opened the door.

"I'm Allegra. Let me know if you need anything else. Another color or size, just give me a shout."

A shout was the least of what I wanted to give her, but I managed to nod before completely losing my grip behind the closed dressing-room door.

What just happened?

I hung up the shirts and sat down on the bench, my face in my hands, willing it to just go away. I'd been floating on a cloud all morning—more specifically, since last night . . . the cottage . . . saying good night in Grayson's car. Every time I thought about one of his slow, deep kisses, it was like a buzz through my body, a yummy ache that could only be filled by seeing him again.

Not like this.

Not like this.

There was a knock at the door.

"Wren."

"Go away. Go away. Go away," I whispered into my hands.

"Wren, please. Open the door," Grayson whispered.

I was instantly flushed, hot. The door seemed so far away.

"Please," he said.

I got up, opened the latch. He came in and shut the door behind him. We stood there, about a foot apart.

Looking at each other.

Grayson's eyes were wary as he studied me. As if I might claw at him. I wasn't entirely sure I wouldn't. I felt duped. All the wonderful feelings I'd been carrying around taunted me now, made the night before feel like a pathetic lie.

"What?" I asked.

"I know this looks . . . bad."

I struggled to take a normal breath.

"Wren, if I knew—"

"Knew what?" I asked, voice catching, my throat so tight it hurt. "That I'd be here?"

Brooke had spent the morning on the phone scouring the tri-state area to find a retired gold Pandora charm she wanted to buy her future mother-in-law for Christmas, before she and Pete headed back to DC for their final exams. Her "shopping quest," as she called it, took us twenty minutes away to the Pandora store in the Staten Island Mall. While Brooke ran to get the charm, I ran to Hollister—not my usual go-to place, but I had a leftover fifty-dollar store gift card from my sweet sixteen that I'd been saving for something special. My date with Grayson seemed like the perfect occasion to blow it on. Even a gal who didn't make NHS could appreciate the irony of the moment.

"You've got every right to be pissed, but I swear it's not what it looks like." The words were laced with sincerity. I hated myself for caving, even tilting in his direction the slightest bit. The image of them leaning together flashed through my mind again.

"And what is it?"

He put his hands up to his face, covering his eyes, praying, maybe, for an answer that would help me not feel so shitty.

His head tilted back as he ran his fingers down his face and heaved an exasperated sigh.

"I'm doing a favor for Luke."

"Luke? Really? Because he has trouble talking to girls."

"I *am* here because of Luke, but I can't . . . I can't go into it right now."

"You touched her hair," I said, stepping back. "The way she looked at you—"

"No, Wren . . . I'm sorry. I wasn't . . . I didn't . . . I'm a total jackass, okay? Don't—"

"Grayson, I need to go. My sister's waiting for me, and I came here to . . ." I couldn't even finish.

He reached for me then, his eyes soft, remorseful. I wanted to believe him, to forget that any of this happened.

"Wren, last night was amazing," he said, touching his forehead to mine, closing his eyes. His hands were around my waist, drawing me in to him. And there was that scent, that earthy, spicy shower-gel thing that took me back to the night before, the way my body had felt underneath his. "You have to know there's nothing I would do to screw that up. Nothing."

I put my forehead on his shoulder. I wanted to believe him. Knew somehow that I could. He relaxed into me, breathing out, pulling me closer. My hands snaked around him. Our mouths found each other, becoming more insistent as neither of us pulled away. We moved until we hit the wall of the dressing room, bodies pressing together, like no time had passed since our after-work tryst. I never thought I'd be the kind of girl who made out in the Hollister dressing room, but there I was, sliding my hands into Grayson's back pockets, pulling him as close as he could get.

"Everything okay in there?" Allegra called.

"Mmm-hmm," I answered, my mouth still on Grayson's.

I heard her flip-flop away. We stopped, straightening up.

"Now what?" I asked.

"I'm going home," he said.

"And your favor?" I asked, not wanting to bring the jeggings-clad Hollister goddess back into it but not wanting to be a complete love-starved doormat either.

"Screw Luke," he whispered, kissing me again. "We're still on for tonight?"

"You *will* explain all of this to me, right?" I asked.

"It's complicated, but, yeah I'll, um, try."

Complicated . . . was this what he was talking about at the cottage?

"See you later then," I said, motioning for him to leave. The thought that he might go back out and continue his conversation with . . . that girl . . . crossed my mind, but I decided to trust him for the moment.

"Later," he said, kissing me. He tugged on his jacket, straightened himself up, and walked out, closing the door behind him.

I turned toward the shirts I'd picked out, catching my reflection in the mirror. My chest was flushed, the echo of Grayson's kiss still making my lips tingle. I took a breath to compose myself and left the dressing room.

Brooke was on a bench out front, sucking down a ginormous cup of lemonade, apparently one of the few things that didn't make her nauseous, Pandora shopping bag next to her.

"Hey, let's go," I said, joining her. When she saw I was empty-handed, she frowned.

"You were in there for half an hour and found *nothing*?" she asked. Another lovely side effect of pregnancy was that she'd transformed into a total bitch. My mother, who, even if she hadn't accepted the fact that she was going to be a grandmother, had at least softened to it, gave Brooke a wide berth and expected me to do the same.

"Wait until you come visit me in January. The shopping in DC is so much better."

"I thought I was coming for a college visit," I said, sitting down next to her. This brilliant idea had been discussed during her and Pete's dinner with the parents. I had the sinking suspicion Brooke was gunning for me to go to Georgetown more for babysitting purposes than higher education, but the thought of an actual college visit—even if it was to a reach school—made me excited. At least I'd have something to tell Mrs. Fiore in our second strategy meeting.

"The college visit will take an hour, two at most; then we'll have fun."

My phone buzzed in my pocket. I slid it out, checked my messages. Grayson.

Sorry. Sorry. Sorry. Sorry. Sorry. Sorry. Sorry.

For someone who claimed to be doing a favor for someone else, he was awfully regretful. I promised myself I wouldn't get so caught up in his kiss that I let him get away with not telling me what this supposed favor was about.

I thought about what Ava had said to me in the hallway at school, how she and Luke just gravitated to each other when they were in the same place. Was that what Grayson and I were doing? Gravitating? Could I handle this relationship if it was just a physical thing?

"You realize that about one percent of the population can wear pants like that," Brooke said, wrinkling her nose and motioning toward the store in front of us.

No surprise, she was talking about *her.* The Hollister girl stood on the porch of the store. She had one of those see-through purses that shop employees needed to carry and kept searching up and down the length of the mall, frowning. The hollow feeling in my gut told me this had something to do with Grayson, and I felt a momentary obligation to tell her that he'd left.

But it was only momentary.

"I hate that store," I said, standing up. "Can we get out of here now?"

Brooke finished the rest of her lemonade with a loud slurp, tossed it in the trash, and we left.

"So let me guess. You're some skating genius too," I said, surprised by Grayson's choice of evening entertainment. I was also secretly excited because, well, I *could* skate. I'd had five years of basic-level training when, once upon a time, I had wanted to be the next Sasha Cohen. And while I'd pretty much quit after my body, as my mother politely put it, filled out, I thought I could pull out a decent scratch spin or something that might at least be a little impressive.

He stood up, the ice skates giving him another three inches of height that made him wobble.

"I think I was about a foot shorter the last time I did this."

"It'll come back," I said as I finished lacing up the rentals.

I hopped to standing, a move that surprised him. "C'mon, let's see what you got."

It was painful. Not inching-along-the-rink-wall painful, but painful. We glided along the ice. Well, I glided. Gray shuffled unsteadily. It was the first time I felt like I had the upper hand, and I wasn't going to let that get away from me. After our third trip around the rink, I crossed in front of him and skated backward, holding both of his hands in mine.

"So about that favor for Luke," I said, trying to playfully bring up the subject. I'd spent the afternoon on the phone with Jazz and Maddie, getting their opinions on Grayson's mall scene. Maddie, who was head cheerleader for Team Grayson since he'd invited us to Andy's party, told me to let it go. Grayson was the kind of guy who girls noticed, and we weren't officially *together*, so for now it was okay. Her take on it made me feel hopeful.

Jazz had the opposite opinion. Suddenly Grayson sounded like the sleazy boyfriend in *Adventures in Babysitting*, the one who cancels his date with sweet Chris Parker in order to date the sexy girl who puts out. I was starting to agree with Mads's opinion that Jazz needed to enter the new millennium and stop living her life according to eighties movies. Even if what she said haunted me a little.

I was somewhere in between, because right there, in that moment, I was holding hands with a dark-haired, brown-eyed boy who looked so deliciously vulnerable, he was worlds away from the slick guy who was doing a favor for Luke in the store this morning. This was the Grayson I knew. The Grayson I wanted to be around. I tugged on his hands to propel him, and he lost his footing.

"We have to talk about this now?" he asked, scrambling to stay upright.

"That's why we're here, is it?" I asked, leading us around a turn. "To completely avoid talking about what you were doing at the mall?"

"Why does anyone go to the mall?"

"You know what I mean," I said, narrowing my eyes at him and speeding us up slightly.

"This is a side of you I've never seen. Very sexy, devious," he said, narrowing his eyes back at me and flipping his bangs away from his face.

I let go of his hands. He was not going to get away with not telling me. No matter how hot he looked when he pulled that bang-flipping move.

"Wren," he said, shuffling a little to get his balance.

I sped away from him, weaving my way through other skaters to put some distance between us. When I caught up to him again, he nearly knocked into a little girl in a sparkly, aqua skate outfit who scrunched her face at him.

"Ready to talk?" I asked, adjusting my speed and grabbing his hand. His fingers tightened around mine.

"Okay, but there's really not much to talk about; I already

told you I was doing a favor for Luke."

"Right, Luke who has trouble talking to girls . . . go on."

He scowled. "I'm serious. He's interested in that girl and just wanted me to talk to her to see if she was, you know, available."

"Did he want to know if her hair was soft too?"

"Wren."

"Isn't he *with* Ava?"

Grayson snickered. "Luke has a pretty wide definition of being 'with' someone."

I let that one sit a minute as our blades scratched across the ice. "Do you?"

"Do I what?"

"Have a wide definition of being with someone?"

His eyebrows rose at the question, but he didn't answer right away.

After a pass around the rink, he spoke. "I've never really been *with* anyone."

"No way!" I said, so loud that a couple skating by turned to see the commotion. After they faced forward again, I spoke. "Really, that can't be possible."

"Skate in front of me again."

I waited until we rounded the edge of the rink to cross over and switch my direction. Grayson's eyes were serious.

"I've been with girls, but it's always been . . . more physical. Short-term."

Physical and short-term. I stumbled. "Okay, you don't have to go into it."

"That's just it. With you? I want to go into it. I want you to know me, but I don't know where to start. Wren, you're so . . . honest and funny and . . . I haven't stopped thinking about you since we met."

I stopped pumping my legs. "Really?"

"Yes. So I'd say my definition of being with someone is tiny. Miniscule, really."

We slowed down. I held on to his hands and broadened my footing as we hit the straightaway. He inhaled, keeping his eyes steady on mine. "I want to be with you. Period."

I bit my lip, aware that we'd come to a full stop as others scratched by on their skates. He kissed me, soft and light, just a whisper on the mouth that left me wanting more. If he was playing me, he was damn good at it.

"I think I like that definition," I said.

"Why don't we get out of here before I crack my skull?" he asked, teetering as someone sped by us.

We returned the rentals, and I made a quick stop to the ladies' room, mostly for damage control, as skating always had the lovely side effects of a runny nose and a glaze of sweat. I took lip gloss from my pocket and freshened up, wondering what the rest of the night held. I tried to focus on the sweet things Grayson had said and not on what he meant by short-term and physical when describing his past relationships.

I left the ladies' room and saw Gray across the lobby. He was leaning against a column and talking to a girl. I'd been gone for *five freakin' minutes*. I ran a hand through my hair, stood up straighter. Talking to a girl or not, he was with me. And I wanted to be with Gray. And it was time to go after something I wanted. This was something—Gray and girls— I was going to have to get used to. As I got closer, I noticed she was a bit older, maybe Brooke's age, and was vaguely familiar. He pointed in my direction. The girl peeked over her shoulder at me.

"Hey," I said.

"See you 'round, Mike," she said, carrying her skates toward a bench.

"Who was that?"

"Waitress at Leaning Tower," he said. "She never remembers my name."

For some reason that made me feel better.

"So where to?" I asked. "Or was that our big date?"

"You can still hang out, right?"

"I'm all yours."

"Great. Feel like going to my house?"

Alone. With him?

"Yes."

MY HEART HAMMERED IN MY CHEST AS I SAT AT the foot of my bed.

I'd never had a girl in my house before.

I'd left Wren and her chai latte downstairs, making up some excuse about wanting to get my iPod so she could hear my favorite song from the latest Coldplay album. In reality I was picking up in my room and figuring out how I could get her to come upstairs, since I pretty much wanted to devour her whole. Pop and Tiff were at a couples bunco night, which proved how desperate my father was to get out. They would be gone for at least a few more hours. And a few more hours alone with Wren sounded like the kind of way I wanted to spend my night.

Only . . . I didn't want to blow it the way I'd blown it that morning at the mall when Wren caught me in Hollister. If that hadn't been a *Grayson Barrett, you've got to stop screwing up your life* kind of wake-up call, I didn't know what was. I thought, or hoped, she bought my explanation, which I worded carefully so I wasn't exactly bullshitting her. Going to see Allegra *was* a favor to Luke. He *was* interested in her . . . or her father's house, but I didn't need to get into that. And I wouldn't. That part of my life was over. Done. Luke and the guys would realize that soon enough.

And then the chick from Leaning Tower calling me Mike at the ice-skating rink. That was like some sort of evil synchronicity in action. Seriously what were the odds? That had been easy enough to play off. I hated lying to Wren. From now on there would be no careful wording necessary.

But Wren . . . she was such a . . . surprise.

Every time we were together, it was like she revealed a little bit more of herself, and I dug it, the not knowing what to expect. The way she made me laugh. The look in her eyes when she'd let go of my hands at the ice-skating rink, proving she had a wicked side. I could spend all day watching her face change expression. And God, I wanted her up in my room so badly, my body was practically buzzing.

So I sat there, clueless, trying to figure out my next move.

Mike Pearson would not be nervous. As Mike I'd go downstairs, tell Wren how hot she looked in her skinny jeans, kiss her until her legs were so weak she couldn't stand, then lead her upstairs without a second thought. But I wouldn't be that way with Wren. Couldn't. This was real. And besides, I wanted to give her something, and being Mike was all about taking.

Luke had given me the necklace to unload in the spring. It was from a hit I hadn't been involved in. That's the way we usually ran it with something personal like jewelry. It was easier to let go of the stuff if you didn't have a direct link to it. I was supposed to bring it to Lenny, our gold guy through Spiro, but I put it off, tucking the necklace away in the top drawer of my desk, where it stayed, forgotten.

Until that afternoon.

It was pretty, unique. A gold chain with a flat charm the size of a dime with the word *love* inscribed in its center. A ruby teardrop-shaped bead and another even smaller circle with a heart etched into it. Simple. Perfect. Even if it had been stolen. I didn't know from where or who, so I reasoned that having it in my possession was just like . . . say, wandering into a pawnshop and picking it out. Right?

And I continued with this train of thought, because I really did want to give her something. Even that morning as I'd raced through the mall, back to the Chrysler, back to Bayonne, swearing never to set foot on Staten Island again, I knew I wanted to make up for it, but how? Flowers? Stuffed animal? Balloon? Yeah, right . . . *Here's a balloon, Wren. Sorry you caught me talking to a hot girl I hooked up with last spring when I was casing her house.*

Nah, jewelry was the better choice. This piece in particular. It said exactly what I hoped to say to her one day, the sort of necklace I'd pick out anyway. With everything that had gone down during my expulsion, Luke would surely have forgotten it. I picked it up again, letting it dangle from my fingers, imagining Wren's face when I gave it to her. Maybe it was a dumb idea.

"Hey." Her voice rang out through my room.

I flipped the necklace into my palm as I saw her in my doorway. The move did not go unnoticed. She brought her latte to her lips, hiding a grin as she leaned against the doorjamb. I shot up from my bed, shoving the necklace into my front pocket. This had been my goal, to get her upstairs, but the reality of it left me speechless.

"Sorry. I just wanted . . . is it okay if I'm up here?" she asked.

"Come in," I said. She put her drink on my desk, sliding her hands into her back pockets as she looked around the room.

"So neat. Like your car," she said, moving past me. "My brother's room is a mess even when he's not there."

"Yeah, got rid of a lot of stuff after, well . . . getting tossed from Saint Gabe's. Gave the room a new coat of paint. Seemed like a good idea," I said, almost embarrassed at the complete lack of something interesting for her to look at. I'd tossed trophies, photos, any reminder of St. Gabe's, into a storage bin over the summer and stowed it in the basement. My walls were blank.

"I like the color," she said, picking up the only picture I had in my room—a photo of me, Ryder, and Grier taken at Jenkinsons' over Labor Day. I walked toward her, looking over her shoulder.

"That's my half brother and half sister," I said, taking in that summery scent of her hair. My body ached to feel her against me. If I didn't make some move soon, I'd start foaming at the mouth.

"Omigosh, look at the grin on her face . . . You must be an awesome big brother," she said, placing it down on my dresser. I laughed. *Awesome big brother.* It sounded pretty cool coming from her.

"How about that Coldplay song you wanted me to hear?"

"Oh, right," I said, going over to my docking station to pick up my iPod. My hands shook. I scrolled through the songs, completely blind to what I was doing. What was I doing? The Trojans I'd bought from the drugstore as a *just in case* practically chanted my name from my side-table drawer. I tossed the iPod onto my pillow and turned toward her.

"I came up here to clean . . . my dirty clothes from the week are shoved under the bed, and I don't even own the new Coldplay album. I have no idea why I said that," I confessed, jamming my hands in my pockets.

249

Her face reddened; she looked down. *Smooth, Grayson.*

"Coldplay was your corkscrew," she said.

"Ha, um, yeah, you're right," I said. We stood there, looking at each other. She wanted to be here. I wanted to be here. *Why was I so freakin' nervous?*

Wren brushed away some stray hair from her eyes, reminding me of the first night I saw her. She had no clue what that did to me, how sweet she looked. Like when she'd saved me. Had I known all along that this moment was coming? The eyes I'd been running toward with such fierce determination were wide open, taking me in.

"Wren," I said, reaching for her. A soft, sharp *plink* caused us both to look down.

The necklace sat splayed on the hardwood floor by her foot. She crouched down to pick it up. Dumb idea or not, the necklace was in play. Neither of us could ignore it.

"Here," she said, handing it to me.

I held it up, the charms dangling in front of her face.

"This is for you."

She furrowed her brow and reached for it.

"For me, really?"

"No, for Tiff, for Christmas. I thought I'd run it by you," I answered, smirking. And when a momentary flash of disappointment clouded her face, I had to add, "Yes, for you, Wren."

She gave me a look then, so open, honest, and thrilled, it just about brought me to my knees. I placed the necklace in

250

her palm. Her eyes lit up when she saw what the charm said.

"Grayson, this is beautiful . . . but why?"

"Why not? I saw it and thought of you," I answered. The last *not-exactly-a-lie* lie I swore to tell.

"I love it," she said.

"Let me put it on you," I said.

She pulled her hair away from her neck. I fumbled with the clasp for a few seconds before finally getting it to latch. Wherever it came from, the necklace was Wren's now. Her hair fell from her hands, sweeping past her shoulders again. She turned to me, holding the charms out from her neck. I raked my hand through her hair. She looked up at me, wrapped her fingers around mine, and gently pressed her lips to the inside of my wrist.

"I love you." The words sprang out so fast, so naturally, I hardly knew I'd said them. They hung there, between us. "I know it's too soon to say that," I said, touching my forehead to hers, closing my eyes, wishing she'd just say something before I blurted it out again. I could feel the L-word, right on the tip of my tongue, ready to tumble out, because it felt so good to finally say it—to mean it.

Wren took my hand and brushed past me, pulling me toward the hall. My mood flat-lined. *Jackass.* Being here was too much, too soon. Why had I opened my big mouth? She stopped short of heading out, closed the door, and leaned against it. The lock made a loud *click* as she pressed it down. I laughed. She tugged me closer to her.

"I love you, Grayson Barrett."

I let it sink in.

My name.

Me.

Wren loved *me*.

A soft, flirty smile lit up her face. "Kiss me already."

I was in love.

Me. Grayson Barrett. Head-over-heels-bona-fide-singing-power-ballads-in-the-shower-texting-Wren-24/7 in *LOVE*.

Four weeks ago I couldn't have imagined having this kind of relationship. But that's how love happens, isn't it? You're just minding your own business, tossing hot dogs in your mouth, and *bam*—you cross paths with a beautiful girl you can't stop thinking about. I felt high. Everything was different.

School became less hellish; the prospect of connecting with Wren afterward made the day fly by. I even participated in class, surprising my teachers who didn't know what to make of the guy who usually slouched so far into his desk, he became one with the seat.

It was a Wednesday, and the object of my affection had a yearbook meeting. We were getting together at the library after dinner, so I could go over arbitrary angles with her. At least that's what we were calling it. It was hard to concentrate when her perfect mouth, ripe for a kiss was only inches from mine.

Naturally good old Sir Isaac and his pesky gravitational law $F = mg$ would have to go and screw it up, since what goes up must come down. I was pretty damn high as I pulled the Chrysler into the parking spot in front of my house, only to come crashing to earth with a thud when I saw Luke sitting on my top step, waiting.

Reality was such a harsh drag force.

I took my time grabbing my backpack, closing the door, and wrestling my house key out of my pocket. I'd called him after the Allegra thing, but it had gone straight to his voice mail. I knew that sooner or later he'd want to talk to me about it. I'd only hoped it was later . . . or never.

"Ah, *amor vincit omnia*," he said, standing as I got to the top of the stairs. He was holding some sort of flowered dish and smirking, black Ray-Bans covering his eyes.

Love conquers all. "Really, why do you say that?"

"My sources tell me you've been picking up a Sacred Heart chick after school, name rhymes with hen. Must be serious. You seem . . . happy."

"'Name rhymes with hen'? Why can't you just act normal about this?"

He pushed his sunglasses up into his hair. "Normal? Really? Grayson, I'm standing here freezing my nuts off with my stepmom's vegan lasagna for your father, and you're as whipped as a housebroken puppy over some girl who saved you from choking. I feel like I'm living in a parallel universe.

253

It's gonna take some getting used to this new you."

I decided to cut him some slack.

"Whipped by choice, my friend," I said, putting my key in the door. "Not so bad; you should try it."

"Ha, I'd rather try this vegan lasagna with a soy-milk chaser," he said, holding up the dish. I stood between the front and storm doors, poised to go in, wondering when he was going to bring up Allegra and what happened on Saturday.

"Are you gonna ask me in?"

"You look like you have somewhere to go," I answered.

"Nope, thought I'd swing by, drop this off before heading to Andy's. I can hang for bit. Remember, like we used to do?"

"Fine, sure, come in."

He followed me. I set my backpack down in the foyer and wandered into the kitchen. Luke opened the fridge, placed the lasagna on the top shelf, and grabbed two Cokes. He tossed one to me and popped his open, taking a long gulp. I leaned against the counter.

"So what's up?" I asked.

"Not much. Coach is still scouting for a new middie, but no one's got your speed or reflexes, so we're pretty much screwed without the Raptor," he said, throwing in Coach's nickname for me. It stung to hear, something I hadn't thought about in a while. "It's a shame Bergen Point doesn't have a team. That must suck for you."

"Yeah, it sucks," I answered, cracking open my soda.

"What are you going to do with your gear?"

"I don't know. I thought I'd pile it in the yard and host a bonfire," I said, wanting to wipe the smirk off his face. "Just ask me what you want to ask me already, Luke."

He swallowed another sip of soda before answering. "Seeing as how you're not into our little arrangement anymore, I thought you could use some cash. Maybe sell your gear. But since you seem to think I'm here for another reason, well, okay . . . What happened on Saturday?"

"Allegra blew me off. I went in, talked to her a little bit, but she wasn't interested, so I left, called you," I said. He fiddled with the flip-top tab on his can.

"Christ, Grayson, you've really lost your edge. You can't lie for shit."

I stiffened.

"I'm not lying."

"Really? Allegra said it was the other way around."

"When . . . how—"

"What? Just protecting our investment. Had to go in and see for myself. Asked her a few questions, that's all. Made it totally casual. I think you're out of your mind to give up tapping that again, but whatever. That house was out of our scope anyway. What I don't get is why you had to lie. It's just me."

Keys jangled, echoing through the hallway as Tiffany and Pop came in.

"Luke! It's so good to see you," Tiffany said, dropping her

gym bag near my backpack and kicking off her sneakers. She padded over to us. Pop followed behind.

"Hi, Mr. Barrett, Mrs. Barrett," Luke said, giving Pop a brisk handshake and Tiff a quick peck on the cheek.

Luke seemed unruffled by our whole exchange. If he had gone to see Allegra himself—why did I have to be involved in the first place? I stewed while Luke, Pop, and Tiff bantered back and forth about the vegan lasagna, Luke not being here in a while, and if his stepmom, Isabelle, was ready for Christmas or not.

"Luke, stay for dinner; have some lasagna," Pop said, widening his eyes at me. I knew vegan anything sounded as appetizing to him as chewing on the bottom of his boot.

"Thanks, but I'm a carnivore, Mr. B," Luke said, patting his stomach. "Have to get going anyway. I'm trying to get Grayson to come to Andy's with me."

"Go, Gray. Don't worry about us," Tiff said.

"I've got something to do later, want to get some homework done first," I answered, glaring at Luke. "Let me walk you out."

"Don't be a stranger, Luke," Pop said, grabbing Tiff's coat and carrying it to the closet while I walked Luke back outside.

"Something to do later or *someone*?" he asked, once we were outside. I closed the door behind me.

"Why are you hassling me if you don't care about the Allegra thing anymore?"

"'Cause I think you should come hang out. It's not the same without you, Grayson. But you're not really the same, are you? I think you're too punch-drunk from steady poontang. How is she, by the way? Quiet in the sack too?"

My fists clenched. Being physical with Wren was so new and . . . private. It took all my self-control not to deck him.

"*Hmm*, not sharing. You are in love. You'll get bored with her, you know," he warned. "And then you'll come looking for us, and we'll be in Amsterdam."

"I won't get bored."

"Yeah, okay." He flipped his shades back on. "Gotta run. Maybe I'll see you 'round. Tell Wren I said hey."

He trotted down the stairs and strode toward his car, a nondescript, black hatchback that Luke's father told him would build his character. *Tell Wren I said hey.* He honked the horn as the car rode down the street. Maybe he was just being friendly. Maybe he would come around to the new me. I went back inside, trying to ignore the overwhelming feeling that this was only the beginning of some sort of trouble.

Something was up.

He'd dropped the subject of Allegra too easily.

Luke was a raptor too.

SIX DAYS, EIGHT HOURS, TWENTY-THREE MIN-utes, give or take a couple of seconds from the moment Grayson Barrett said those three little words. Common sense told me things were progressing way, *way* too fast, but my heart was enjoying the ride too much. In over my head? More like drowning and loving it.

Which was probably why heading to St. Lucy's to spread holiday cheer felt like a fun, festive thing to participate in, even if I'd been backed into doing it. Afterward I was supposed to go with Grayson to his mother's in Connecticut. *I need you there,* he'd said. There was no question in my mind that I would go. Thankfully the parental units approved, but it didn't stop Mom from grilling me on the car ride to Sacred Heart.

"Where in Connecticut does Grayson's mother live again?" Mom asked.

"I don't know, something with a D . . . Darien, maybe?"

"Something with a D, Darien maybe," she repeated. "I'm letting you go out of state with a strange boy, and you don't even know where you're going?"

"He's not a strange boy," I said, texting him my mother's question. "He's your employee, my friend, and I saved his life. We have a history."

"A history? Wren, it's barely been a month. Aren't things progressing a little fast? You're meeting his mother?"

"She's having a tree-trimming party, Mom. It's not like a special dinner just to meet me. And yes, it's Darien," I answered, reading Grayson's text but quickly shutting down the window. The rest of the message was not something I wanted to share, but it made me grin so wide, my mother raised her eyebrows in response. How could he make me blush with a text? Seeing him couldn't come fast enough.

"Remember to call me when you get to his mother's house!"

"Yes, Mom. Thanks for the ride," I said, leaning over and giving her a peck on the cheek. I slid out, closed the door, and headed for the parking lot, where I could already see a group huddled around Ava. She was wearing a sparkly Santa-hat headband, which looked totally adorable on her flat-ironed style, and she knew it.

"It's about time," she said, handing me a bag. I pulled out a hat shaped like a Christmas tree. To further the tackiness, one push of a button, and it danced on your head.

"You're not suggesting I wear this?"

"C'mon, it's a holiday party."

"Are you trying to get someone to wear that asinine hat again?"

Luke Dobson stood behind Ava. Maybe it was the overcast gray-lit morning, or maybe it was my viewing the world through Grayson-colored shades, but he seemed less imposing than he had at Andy's house. I met his gaze.

"Perfect word," I said.

Ava huffed and handed me a jingle-bell necklace instead. "At least wear this, and hand out some of them to the guys on the bus."

"Great," I said, accepting the handful of necklaces. She took one and dangled it in front of Luke.

"Not happening."

"Luke, c'mon," Ava pleaded.

"I'm wearing red," he said, unzipping his ski jacket. "That's festive enough."

I laughed.

"See, Wren agrees."

"Fine," she conceded.

"Okay, people, let's move it, on the bus," Mrs. Fiore said, clapping her hands to call us to attention. A large man in a Santa hat poked out his head from the bus doorway and waved us on.

I waited as the others piled onto the bus, then walked to the back and handed out the necklaces. A few of the St. Gabe's boys made snarky remarks, mostly about jingle balls. I pretended not to hear and kept moving down the rows of seats. The engine sputtered to life. I held on to the seats on either side of me as the bus lurched forward.

There weren't many seats available. To the left of me, Luke was sprawled out, head against the window. He caught my eye and motioned next to him, adjusting his position so there was more room for me. I wondered where Ava was, then spotted her up front, sitting next to Mrs. Fiore and pointing to something on her clipboard. I plunked down next to Luke, knocking into him pretty forcefully as the bus exited the parking lot.

"Sorry," I said, sliding away from him. He didn't say anything, just locked eyes with me, his lips upturned slightly. I caught myself staring. *That mouth. He really knows what to do with it.* I mock-coughed into my fist and peered out the window as the bus ambled along the boulevard. Someone began a holiday sing-along. Luke muttered, "Hell, no" and hunkered down into his seat.

"So how did you like Andy's house?" he asked.

"It was cool," I lied.

"You skipped out pretty early, no?"

The fact that he'd noticed was unsettling. "Yes."

"Why?"

I shrugged.

"Let me guess, you're more of a one-on-one kind of chick."

"Not really."

"Too bad for Grayson then."

My body clenched in response.

"Did you get a chance to meet Gray's other friends?" he asked.

"A few, I guess. Why?"

"We're all, well . . . curious about the chick he's been hanging with instead of us."

"Could you stop referring to me as a chick?" I inched away from him, ready to spring up for a different seat.

He tugged my coat sleeve, urging me back.

"C'mon, stay. Here, I'll take this," he said, taking the remaining jingle-bell necklace from me. His fingertips grazed my palm, a move I felt down to my toes.

"Really, just trying to get to know you."

"Whatever," I said, digging my hands into my pockets.

"Now who's dissing who?"

"I'm not dissing you, Luke."

"Whateverrrrr."

I wondered if he was being sincere or not. If he was Grayson's friend, he must have been okay on some level, right? And if I put up with him, maybe he'd prove to be a wealth of information. There were some definite blanks about Grayson that he could fill in.

"So you, Andy, and Gray all went to Saint Gabe's together?"

"Yep. We used to be tight. Kind of partners in crime," he said, shifting in the seat. "Has he ever mentioned Brinker Hadley or Mike Pearson?"

The names sounded vaguely familiar.

"Brinker Hadley? *A Separate Peace*, right?"

His eyes changed, softened the tiniest bit. "You've read that?"

There was an edge of disbelief in his voice, which bugged me.

"Yes, last year. It's one of my favorite books."

He ran a hand through his hair, pushing it back from his face. "Interesting."

"What's interesting?" Ava stood above us in the aisle.

"There she is," Luke said.

"So now you're wearing a bell?" she asked, gesturing toward his chest.

Luke picked it up and shook it. "Wren asked me nicely."

I took Ava's arrival as my cue to get another seat. She mouthed, *Thanks*, as I walked up the aisle. There was something about the gesture that reminded me of St. Vincent de Paul Ava. Maybe it wouldn't be impossible to be friends again. I thumped down into the first available seat, next to a girl who pressed against the window when she saw me. *Freshman.*

The morning was going to crawl by. A text to Grayson was in order.

No sooner had I typed in the message than Mrs. Fiore ripped my iPhone from my hands. I gasped, reaching for it as she shoved it into her shoulder bag.

"I was only going to use it on the bus."

"You won't miss it for two hours. These seniors look forward to this visit all season. We need to give them our full attention," she continued, now loud enough for all to hear. "Does anyone want to join Ms. Caswell in relinquishing their phone?"

"Oh, snap," someone sounding suspiciously like Luke said from the back. I slunk down in my seat. Ten minutes later we arrived at St. Lucy's.

The rec room was decked out and ready for our arrival. Multicolored Christmas lights hung around the perimeter, and the focal point was a six-foot artificial tree that had so much tinsel on it, it almost looked like it was made of silver. The room was dry and hot, with a faint medicinal odor. We dumped our coats in a walk-in closet off the kitchen and went out to mingle, offering coffee and tea to the residents while Michael Bublé crooned on a Christmas CD in the background.

I chatted up residents with holiday small talk—the recent snow, favorite Christmas songs, whether or not their grandchildren were going to visit, which at times broke my heart.

So many of them seemed forgotten. I noticed one woman in a wheelchair, sort of off by herself at the end of the long table where Ava was teaching some of the residents how to make pom-pom wreaths, and walked over to see if I could get her anything.

"Tea," she said softly. Her hair was the color of straw, all drawn up in a messy bun, and her face was plump, cheeks drooping into soft jowls that shook when she spoke.

I returned with a Styrofoam cup of tea, steam swirling above it as I set it down on the table in front of her. "Here you go," I said, smiling.

She glared at me and swiped the cup sideways off the table. I hopped out of the way just in time, barely missing the scalding fountain of tea that would have sprayed across my jeans.

"Don't want no tea," she sputtered, frightening the residents closest to her. "Who the hell are you?"

Sweat trickled down the back of my neck as the woman stared at me with curious gray eyes that appeared slightly unfocused, like it wasn't really me she was seeing. I touched my necklace, holding the love charm between my thumb and forefinger, a habit that had become instinctive in the last few days. A hand on my shoulder brought me back to the present.

"Everything all right?" Luke asked.

I moved the charms across the chain a few times before letting them drop. His eyes danced across my chest, taking in the necklace, then back to my face.

"Yeah, thanks," I said. Mrs. Fiore and a heavyset female attendant dealt with the situation. I cleaned up the mess. The attendant spoke to the woman in the wheelchair in a less comforting tone than I would have imagined to be appropriate.

"Rosie, that wasn't very nice. This young lady is here to help us," she said, motioning at me.

Rosie cried, bringing both hands up to hide her face. I felt terrible. Mrs. Fiore patted Rosie's back, then came over to me. The attendant whisked her out of the room.

"I'm sorry," I said.

"It's okay, it happens sometimes," Mrs. Fiore said. "Why don't you join the party?"

I hung around Ava's craft table, but it only further depressed me. At one time these adorable old people, as Ava called them, were our age, with their futures ahead of them. I thought of my own grandpa, how he'd fought in the Korean War, all those old black-and-white photos of him and Grandma, how dramatic everything looked, how dressed up they got for something as simple as a picnic at the lake. I couldn't imagine them here, making pom-pom Christmas wreaths and never getting any visitors. Wasn't there something more we could do?

One of the St. Gabe's guys played "Jingle Bell Rock" on the piano, which got the residents clapping along. Across the room Luke chatted with a red-haired woman in a reindeer sweater. He tossed back his head and grinned, enthralling the woman. If I couldn't see she was in her nineties, I might have imagined he was hitting on her. For that matter, he still might have been. He took the bell from around his neck and placed it around hers. She beamed up at him from her seat. Maybe he did have some hidden depths. He certainly dealt with people better than I did.

"It's cake time," Ava announced, striding up to me while wielding her clipboard and crossing off something else on her to-do list.

"I'll cut," I answered, jumping at the chance to feel useful.

The kitchen was cooler than the rec room, and quiet. My Camelot skills came in handy, and I attacked the cake like a surgeon, cutting thin slices while another girl scooped vanilla ice cream onto them. The volunteers lined up to carry out cake to the residents. There was a small slab of cake left that I pushed to the side, waiting for Mrs. Fiore's orders on whether to save it or trash it. I picked up the metal server and ran it under warm water, working the icing off with my fingers.

Luke sidled up to me and placed the extra cake he was holding on the counter.

"Hiding out?" he asked, facing me.

"That obvious? I sort of suck at volunteer work, don't I?"

"Nah, I think it takes substantial talent to make an old lady toss her tea across the table. Frankly I was impressed."

"Funny," I said, genuinely cracking a smile. "And you

looked like you were about to get lucky with that redhead."

His eyes lit up as he smiled, completely transforming his face. He was unnervingly scorching when he wasn't pouty and brooding. "You should have heard what she said to me."

"Giving her that bell was sweet. You made her day," I said, scraping some stubborn icing off the other side of the cake server and shaking off the flustered feeling that sprung up when he looked at me that way.

"It has to suck, you know? I mean, if I'm ever stuck in a place where the highlight of my day is a sing-along and some red-velvet cake, well, fuck, just put a pillow over my head and put me out of my misery."

I laughed, a loud pop of a laugh that surprised me. "You're awful."

"Although this cake," he said, pinching off a piece from the leftover cake and popping it into his mouth, "is pretty damn good."

"Looks yummy," I said.

"Here," he said, grabbing another bit and holding it against my mouth. "Try it."

The icing touched my upper lip. My hands were still under running water, and I had no choice but to open my mouth or the piece would have tumbled down the front of my sweater. Luke's thumb grazed my bottom lip. The air in the room became dense, hot, as his eyes held mine.

"Good, huh?"

I broke his gaze, mumbled *mm-hmm* as the cake melted in my mouth. My fingers were pruney from the water. I turned off the faucet and shook my hands dry. Luke handed me a paper towel.

"That's an unusual necklace," he said.

"Um, thanks," I replied, focusing on drying the cake server and putting it away.

"Do you mind?" he asked, reaching toward my neck. Before I could say anything, Luke had the charms in his hand, gently tugging me toward him. I had no choice but to follow, afraid the necklace would break otherwise. His face was calm with concentration as he studied it.

"Love," he said, directly to me. "Grayson gave this to you?"

"Perceptive," I replied, to which he arched an eyebrow. "Now could you let go?"

He held on to it a second longer, then let the charms fall to my collarbone. I went back to cleaning up, hoping he'd take the snub as a sign to leave.

"I was with him when he got that."

"Right," I said. The likelihood of Grayson and Luke going jewelry shopping together was absurd.

"Seeing Grayson later?"

"Yes. He's picking me up from school."

"Could you tell him I need to speak to Mike Pearson?"

"If you're his best friend, why don't you just call him?" I asked, walking past him and throwing the cake plate into the garbage can. When I turned around, I was nose to nose with the Polo insignia on Luke's red sweater.

"Because it would mean more coming from you."

My curiosity was piqued, and against my better judgment, which would have been to just freakin' walk away, I asked, "Does this have anything to do with the favor he did for you?"

Luke's face contorted in confusion; he tilted his head to the side. "Favor. For me?"

Even though I'd tried to give Grayson the benefit of the doubt, I still had the feeling he was holding something back. As much as I hated bringing it up with Luke, I forged ahead, hoping to get some more information.

"You know, the girl at the mall?"

He looked past me, blinking a few times before his full lips curled in understanding.

"Allegra? The hot chick about yay high," he said, putting his hand up to his chest to show her height, then cupping both his hands to mime boobs. "Rack like that? So you know about her?"

My legs felt like liquid as all my worst fears danced in my head. I stared down at my feet and bit the inside of my cheek.

"Come on, you believe Grayson was doing me a favor? You're smarter than that."

"Leave me alone." I shoved past him.

"Wren, chill. I'm not surprised Grayson wouldn't talk to you about hooking up with that girl. Hell, I'm jealous for you."

"Don't be," I snapped, frantically looking for something to do, but the kitchen was clean. The last thing I wanted to do was go back and pretend to be in a holiday mood, but that was better than staying with Luke. He stepped closer, putting his hands on either side of the counter, cornering me before I had the chance to move away.

"Hey," he said, softer, his head hung low, his mouth by my ear. "I wasn't trying to upset you."

"Sure you were," I said, shifting to glare at him.

"This is between me and Grayson. You just happen to be in the way."

"Let me fix that."

"Wren, wait," he whispered, blocking my exit.

His face was so close, I could make out the different shades of brown and green in his eyes. He broke our gaze, glancing down at my mouth. The tip of his nose brushed against my cheek as his lips touched mine. The kiss was soft, and it caught me off guard. Instinctively I closed my eyes as my mouth melted against the warmth of his, but then I pushed him away, trembling with anger. Our lips parted with a soft smacking noise. The swinging doors opened with a groan, causing us both to jump.

Ava. Her mouth formed a small, surprised O. Had she seen?

"The guy from the paper is here," she said, her voice small, echoing through the quiet kitchen. "He wants to take a group picture." The last sentence trailed off as she calculated the scene.

"We were just talking about Grayson," Luke said, sauntering over to her. He threw an arm around her shoulder. "How we should all hang out."

Ava closed her eyes and shivered. "Whatever. Let's just take this effing picture and get out of here. I've filled my community-service quota for the decade."

The two of them disappeared through the swinging doors, and I crumpled. There was no way I was going to take a group picture—the thought of this event being commemorated in any way made my skin crawl—but then Mrs. Fiore poked her head into the kitchen.

"Come on, Miss Co-chair. You're needed!" she said. She was wearing the hat with the dancing Christmas tree and looked just this side of crazy. Before I could protest, she hurried me out to the group huddled in front of the tree and placed me right next to Luke.

When the photos were done, and the spots in my eyes from the flash evaporated, I was the first to pull away from the group.

"Wren," Luke said, putting his hand on my shoulder.

I swatted it off. "I'll talk to Grayson; just get away from me."

"You closed your eyes," he said as I walked away.

I stopped, a stream of students and residents continued flowing around me.

"What?"

"When we kissed," he said, coming closer to me. "You closed your eyes."

My jaw dropped. I jerked my head from side to side to see if anyone had heard what he'd just said. Someone plunked a few keys on the piano, and Mrs. Fiore told the students to form a line to get their coats.

"We," I said as low as I could, "didn't kiss. You kissed me. And I pushed you away, and—"

"And you closed your eyes, and for a second you just went with it," he finished. "All I'm saying is I thought we kind of rocked it, and I think you'd be lying if you said different."

How could I answer that? Closing my eyes had been a reflex, pure and simple. I *had* been curious, but it was the same sort of curiosity that drew me to the edge of the second floor of the mall, wondering what it would be like to toss myself off. I'd never do that, never go over the railing because I knew it would hurt and I'd break something or die right in front of Old Navy. Still, I'd kissed Luke. So there I was. *Splat.*

"You're deluded," I answered, walking away to get my coat.

He easily kept up with me, and we stood at the back of the line, inching up as each person retrieved his or her belongings.

"When you have that conversation with Grayson, and you're feeling really awful about that hot chick from the mall," he said, "just, you know, keep me in mind, if you want a revenge hookup."

"How can you talk like that? You're *with* Ava. I thought you were Grayson's best friend."

For a moment I could see that I'd hit a nerve. On some level his friendship with Grayson mattered to him. Whatever he was playing at now had nothing to do with friendship. Ava came by and shoved his jacket into his chest. He raked his teeth across his lower lip. The glimpse was gone. He stood up straight and put one arm through the sleeve of his jacket.

"All's fair, Wren," he said, walking away, jogging to catch up with Ava, who glared over her shoulder at me. So much for rekindling our BFF status.

I grabbed my coat, avoiding further contact with anyone, and scored a window seat on the bus ride back to Sacred Heart. Mrs. Fiore returned my phone. I had five texts from Grayson. Normally I would have torn right through them, but I rested my head against the window, trying to make sense of all that had happened.

Luke's knowledge of the *mall chick . . . Allegra . . .* burrowed under my skin, giving new life to the fears that I'd squelched about Grayson. There was something he wasn't telling me.

He'd hooked up with her? That thought alone made every nerve in my body sizzle with jealousy. I'd had a gut feeling he'd been doing more than a favor for Luke, but ignorance was bliss. I swiped a few tears away before the bus steered into the Sacred Heart lot, where I saw him perched on the Chrysler. Completely oblivious to the hell I was about to give him.

TWENTY

GRAYSON

I STARED DOWN THE STREET, SHIVERING MY ASS off as I sat on the rear bumper of the Chrysler. Waiting. We were due at my mother's in about three hours. Why wasn't Wren returning my texts?

The wheezing sound of bus brakes got my attention. The bus chugged down the street and into the Sacred Heart lot. My pulse sped up at the thought of seeing her. She'd told me just last week how she loved to walk out of school and see me there.

Me. Grayson Barrett. Boyfriend.

She was the first to get off the bus. Hopping down, she walked with quick, short steps. The hood of her coat was up, the fuzzy fur trim blowing back with her movement. She pulled the hood down, shook out her hair. The corners of my mouth turned up at the sight of her, but as she got closer, I knew something was wrong. Her mouth was a tight, glossy line, and that spot between her eyebrows was creased.

"Hey, you," I said, opening my arms to give her a squeeze, hoping that would help. She stopped about three feet away from me, arms crossed and eyeing me like coming closer would be painful. Her mouth opened and a puff of white escaped, drifted away.

"What's wrong?" I asked.

"Why don't you ask your friend?" she said, her voice catching.

"Friend? Wha—" I stopped, my eyes fixing on Luke. He had his arm around Ava and was talking to a guy I recognized from St. Gabe's. What was he doing here? *You know I wouldn't mind having that conversation with her.*

"What did he say?" I asked, trying to control the rage snaking up in my chest.

Wren shook her head, lips trembling. Silent. This was bad.

My feet took off before my brain was up to speed. Luke and Ava saw me from about a foot away. She let out a yelp as he pushed her out of the way. I freight-trained into him, and we both tumbled down to the pavement, rolling over until we stopped, splayed apart from each other not far from the curb.

"Barrett, what the hell?" he yelled, and scrambled to his feet.

I had one knee up and one still on the ground when the

bottom of his shoe made hard contact with my shoulder, shoving me back. My palms scraped the pavement, and I crab-walked backward, practically knocking over Ava, until I got my footing and stood up, ducking just in time to dodge Luke's fist. I grabbed hold of his jacket, and we spun before I slammed him into the wrought-iron fence that surrounded the front lawn of Sacred Heart. Someone screamed.

"What did you do?" I asked, gathering up the slack of his jacket in my fists and slamming him against the fence again. It knocked the spit out of him, but he brought up both arms in between mine and broke my hold, shoving me away. I stumbled back, fists at the ready.

"I did you a fucking favor," he said, squaring off his shoulders. We circled each other, catching our breath, until Luke lunged toward me. I sidestepped him, letting his momentum carry him past me, but he turned sharp, and his fist clipped my chin. The sting spurned me on, and I landed a punch square on his cheek, my knuckles throbbing. He rubbed the spot where my fist had made contact and laughed.

Grunting, I charged him. He braced himself, chest slamming into mine. We butted against each other, the force making us momentarily still.

"Grayson! Luke! Stop." Faceless voices shouted our names as we spun slowly, pushing into each other, neither one of us backing down.

278

"What . . . did . . . you. . . tell . . . her?" I asked, stammering between shoves.

"The . . . truth," he said, his voice rough with struggle.

Fuck.

I backed away, and Luke fell forward into Ava. She pulled on his jacket, but he batted her off, coming at me again. Adrenaline numbed me from the fight, but twinges of pain prickled through my palms, chin, and shoulder. I steeled myself for his assault. He came at me again, and our arms were around each other, each grappling for the upper hand.

"Why are you doing this?"

"That's my property around her neck, Barrett."

"Drop it. It's over."

"Who said you get to say when it's over?"

"Enough!" a high-pitched voice squealed. We were moving apart from each other but still jabbing. A two-ton guy in a Santa hat was behind Luke, holding him by the elbows. Luke squirmed but finally relented. An older woman with frosted hair and stale coffee breath was in my face, hand up, urging me to back off. I tried to get around her, but she got in my face again with another shrill command of, *"Enough!"*

"Barrett, dude, calm down."

The guy from St. Gabe's had me by the back of my jacket. I twisted away from him.

"Who are you?" the lady asked.

I stepped back.

"You weren't even on the bus . . . why are you here? Where did you come from?" she demanded.

"He's with me, Mrs. Fiore," Wren said, coming to my side and grabbing my hand before I could answer.

Ah, the Harvard-stomping guidance counselor.

"Miss Caswell, this is Sacred Heart property, and you're still representing this school and the Spirit Club. I won't tolerate this. What's your name?"

"Grayson Barrett, ma'am," I answered, standing up straight.

"I'd better not see you within a five-block radius of this school for at least a month, Grayson Barrett, or I'll call the police, do you understand me?"

Luke stood by Ava, triumph on his flushed face.

"Don't forget, Wren," he said.

She flipped Luke off. He pouted and put his hands over his heart in mock hurt, finally scowling at me. My blood boiled. I started toward him again, but Wren dug her nails into my raw hand so hard, I winced.

"Grayson, please, just stop," Wren said, keeping her grip on me. When we got closer to the Chrysler, she let go of my hand. I walked over to the passenger side, to open the door for her. She stopped in her tracks.

"Wren, I can explain," I said, my voice unsteady. Not

knowing what Luke had told her, I wasn't sure what kind of explanation I could offer.

"Do I want to hear it?" she asked. "Whatever it is, it must be really awful for you to go at him like that."

My brain went numb. I put my hands in my hair, tugging at my roots, closing my eyes.

"Why did he say his property was around my neck, Grayson?"

"You heard that?"

"He was looking over your shoulder at me when he said it," she said.

"Wren, please, let's just go somewhere and talk. I'll explain, I promise. What did Luke mean by, *Don't forget*? Don't forget what?"

"He needs to speak to Mike Pearson. He said it would mean more coming from me. What does that even mean, Grayson? Who is that?"

I'd heard that when you die, you see your life flash before your eyes. It hadn't happened when I'd choked, but it happened now. Only, it was Mike Pearson's life that flashed before me. Faces of girls I thought I'd forgotten and houses we'd swiped stuff from all rushed before me as I stood in front of Wren, wondering what I could possibly say to make her understand I'd changed.

"Grayson, please, who's Mike Pearson?"

Of course Luke would know exactly what to say to Wren to make it lethal. I jammed my eyes shut, tried to right the sensation I had of free-falling down a deep dark hole, and took a deep breath.

"Me, Wren. I'm Mike Pearson."

Her eyes turned a brighter shade of blue when she cried.

We sat in the Chrysler, behind the A&P only a few blocks from Sacred Heart. My confession flowed easily, as if I'd only been waiting for the right time to tell her. I left out names and places, details I'd either forgotten or forced myself to forget. I didn't tell her about Andy, Dev, or Logan specifically, just that I had other friends involved. But I told her how we'd worked, how *I'd* worked. There was no spin-doctoring, no *not-exactly-a-lie* half-truths. I felt so detached, it was like I was telling someone else's story. I blocked out her occasional sniffles, trying not to look at her, because every time I did, my heart imploded a little more.

After I finished we sat in silence, broken only by Wren's occasional sobs. I wanted to reassure her that I had changed, that what I had with her was all I wanted, but I sat frozen. The longer we sat, the more scared I became of what she was going to say.

"Did you sleep with any of them?"

I breathed out, closed my eyes, and leaned back on the headrest. There was no turning back from this.

"Two of them," I whispered.

"Allegra?"

"Last spring, Wren. Yes. Before I knew you."

She looked out the passenger window, her breath forming moisture on the glass.

"W-w-what were you doing at the mall?" she stammered, a curtain of hair hiding her face. "Were you planning on hooking up with her again?"

"No." I reached for her, but she shrank away.

"Then what?"

"Luke threatened me. He said he'd talk to you if I didn't go talk to her." Christ, it sounded so dumb. What exactly would he have told her? I'd been with girls? The excuse justified nothing.

"He really has that kind of power over you?"

"Fuck no," I said, looking at her.

"You didn't have to go there—"

"Wren, what we have—"

"We have nothing."

"Don't say that. That other stuff . . . that happened before we met. What we have is real."

"I saw the way she looked at you, Grayson. Don't kid yourself . . . that was real to her."

Wren's words, her eyes, were a knifepoint. All this time I'd justified my actions by pretending to be someone else, but my role in our scamming had been more detestable than stealing

283

goods. Gadgets? Necklaces? iPods? All that stuff the guys took could be replaced. Luke and I were guilty of something way more damaging. Stealing trust. That wasn't something you could pick up at Target or Best Buy. There was really nothing I could say to repair this, but I had to try.

"I'm sorry, Wren. I can't change what I did, but it's not who I am anymore. Not who I want to be. I'm not Mike Pearson. I haven't been for a long time."

"Do you know how ridiculous that sounds? I can't even believe I'm having this conversation," she said, shaking her head.

She opened the passenger-side door. I grabbed her elbow. "Wren, please."

She stared at my hand, then back up at me; the sadness in her eyes sent a shock wave through my body.

"I have to go," she said, sliding away from me.

"Please don't," I whispered. She slammed the door, sending the air freshener spinning, wafts of cinnamon spreading through the car. She walked a few feet away, stopped, and came back, hand poised to open the door, but then she took off again.

I got out of the car. "Wren!"

She kept running, her hair a light brown wave behind her. I got back into the car, ready to put it in Drive, but stopped.

"You fucking idiot," I cursed myself as I clutched the wheel. I'd confessed the short, pathetic half-life of Mike Pearson. It hadn't felt good or cleansing or like any of that psychobabble parents and teachers feed you about how the truth shall set you free. It felt like shit.

When I put the car in Drive, I had no clue where I was headed. I thought of hitting Andy's to see if anyone had known what Luke was up to but decided against it. What did it matter if they knew? The damage was done, and there was no way I wanted Luke to find out he'd gotten the best of me. Staying away was the perfect strategy, even though I wanted to track him down and kick the living shit out of him.

So I drove past the town limits and onto the turnpike. The sound of the wheels on the road became a tranquilizer. I wasn't conscious of where I was heading; all I knew was that I wanted to drive—as if the simple act of getting away from Bayonne would let me leave my past behind. Which was a joke, because my past may as well have been sitting in the backseat, reminding me why I didn't deserve Wren in my life.

This was all for the best, because clearly there was something wrong with me. I'd had every advantage I could possibly have had, and I threw them away in search of . . . what?

Nights of meaningless sex?

Extra Taco Bell cash?

A graduation trip to Amsterdam with my friends?

Why had I gone to see Allegra? To prove to Luke I was willing to fight for what I wanted? Wren did not deserve to be in the middle of this. Who was I kidding? She wasn't in the middle anymore. She was gone. And that had been Luke's goal all along. Wren was right—he did have some sort of power over me.

When I pulled off at the Darien exit, I was almost surprised. Was this really where I wanted to be? I parked on the street outside my mother's and grabbed the bin of Christmas ornaments from my trunk.

My heart raced as I trotted up the small stone steps. The tip of my sneaker caught on the top step, and I tumbled forward, helpless to stop my fall. The bin flew from my hands, crashing a good three feet away. I followed, landing with a thud on my elbow, belly down, my skull an inch from being cracked. The front door squeaked opened.

Footsteps.

"Grayson?"

A pair of brown loafers and a smaller pair of light-up sneakers appeared in my line of vision. Two surprised blue eyes met mine.

"He's bleeding!" Ryder yelled, tearing off back into the house.

Laird crouched down and reached out to examine my face. I flinched but stopped when I saw his look of concern. I was tired, all my fight gone. There was no need to struggle against this. Laird wanted to help me. I'd been nothing but a prick to the guy, yet he still wanted to help me.

"Grayson, he's right, you're bleeding."

"I'm fine," I said, propping myself up, a little dizzy from getting the wind knocked out of me.

"Let me just take a look," Laird said, tilting up my chin to see the left side of my face. His brows drew together.

"You didn't get this from falling, did you?"

I stared down at the walkway.

The door opened again. Ryder dragged Mom toward me; she went from smiling to stricken the moment she saw I was on the ground.

"What happened?" she asked.

"I, um . . ."

"He fell, nicked his chin, nothing a bag of frozen peas won't fix. Think you could hook him up, Ryder?" Laird asked, holding out his hand to me. I grabbed it and pulled myself upright.

I brushed some dirt off my jeans and inspected the damage. The top of the bin had popped off in the fall; a few of the antique ornaments lay on the stone path, shattered.

"I'm sorry, Mom, I—"

"Don't worry about it. Are you all right?"

She brushed some hair away from my face.

No. I was not all right. I was broken and screwed-up. And as I stood there, feeling Wren's absence, all I wanted to do was bawl like a five-year-old. *You must be an awesome big brother,* she'd said. I wanted to be that guy she saw in the picture.

For her. *For me.* Big brother to Ryder and Grier. The son my mother and Laird bragged about. I'd pushed my mother's family away out of some sense of duty to Pop, but he'd moved on. They all had. Except me.

"Yeah, fine," I said.

"I'll get this," Laird said, walking over to the mess.

"Laird," I said. He picked up the top of the bin and turned to me.

"Thanks."

He grabbed the rest and walked toward the house. "Get those peas on that soon. It'll stop the swelling."

"Your father mentioned you were bringing a friend," Mom said.

"She, um, couldn't make it."

"You sure everything's okay?"

"I wanted you to meet her," I whispered, wrapping my arms around her. My chin rested on top of her head. When had she shrunk?

"Next time," she said, pulling away and beaming. "Grier has been talking about you all day. Come on, there's a ton of food."

"Sounds good."

TWENTY-ONE

I RAN.

Mostly because I didn't know what else to do.

Maybe I was trying to outrun Grayson's Mike Pearson confession.

Or maybe I was trying to sprint away from the awful feeling that I'd been humped-and-dumped again. At least, this time, I was the one doing the dumping.

Whatever the reason, I booked it like I'd never had before.

Five blocks, *long blocks*, after I'd left the A&P parking lot, a jagged pain seared up my right side under my rib cage, letting me know how *not* a runner I really was. I doubled over in the middle of the sidewalk, hands on my knees, panting. I collapsed onto the front steps of a large yellow house. I leaned on the slightly rusted railing, sucking in gulps of frigid air until my breathing became almost normal.

The pain grounded me in the moment. I could focus on my breath and not on the haunted look in Grayson's eyes when I'd left. The look that made me feel like I was abandoning him, when, let's face it, he sort of deserved to be abandoned. Giving me a stolen necklace?

No matter how much time had passed since it had been taken—the necklace belonged to someone else. Someone it probably meant something to. Like it meant to me. I tore open my scarf, reached for the chain, and stopped just short of yanking it off my neck. I undid the clasp and tucked it into my coat pocket.

I trudged on, finally realizing what it was I was running from—the urge to go back to Grayson. I still felt that magnetic pull, this sense of belonging with him . . . and I hated it. I couldn't go back to him now . . . possibly ever.

I'd known there was more to Grayson. Some part of himself he kept hidden. These were things he did before we were together. Could I really hold that against him? Everything that had happened between us up until this moment had been genuine. Hadn't it?

But . . . Allegra. The mental picture of them leaning toward each other; the way she'd looked at him. That would take a while to get out of my head, whether or not it meant anything. I wasn't entirely sure the fact it was meaningless to Grayson made me feel any better. Was he capable of being so heartless?

I couldn't go home either. My mother would grill me about my change of plans, and I wasn't ready to face that kind of interrogation. There was one place I knew I could go, no questions asked.

Maddie opened the door, eyes popping as she pulled me in.

"Wren, what the hell? Were you running?" she asked as I whipped off my coat.

"Kind of," I answered, trying to catch my breath. "Jazz is certifiable if she's willing to torture herself like that."

"No argument here," she said, holding out her arms for my coat. The acrid smell of hair dye hit my nose. Maddie's mom was in the kitchen with a styling client. She gave me a quick wave with a small brush covered in thick, white highlighting goop. There was another scent too—craft glue—and as Mads hung up my coat and pointed me toward the dining room, I saw Jazz sitting there sprinkling glitter over something. She stopped when she saw me, like I'd caught her doing something wrong.

"Hey," I said.

"Wren? What are you doing here?"

Maddie sauntered into the room. "She's caught the running bug, Jazzy."

"No freakin' way," I answered as my breathing finally returned to normal.

On the dining room table, there were three rows of cardboard-cutout teacups with names in script across the rims. They'd been in the middle of a project.

"We're working on this for the NHS mother-daughter Christmas tea."

"Yeah, I maintain a 4.0 average so I can make glittery tea-cup place cards. I'm so proud," Maddie interjected as she sat back down on the dining room chair, one leg curled beneath her. She pulled on the sleeve of her oversize black sweatshirt, revealing a sliver of shoulder, and grabbed a Sharpie.

I picked up one of the place settings. *Jasmine Kadam*, it read in fancy calligraphy that I knew was Mads's handiwork. My emotions were raw, right at the surface. I wanted to crush that stupid, glittery teacup in my hand, hating the fact that I didn't have one of my own. *Try again next semester.* What if I didn't get in? There were no guarantees.

But there were no guarantees in life either, were there? The Camelot. My sister, Brooke's, perfect life plan. Grayson. Even my friendship with Mads and Jazz was changing, evolving. With the NHS they were part of something I wasn't—and maybe never would be.

One thing I could guarantee was that I wouldn't be denied entry into the NHS because I was quiet. Quiet could be a lot of things—fierce, thoughtful, compassionate—but never deficient. That teacher evaluation was just a piece of paper. I had to stop letting it define me.

"You both should be proud. It's an awesome accomplishment," I said, my voice high-pitched as I put down the place card on the table. "Much better than being a part of the lame-ass Spirit Club. I made a woman throw her tea at me and cry at today's service project."

"Aren't you supposed to be with Grayson?" Jazz asked. Her question cracked my cool facade. The tears flowed freely, right in front of their baffled faces. I sniffled and sat down in the chair at the head of the table.

"I think we broke up."

"Why didn't you say something?" Mads asked, coming over to me.

"What happened?" Jazz asked, right behind her.

I didn't want to lie, but how could I tell them the truth? What Grayson had confessed was so surreal, I could hardly wrap my mind around it, let alone explain it. What would they think of him?

"I don't want to talk about it here," I said, motioning toward the kitchen, where Maddie's mom was singing softly along with "Livin' on a Prayer" as her client gabbed with her about an upcoming baby shower she was attending.

"Break time," Maddie said.

"We have only five more to go," Jazz said.

"Let me help," I said, grabbing a bottle of silver glitter.

"You sure?"

I stood up and shook the glitter over Maddie's head, laughing. "Yep!"

"So that's the way you want it," she said. "I think gold is a good color for you." She grabbed a different bottle and shook it at me.

"Are you guys completely out of your minds?" Jazz asked.

We both turned on her; she backed away, laughing. "Please don't."

"Beg," I said, glitter poised over her head. She darted between us, grabbing her own bottle.

"I'm faster than both of you, so go ahead, try it."

"Take the right," Mads said. We cornered her, and suddenly there was a frenzy of glitter. The three of us sparkly and laughing.

"Girls!" We stopped.

Maddie's mother stood in the doorway. "You *will* clean that up!"

"Yes, Mom," Mads said, giving one more toss of glitter in our direction.

"Better save some for the teacups," Jazz said.

We made quick work of the rest of the place cards. When we were finished cleaning ourselves and our mess, Maddie disappeared into the kitchen, coming back with bottles of water and a huge bag of pretzels. We retreated to her room. I plopped down on the leopard-print comforter. Jazz sat cross-legged in front of me on the hot-pink shag carpet, looking as though she were waiting for story time at the library. Mads sat behind me and played with my hair.

I told them about the Spirit Club debacle and Luke. How he'd hinted Grayson had hooked up with the girl at the mall. The kiss. I told them about Grayson's confession, almost regretting that I'd revealed too much when I saw Jazz's horrified face. The story of my strange morning poured out and ended with my sprint out of the A&P parking lot. I reached for the charms on my necklace as I spoke, my fingers grasping at the empty space.

"Your necklace! You gave it back?" Jazz asked, noticing.

"Not yet. I can't believe he gave it to me; that's pretty unforgiveable, right?"

A moment passed before either of them replied.

"Wow, Wren, you weren't kidding with the brainathiminal thing," Jazz said. "What are you going to do?"

We both looked at Mads, who was finishing up a tiny braid in my hair. "What?"

"Well?" I asked.

"You're not going to like what I have to say."

"I know—I'd be stupid to ever trust him again."

Jazz nodded.

"Um, no. I was going to say I thought it was kind of . . . hot."

I pulled away to face her.

"Explain," Jazz demanded.

"I didn't say I *approved*. What he did was awful, but he sort of got karmic payback getting kicked out of school. Don't you think? And, well, he hasn't done any of this in a while, right? Like months. A guy with a past is hot. And he wants to change . . . with you. The only things he's guilty of are giving you that necklace and flirting with a girl he hooked up with last spring before he even met you."

"The necklace is bad, Mads," I said.

"And how does Wren know anything else he said was true either?" Jazz asked.

Mads wrinkled her nose at Jazz. "I'm not saying he doesn't deserve to be a little tortured over that necklace. That was a total brain-fart, dick of a move, but . . . Grayson is basically a good guy. Look at his car. I know you guys laugh that I pay attention to that stuff, but a car can tell you a lot about a person. That car tells me he doesn't take himself too seriously. He's not into labels. That's not the car of someone who's trying to put one over on you."

"I guess," I said, smiling a little, thinking of that Home Sweet Home air freshener. Definitely not the accessory of a player.

"Wait a minute. There was one detail of this morning's story that needs further review . . . the part about kissing Ava Taylor's boy toy?"

"Oh, um, he kissed *me*. And it had more to do with pissing off Gray than, like, really wanting to hook up."

Maddie gave me a dismissive snort. "Is he hot?"

"Would definitely cast him as the sexy, troubled bad boy in my movie," Jazz answered.

"Jazz."

"Holy shit, the girl does have hormones," Maddie said.

"It was a territorial thing, completely," I answered.

"Why would you think that? Wren, you're pretty scorching yourself. Who cares if he kissed you to piss off Grayson? The way I see it, you had two smokin'-hot guys fighting over you in front of Sacred Heart . . . more importantly, in front of Ava Taylor. You're like my hero today."

Maddie's take on the situation might have been out there, but it gave me some hope. Maybe it would be possible to forgive him.

"I know the two of you don't approve of my . . . fixation . . . with Zach. And I know the cons list sure outweighs the pros on some days, but when he's with me, he's *with* me, completely. And his kisses freakin' make me melt into a hormonal puddle of hotness."

"What does you being horny have to do with Grayson?" Jazz asked.

"What I'm getting at is—so what if he's been with other girls? It only means he's experienced. You've been with other guys—is he all jacked up over that? We're sixteen . . . this is how it's supposed to be. I've seen you and Grayson together, Wren. He's completely into *you*. Focus on that instead of thinking about things that went on before you met."

"Easy, in theory," I said.

"And now that we have all that figured out, I need you to do something for me," she said, pulling me off the bed.

"What?" I asked.

Maddie ran her fingers through my hair again. "Time to play."

In homeroom on Monday morning, Sister Raphael called me to the front of the room and handed me a slip of paper that read:

Please see me immediately . . . Mrs. Fiore.

Crud. I was hoping the fistfight had been forgotten. Seeing as I hadn't been directly involved, I wasn't sure what she could do. Give me detention for watching?

Enduring the weekend had been punishment enough. I'd fought the urge to call Grayson pretty much up until I'd arrived at school. He didn't call or text, but I had the feeling he was giving me space. Luke, on the other hand, had texted me twice. I wasn't sure how he got my cell number, but considering he'd been arm-in-arm with a certain clipboard-holding adversary who must have had it on one of her lists, I didn't need to be Veronica Mars to figure it out. The first one asking, *R U Ok?*—like he cared. The second one simply read: *you closed your eyes. . . .*

Mrs. Fiore was at her desk, zebra-print half glasses perched on her nose, Precious Moments coffee mug in her hand. The weather outside her window was dismal and gray, making the fluorescent lighting in her office seem more unnatural. Every wrinkle and imperfection was magnified under the greenish tint. I stood in front of her desk, ignoring the impulse to hurl and thinking of something polite to say.

"Sit," she said, gesturing toward one of the orange monstrosities.

I put my books on the floor beside the chair and sat down on the edge of the seat.

"You changed your hair," she said, tilting her head to one side.

"Oh, my friend Maddie did it over the weekend," I said, running my fingers through my freshly ombré-highlighted hair. Mrs. Fiore eyed the blue streaks that Maddie had insisted on adding around my face to make a statement. Mads swore she'd fix it if I didn't like it, but I thought it made me look . . . edgy. It felt right, but sitting there under Fiore's judging gaze, I twirled a section around my fingers, trying to hide it.

"It's interesting," she said finally. "But we both know I didn't bring you in to talk about your hair. We need to discuss what happened over the weekend at the Spirit Club event."

"Mrs. Fiore, I'm sorry about the fight, it won't happen—"

"This isn't about the fight, Wren, although I think I understand why it happened," she said, leaning back in her chair. My heart stopped. What did she know?

She swiveled in her chair before smoothing out her desk blotter. "I know it's fun working with the boys from Saint Gabriel's, but you're still representing the school."

"I . . . um . . . what is this about?" I asked.

Mrs. Fiore took off her glasses and leaned toward me.

"I know about your hookup."

Hookup sounded so wrong coming from her mouth; she could have flashed me, and I would have been less shocked. My throat tightened as I thought about Luke—even though a forced kiss didn't qualify as a hookup in my mind.

"Mrs. Fiore, I didn't hook up with anyone," I said.

She leaned back again. "Wren, I have several people who told me otherwise."

"Several people? That's insane."

She narrowed her eyes. "So you weren't next to the boy in question on the bus? Or in the group photo? The same boy who was in a fight with your friend?"

I gripped the edge of my seat, grasping for some way to explain without spilling my guts. "It's not like it sounds. He kissed *me*."

"Are you saying this wasn't . . . consensual?"

Luke was a shit, but I wasn't about to make *that* big a deal out of it.

"No."

"Then what *are* you saying?"

The tone of her voice got under my skin; it was the same

tone she used for her no-Harvard comment to my Honors Lit class, like she knew better than me. "I'm saying it's none of your business. Why are you even hassling me about it?"

"Yes, it is my business."

"Who told you about this? Ava?"

"That doesn't matter," she said.

"Yes, it does," I said, standing up. "You're accusing me of something that didn't happen, so what you're really saying is that you believe her over me."

She stood up. "But something *did* happen," she said, jabbing the top of her desk with her index finger. "You just admitted it. If this is how you carry yourself outside school, that's your business—but you were on my time. That's the real issue. And I take our commitment to Saint Lucy's seriously."

"*Seriously?* Really? You think making a wreath out of pom-poms was fun for those people? That stops being fun after preschool. There's nothing better we can do with our time there?"

"Sit down, Miss Caswell."

My heart raced as I caved and dropped down into the chair. I'd never raised my voice to a teacher before.

"I could easily give you a detention over this," she said, still standing. "But I won't. Just a warning." She sat down and looked at me, waiting. This was the most in-depth "gettin' real" conversation I'd ever had with Mrs. Fiore. If there was any time to speak my mind, it was in that moment.

"Why don't you think any of us are going to Harvard?"

She flustered. "I didn't mean it the way you're implying."

"Well, it sounded pretty clear. I don't want to be told what I *can't* do before I even start trying."

She ran her fingers across her lips, then rested her chin in her hand. "The truth is that the majority of you won't go to an Ivy League school, and that's fine. There are so many options out there. Different paths. It's my job to let you know what choices you have, help you find your way. Although I don't think *your* best path would be making the Vatican out of toothpicks."

I laughed. "I wasn't serious about that."

A smile played at the corners of her mouth. Was she joking with me?

"I know. You do sound passionate about Saint Lucy's though. You really thought the craft was—"

"Lame."

"What would you have done instead?"

What got to me the most was how forgotten the residents seemed to be.

"I don't know, some of them just seemed happy talking, but maybe we could connect them with their families. Write letters. Help them make phone calls or something."

"The Spirit Club makes monthly visits to Saint Lucy's. These are voluntary, so you can imagine the turnout. A lot of the students who visit there just do it for the service hours.

You have some interesting ideas, Wren. Maybe you could—"

"I'd like that. A lot better than decorating the hallway too."

The bell for second period rang, and a flurry of activity—doors opening, footfalls, chatter—went on outside the door. Mrs. Fiore grabbed a pink pad. She signed the top sheet with a flourish, peeled it off, and handed it to me. It was a note letting my second-period teacher know why I was late. I grabbed my books and stood up, ready to leave.

"Wren, wait," she said. "Thanks for commenting on my speech. I never realized . . . how that might have sounded. Nice to know someone was listening."

Was I actually having a friendly conversation with Mrs. Fiore? I wasn't overthinking or worrying about what I said before I said it. We might not be giving each other mani-pedis anytime soon, but it was a start.

"Thanks for not giving me detention, Mrs. Fiore."

The hallway was mostly empty. A few stragglers scurried as the warning bell for second period sounded. The good feelings from my momentary victory with Mrs. Fiore faded. This incident had Ava written all over it. But why wouldn't she just confront me? I wondered what Luke had told her about what she saw—probably twisting it around to where I forced myself on him. I wondered if some guidance counselor was torturing Luke for his behavior. Probably not.

I sat through my next two classes, barely absorbing the lessons, hoping for the opportunity to question Ava before

Honors Lit began, but she slipped into her seat as the bell rang, not even a glance in my direction. At lunch I stormed into the cafeteria on a mission, barely dropping my books with Mads and Jazz.

"Wren?" Mads called after me.

Ava, flanked by her usual posse of worshippers, was placing a supermarket bento box of sushi on the table as I approached. Darby Greene tapped her shoulder and whispered something. An uncomfortable couple of seconds passed where no one seemed to think it was necessary to acknowledge my presence. Ava finally looked up as she slipped the chopsticks out of their red wrapper. Her eyes zeroed in on the blue streaks in my hair.

"Nice hair. What, did you do a Smurf over the weekend?"

Oh, how I wanted to smash a California roll up her nose. Darby raised her eyebrows and took a slow sip of her Diet Coke, daring me to strike back at Ava. Jazz and Mads were suddenly next to me. Their support fueled my fire.

"No, I did Luke Dobson," I said, letting his name roll slowly off my tongue. "And you know, you're right, he *can* do some pretty amazing things with his mouth."

Jazz gasped. Ava froze, chopsticks poised.

"Nice one," Mads whispered.

"So can we talk now?" I asked.

Ava tossed the chopsticks on the table. She stood up with such force, the green plastic caf chair fell behind her, startling a girl at the next table, who hopped up when it hit the floor.

"Let's go." She barreled past me.

I followed Ava as she pushed through the swinging doors into the empty locker bay next to the caf. The deep bellow of someone practicing tuba echoed from the music room. Ava faced me, her eyes sharp.

"So, what?" she asked.

"Why did you tell Fiore I hooked up with Luke?"

She crossed her arms and stared at me, not giving an inch.

"Don't pretend you didn't do it. You were the one who walked in on us in the kitchen."

Her nostrils flared, her eyes calculating and cold. "Us? There is no 'us' when it comes to you and Luke. If you think for one minute he enjoyed that . . . pathetic."

"Didn't feel that way when he kissed me."

She nibbled her bottom lip fiercely. I stood firm, hands on hips, waiting for a response. We held each other's glare, neither daring to blink. Finally Ava grunted a smug-sounding *humph*.

"Wren, I'm sure you've enjoyed your tour of A-listdom, but it's over. So just drop it and go back to your nonexistent, sad, little social life."

"A-listdom? What are we, twelve?" I countered. "If your *gravitating* with Luke is what you call A-list, then fine, count me out. The way you two treat each other? What kind of relationship is that? At least I know I have real friends."

305

"I'm talking about Andy's party and the laughable pairing of you and Grayson Barrett. You do realize that's the only reason Luke was even talking to you, right? You think it was an accident the seat next to him on the bus was empty? Or that I even wanted you there as co-coordinator? You've been played, Wren. *Played*. Let me guess, you and Grayson broke up? Imagine that."

The meaning of what she'd said made my breath catch in my throat. Her mouth curled into a victorious smirk. Saturday played in reverse through my mind. The kiss. The empty seat on the bus. The way Luke had been there when I'd arrived that morning for the St. Lucy trip, joking with me. Had it really reached as far back as Ava inviting me to lunch in Mrs. Fiore's office?

Still . . . I'd seen her face when she'd walked in on us, and her reaction just before in the cafeteria. Ava had many talents, but she wasn't *that* good of an actress. No matter what hurtful crap came out of her mouth, I realized how much of a sore point it was for her that Luke had kissed me.

"So Luke's offer of a revenge hookup was just something he did because he was playing me? I guess his texts over the weekend were about playing me too. And I bet he got my cell number from you, because I didn't give it to him. Sounds like you're being played too, Ava."

"I'm done with you," she said, shaking her head and walking away. She turned back sharply, jutting out her hip, and continued, "Where do you even come off saying that to me?"

"Just wondering if you really know him."

"Because you do? Please. How well do you know Grayson? Guess you won't have to worry about that anymore."

"I know Grayson really well, and this stupid little drama you created did nothing to change that, Ava. We're closer than ever. So make sure you tell that to Luke. Or maybe I'll just text him myself."

I brushed past her, buzzing with anger, and pushed open the doors to the cafeteria. Maddie and Jazz were cleaning up as I approached the table. I sat down, head in my hands. I wondered if Ava knew the truth—the *whole* truth.

"Everything okay?" Mads asked.

Then it hit me. Luke had played Grayson too. He'd known exactly what to say to get under my skin and knew it would lead to our breakup. Why he felt it necessary to go that far, I wasn't sure. Maybe he was just sadistic.

The one person who could understand what was going on was Grayson. I'd told myself I'd wait until things cooled down to contact him, but I didn't want to wait anymore. Besides, I hadn't told him what had happened at St. Lucy's. What if Luke said something to him first? I had the sudden, overwhelming urge to speak to him.

"Jazz, you need to cover for me in Chem last period."

TWENTY-TWO

I WAS A ZOMBIE.

Not the flesh-hungry, decimating-the-world, take-'em-out-with-an-AK-47 type of zombie.

I was a walking void in a skin suit.

I could not stop thinking about Wren or the way she'd run from me on Saturday. There were no corners of my mind to hide away in. No thrash punk angry enough to pound away my troubles on the drums. Nothing but the raw pain I felt any time I thought about what a colossal screw-up our short-lived relationship had become.

My mother's house had been . . . comforting. Playing with Ryder and Grier managed to occupy my mind, made me feel like things weren't dire. I was their *awesome big brother*. Wren helped me see that. Laird apologized for the way Cooper had put me on the spot at Thanksgiving. We even spoke about what strings he could pull at Columbia for me. It was a reach at this point, but it was something to focus on. It was the first time I was almost bummed to leave their house.

The ride home was torture. Going home to more silence was a depressing option, so I went to Andy's, just to see if he or anyone else knew what Luke had done . . . or what he was planning to do. I'd found Andy, stoned and strumming his guitar alone in the basement. Luke had already filled him in on what had happened earlier in the day.

"Are you expecting him anytime soon?" I asked, not wanting to run into him just yet for fear I'd ram his head into the bar.

Andy shrugged. "Didn't say."

"Why is it so important I'm still a part of this?"

Andy stopped strumming and looked at me with glazed eyes. "Dude, I don't know. I say we just cut our losses and throw an epic party with the money. But you know Luke. He wants things to be like they were before you got kicked out, and when he wants something . . . he's a prick till he gets it. No one's allowed to be happy if he isn't."

Even stoned, Andy nailed the situation.

School on Monday offered relief. At least I could lose myself in velocity and acceleration. Problems my mind could plug into and figure out instead of brooding over Wren. When school was over, the screw-up reel in my head played again.

Could I catch Wren at Sacred Heart? Should I even bother? Why couldn't there be some theorem to help me with that?

I shuffled along with the rest of the Bergen Point inmates as we spilled out onto the gum-stained pavement. The day was bright but colorless, like living in a black-and-white film. I dug into my pocket and grabbed my keys, debating where to go instead of heading home to stare at my ceiling. In the middle of the crosswalk, I stopped short, sure I was hallucinating the figure leaning against my bumper.

The crowd continued past me. Some guy knocked into me and mumbled, "Douche." The crossing guard blew her whistle with the ferocity of a football referee and motioned for me to get onto the sidewalk. The hallucination was still there.

She stood out against the colorless day, improbable and beautiful. A wildflower in winter sprung up from a crack in the concrete. I inched my way closer and kept my eyes on hers, as if one wrong move or thought would make her evaporate. She lowered her gaze and bit her lip. So many feelings rushed through me . . . relief, fear, love . . . Wren being there meant something. Good or bad, I wasn't sure.

"I almost gave up," she said. "I walked through the parking lot twice, looking for your car, and figured maybe I missed you, so I walked up this block to head to the bus, and I found it, and . . ."

"Here you are."

"Grayson, I still don't know how I feel about the other day.

310

It's just what you told me? The whole morning . . . the fight? It was a lot to take in."

"A complete mindfuck," I said.

She laughed. "I guess you could call it that."

I leaned next to her on the bumper, dropping my backpack at my feet.

"I never meant for you to find out like that."

"You never meant for me to find out."

What could I say?

"Grayson, I get it. There never would have been a good time. . . . But I guess I'm glad I know."

"Really?"

"Not sure," she said, chuckling. Adjusting her position she faced me, hip against the bumper, and tucked some hair behind her ear. The blue hair suited her. I had to stop myself from touching it. The first move needed to be hers. She dug into her coat pocket.

"Here—I've been carrying this around since the weekend," she said, the necklace dangling from her fingers. "I can't keep it. Obviously."

I grabbed the physical reminder of just how royally I messed up and shoved it into my own pocket to deal with later. "Giving you that necklace was the stupidest thing I've ever done."

"Nah . . . taking me skating was a pretty bad move, considering how terrible you are on the ice," she said, tugging the open collar of my jacket. I turned toward her.

"Wren . . . the only thing I could think about all weekend was that look on your face when you left . . . how much I hurt you. I'm so sorry. I know what I did was wrong, all of it, and I wish I could change everything. You deserve better than this. I don't expect you to just . . . trust me . . . but that's not me anymore. I would never do anything to hurt you."

"I know that," she said, moving closer to me.

"Being with you is all I want," I whispered. "Forgive me, please." My forehead grazed the top of her head. I took in the summery scent of her hair and allowed myself to feel the barest hint of a hope.

"I do," she whispered, bringing her face up to mine.

Our lips touched, lightly at first. When I was sure she wasn't going to pull away, I wrapped my arms around her, felt her arms snake around me.

"Sacred Heart girls—easy access!" someone yelled.

Wren laughed into my mouth and stepped back to take in the mob scene herding up the street.

"I'm not a very good Sacred Heart rep."

"Yeah, you are," I said, running my fingers through the blue part of her hair.

Wren folded her arms across her chest and winced.

"Grayson, I never told you my side of Saturday."

"You have a side?"

"Why don't we go somewhere warmer to talk?"

Somewhere warmer was a booth in the back of our diner. Coffee for me, cocoa for Wren, and a huge slab of the World's Best Boston Cream Pie to share.

We sat side by side, shoulders touching. She hadn't said a word on the ride over. The miracle of her being there with me, of even talking to me, still hadn't worn itself out, and I didn't want to jeopardize it. I took a forkful of pie and held it up for her. She opened her mouth, sliding her lips across the fork and grinning as she tasted it—an unintentionally sexy move that left me wishing we were somewhere more private.

"So, Saturday . . . what happened?" I asked, digging the fork into the pie for a bite of my own.

Wren dabbed the corner of her mouth with a napkin. She folded a knee up onto the bench of the booth so that she faced me. Finishing my bite of pie, I gave her my full attention.

She fumbled with her coat, reached into the pocket, and pulled out her phone.

"I had a fight with Ava today."

"About what?" I asked, alarmed. Was Ava in on this too?

"Well . . . she told Mrs. Fiore I hooked up with a guy from Saint Gabe's during our service project. Even had people back up her story."

"That's a crock, right?"

She leaned on her elbow and rested her forehead into her open palm. The pie felt heavy in my gut. Her hand slid down her face before she looked at me between her fingers.

"Luke kissed me."

"Excuse me?"

"It happened really fast. He kind of cornered me before I could stop him. . . . I wanted you to hear it from me."

It surprised me that Luke hadn't offered up that information himself. It would be just like him to prod me with some random text like, *Wren's lips taste like candy, bro.*

"And Ava told me today that the whole thing—me being there to help out—was all just so Luke could, I don't know, piss you off or keep tabs on you or something."

"Classic friggin' Dobson," I said, mashing the edge of the pie with each word.

"Why would he do this?"

"He wants me to be, ah, active again."

"Active? You mean . . ."

"Find hits."

"Oh. Like Allegra," she said into her cocoa mug, before taking a sip.

"Wren, stop."

I reached for her hand as she put down the mug. There was a moment of hesitation on her part, her hand unyielding. Then she softened. I entwined my fingers with hers, finally relaxing, when she gave my hand a squeeze.

"Luke isn't going to drop this, is he?" she asked.

"Probably not," I said.

She pushed her phone toward me, showing me her message history.

You closed your eyes.

He texted her? My throat tightened. "What does that mean?"

"It's what he said to me after . . . he, you know . . . kissed me."

"You closed your eyes?" I asked. It wasn't fair of me to be angry. I knew it, but I couldn't help it.

"Don't even go there, Grayson. It lasted, like, a second, if that, and I shoved him away."

"Wren . . . I didn't mean . . ." I said, not wanting to lose her again. "It just makes me . . . want to hurt him. That's all."

She growled, buried her face in my shoulder. "Me too. Ava . . . *ugh* . . . it was like she got off on telling me how they tricked me. We have to do something."

"I'll take care of it."

"Grayson, I'm sick of people . . . underestimating me. Thinking they can walk all over me because I'm not some loudmouth bitch."

"Luke likes to mess with people. It will drive him nuts if we ignore him. Trust me."

"He said to keep him in mind if I wanted a revenge hookup."

I laughed. "Yeah, right. Want me to drive you to his place?"

"I'm serious. Why don't we just . . . I don't know, set him up somehow. . . ."

"Wren, he would see it from a mile away."

"So that's it, you're just going to let him get away with it."

"No, I don't want you involved."

"I already am. They used me to get to you. Luke wanted us to break up, and . . . well, we almost did, didn't we?"

"Wren."

She grabbed her phone, typed a message, and hit Send.

"Well, better think of something . . . fast," she said, pushing the phone back to me, that devious smile from the ice rink crossing her lips.

Luke—Still have your property . . . want it? Wren

The die had been cast.

LUKE WAS TEN MINUTES LATE.

I surveyed my house, praying my mother wouldn't look out the window. She and Dad were having a much-needed "date night in," complete with the latest rom-com from Redbox and takeout from their favorite Spanish restaurant. And while that hadn't been part of my plan, having them busy with their own stuff made it much easier to slip out, no questions asked. As far as they knew, I was waiting for Maddie and Zach to pick me up, not having a faux-revenge hookup with Luke at the love shack. I was grateful it hadn't occurred to them to wonder why I'd stand outside in below-freezing weather.

The plan was simple: entice Luke to the cottage, where Grayson and Andy were waiting to talk to him, sort of like an intervention. Grayson wasn't into it at first; he thought Luke wouldn't fall for it. But the more we talked it out, the more he came around, thinking that maybe the element of surprise would make Luke vulnerable. And, okay, I wanted to prove that I could play this game too, to send a message. He had toyed with the wrong quiet chick.

"Wren."

I startled. "Are you part ninja?"

Luke was in his varsity jacket and dark jeans, mane of hair loose around his face. He seemed pleased with my reaction.

"No, thought I should meet the parents and all that, so I parked."

This was already not going the way I imagined.

"Kidding," he said, holding out his hand. I hesitated, then put my hand in his. His fingers wrapped around mine, warming me up. Could I really do this?

"Just trying to be a gentleman," he said, leading me up the block to his car. "For now."

I ignored his comment, but it put me even more on edge. He opened the passenger door, and I slid in, trying to work up the nerve to introduce step two of my plan. He got in and put the key in the ignition.

"So . . . where to?"

I took out the key to the cottage from my pocket and dangled it in front of him.

"You got us a room? Eager."

"Ha . . . It's for the cottage . . . at the Camelot . . . one of the perks of being the owner's daughter . . . so we can be . . . alone."

"There's no one home at my house," Luke said, the corner of his mouth curling into a slow smile that made me momentarily forget that being alone was not the goal of this conversation.

I held my breath, grasping for an argument.

"Well, the cottage is the first place Grayson and I . . . you know . . . hooked up, so I was thinking it would mean more if we went there. Kind of . . . poetic, I guess."

"Hmm . . . poetic," he said, charging the engine. "The cottage it is then."

The Camelot was only a ten-minute drive from my house but that night it felt like an hour. We caught every red light. I stared out the window, trying to think of some casual conversation to fill up the time. Just when I was about to ask him about school, he spoke.

"Heard about your catfight with Ava the other day."

"Really? I'm sure she exaggerated."

"She told me what you said. About me. Didn't realize what a dirty mouth you had. Have to say I kinda like it. The blue streaks too. Very, um, Katy Perry."

I did Luke Dobson.

"Oh, huh, that." My skin became molten. "I said that to piss her off."

"Well, it worked," he said, signaling to turn up a side street.

"We're not speaking."

"Sorry about that . . . I guess," I said.

"Ha. Right. Don't be. I'm a bit player on Planet Ava. When she needs me for something, she'll be back." He gunned through a yellow light, then slowed down a bit after we passed the intersection. "It's Grayson she's really after, even if she thinks I don't know it."

I sat with that information for about half a block. Did he just say that to mess with me?

"Didn't she do all that . . . set me up . . . for you?"

He tapped the steering wheel with his index finger. "You don't get it, do you? She's, like, bat-shit-crazy jealous of you. She wasn't helping me; she was helping herself."

"No . . ." I said, trailing off as I mentally walked through my moments with Ava in the past month. *She kind of stalked me last year,* Gray had said. Her dis in the hallway; the way she'd looked at me at Andy's party, being so smug when she'd thought we'd broken up. I thought she was just being mean but . . . jealous?

"But," I said, "she was with you."

"*With* me? Nah. It's not like that."

His posture softened as he shifted in his seat. There was something unguarded about his words. Maybe he was good at manipulating people, but Ava wanting Grayson bothered him, I could hear it. He didn't appreciate being . . . what? Second-rate? Luke, who could probably have any girl licking

320

buttercream frosting off his cleats, couldn't have Ava, not the way he really wanted.

"Don't judge me with those baby blues, Wren."

"Not judging. It's just . . . you don't seem like the kind of person who would put up with that."

"How is it any worse than putting up with a guy who boffed half of New Jersey and gave you a stolen necklace? We're all willing to overlook a few things when we get what we need, right? Ava filled a need, and we had a few laughs. What's your payoff?"

"I don't really look at it that way."

"Sure you do. I bet Grayson makes you feel . . . special. He was always good at that."

His observation jabbed me in a raw place. I'd come to terms with Grayson's past . . . sort of . . . but I didn't like to be reminded.

"He doesn't make me feel much of anything now."

"Where should we park?"

I'd been so caught up in what he'd been saying that I hadn't noticed we reached the Camelot. A car parked in the empty lot would be like sending up a flare, so I directed him to a spot on the block next to it. He turned off the car and leaned back. I reached for the door handle, felt his hand on my knee.

"How 'bout a little warm-up?"

"What?" I asked, slouching back into my seat.

"Or are you having second thoughts?"

You're supposed to want to be here.

"No, no second thoughts."

"C'mere," he whispered, reaching for me.

This was not real. Luke's fingertips on the nape of my neck, pulling me toward him, the gentle way he spoke. This was a show, a play. My mind fed me all sorts of ways to detach—Maddie's notion that this was what being sixteen was all about; Grayson's warning about the *Dobson mindfuck*—but my body told me a different story.

Luke swept his lips across mine, soft, surprising, his tongue tracing the curve of my mouth, seducing me to open up. I closed my eyes and let him in, the spearmint taste of his mouth making my lips tingle. Me. Melting into a hormonal puddle of hotness.

This kiss made me want to kiss him back.

And I felt sick. For me. For all the girls who had fallen for him, for this.

Did he feel *nothing?*

I broke away before my body betrayed me even more.

"Luke, why don't we take this inside?"

"Why don't we forget this and go to a movie or get a steak . . . or drive somewhere till we run out of gas?"

I ran my finger down the front of his jacket, tugging on one of his pockets. "Don't you want to um . . . hook up?"

"I like you, Wren. Not everyone gets in your head, do they? They have to earn it," he said, snaking his hand into my hair. He kissed the tip of my nose, my cheek, my lips again. "I'd like that payoff."

He couldn't possibly be sincere . . . and even if he was . . . this was Luke. This was . . . wait . . .

"You're doing the Brinker thing, aren't you? Wow . . . you're good."

He backed off, chuckled to himself, and took the keys out of the ignition.

"Grayson told you everything."

"He told me enough."

His eyes held mine, steady, sure. "If I was doing the Brinker thing, you'd be undressed already."

I swallowed. "Well, then, let's go."

I was out of the car before he could say anything else. He grabbed my hand as we walked toward the cottage. We were almost to the front door when he stopped short. The momentum made me jerk back and face him. He walked toward me, forcing me to walk backward a bit.

"How far are we going to take this game of chicken?"

Five seconds away from Grayson. Ugh.

"What?"

He put his hands on my waist, pulled me to him again.

"Wren, c'mon. You're not the casual-hookup type. Grayson

323

and Andy are right behind that door, waiting to what? Kick my ass?"

"I don't know what you're talking about."

Without warning he brought his face close to mine, as if he were going in for a kiss. I could feel the heat of his mouth, inches away.

"What's so fucking great about Grayson Barrett?" he whispered.

"Luke!" Grayson shouted behind us. Urgent. Angry.

Luke smirked and stepped away, "He's so predictable."

My hand went up to my mouth. He'd known. He'd known the whole time.

Grayson pushed Luke away from me. "Are you okay?"

"Dude, we were holding hands."

"Shut up," he snapped, then looked at me.

"Let's just get inside," I said.

"After you," Luke said.

"No, after you," Grayson said, draping his arm over my shoulder. Luke sauntered through the front door. We followed.

My stomach sank; I just wanted this to be over. Gray closed the door behind us. A small table lamp cast shadowy light across the room. I thought about Eben's warning about keeping the lights out, but I knew it wouldn't fly. Besides, who would see us? No one was over at the Camelot, so as far as I could tell, we were good.

Luke stood in the middle of the room, hands in his pockets. Grayson stood in front of him, arms crossed. Andy and I leaned against the wall near the kitchen, as if we were waiting for a show.

"Okay, Barrett, I'm here. Now what?"

"I want out, Luke."

Luke rolled his eyes. "And we're talking about this in front of her, why?"

"You're the one who brought Wren into this, thanks to the shit you pulled the other day."

Luke looked at me, then at Andy. "Get her out of here."

Andy pulled back my arms until it felt like they'd come out of their sockets. I lurched forward, trying to break away, but he had me in an impossible hold.

"Foley, what are you doing?" Gray asked.

"You didn't think he'd tell me what was going on?" Luke asked, moving closer to Andy and me.

"Gray, dude, I'm neutral. Kiss and make up already. I've got a house party to hit by ten," Andy said.

"Let me go." I tried to wrench free from Andy. He tugged me back. Grayson took a step toward us, and Luke blocked his way.

"I'll give you the necklace. Why don't we just call it even?"

"Class act giving it to Wren, by the way. No. I want

something bigger. What about those Marshall amps back there? Are they shit or vintage? What do you think we can get for them, Andy?"

"No!" I said.

"Not sure, can't tell, maybe a couple hundred," Andy said, behind me.

"You can't have them," I insisted.

"Or," Luke said, "maybe Wren should join us. Might shake things up, having a chick on the team. She was quite convincing. I think we may have shared a genuine moment."

Grayson was on him in an instant. They tumbled into the end table, knocking over the lamp, which landed with a crack and went out. I screamed. Andy pulled me away from the commotion. I fought him the whole time, grunting, leaning forward, thrashing back, trying to kick my legs up or gain leverage on the wall as he pulled me into the kitchen and away from the door frame.

"Let . . . me . . . go," I said, struggling. "They're wrecking the place."

"And what are you going to do about it? Just let them hash it out. It'll be over soon."

I huffed while a blur of Grayson and Luke passed before the doorway, followed by another loud rumble against the wall. *Over soon* was not something I was willing to wait for; they had to be stopped.

326

"Sorry, Andy," I said, stomping down on his toe as hard as I could.

Andy dropped an F-bomb as he let go. I scurried out of the kitchen just as a loud *crash* erupted in the sitting room. Grayson stood in the center of the room, doubled over and gasping. Luke popped up from behind the love seat, brushing glass off his sleeve from the front window. I tried not to think about how I was going to deal with that and instead crouched down next to Grayson.

"Are you okay?" I asked. There was a dark, glistening trickle coming from his nose.

"I'm fine. Wren . . . get out of here . . . now."

"You're bleeding," I said, moving the hair away from his face.

He stood up and grabbed my shoulders. "Please, just go."

"Yes, Wren, get out of here," Luke said, behind me.

I spun around and stood firm in front of Grayson.

"Stop, already," I said.

"Move away," Luke growled, coming closer.

"Dudes, really, enough," Andy said, finally emerging from the kitchen. He stepped toward Luke but was greeted with a punch. He staggered back, holding his nose.

"Just take the amps, go!" I yelled.

Luke bared his teeth. Grayson gripped my shoulders from behind, shoving me out of the way.

Beams of light swirled across the floor, onto the ceiling, on Luke's bloodied face, in my eyes.

I put up my hands and tried to squint the pain away, but the light got brighter. I felt Grayson's hands around my waist, pulling me to him, and heard a loud, deep voice yell:

"Break it up!"

NO FEAR, AND SILENCE.

That was always our contingency plan—because when you're swiping goods, taking the profit, and planning a monthlong party in Europe, you needed to know how to deal if the cops ever got involved. Sounds simple, until reality hits and you realize that fear part? You've got no control over it.

I stood about a foot away from Wren, hands over my head, willing my jackhammer heart to slow down. I wanted to hold her hand, tell her this was all going to be okay, but really? Another siren blared outside, short and loud. I didn't know how many police cars were outside, but from the glow of the red and blue lights flashing strobic across our faces, my guess would've been a very unscientific shitload.

Luke and Andy were on the other side of me. Luke didn't

look particularly concerned—with the exception of the blood on his face and his hands in the air, he could have been waiting to get a haircut. Andy, on the other hand, looked as fragile as a preschooler about to hurl. He winced as he was patted down.

A cop pulled something out of Andy's front pocket.

"What's this?" he asked, bringing up a Baggie to his nose.

Andy made a series of spluttering noises and looked over at us. The cop shook his head and reached for his cuffs.

Luke and I shared what was probably the first and last look of friendly agreement in a long time. I imagined the collective thought bubble over our heads would read:

Fucking. Bonehead. Stoner.

I wanted to pummel Andy. Shake some sense into him. It was stupid enough for him to rat to Luke about what we were doing, but carrying a freakin' dime bag around like a pack of gum? Luke muttered and looked up toward the ceiling. Andy was cuffed. We were screwed.

There were more voices and footsteps coming toward the cottage. Someone whistled long and low. Mrs. Caswell's face appeared behind the shattered window, her eyebrows jagged lines of anger as she took in the empty space. She said something to one of the officers outside and put her phone to her ear.

Then Mr. Caswell walked in, followed by two more officers.

The officer closest to the door saw him and smiled. "Jimmy?

Why'd they send someone from the prosecutor's office?"

"Not here officially, Mike. Just here. Family business," he said, patting the officer's shoulder before taking a look around.

"Your father's with the prosecutor's office?" Luke whispered, peering over at Wren. She wrinkled her nose at him.

"Unless one of you wants to explain why you're here, I'd keep silent," said the younger cop who'd cuffed Andy and was standing beside him.

"Sorry, sir," Luke said.

Mr. Caswell took in the damage, looking from the window to the lamp to the fallout on the floor. He crunched some broken glass with his foot and kicked it aside. Then he folded his arms and stood in front of us, eyes on fire like the fucking Chernabog.

That should have been my cue to tell him this was my fault. That I'd pay for the glass. That I'd steam clean the carpet. That Wren was the most innocent party in all of this.

Except my nuts pretty much slithered down my leg and crawled out of the building when his eyes landed on me. *Your father was defensive tackle. No one could get by him.* All I could think of was Pop's description of Mr. Caswell. Fitting. Safe to assume my marginal cater-waiter skills would no longer be needed at the Camelot.

"Would someone like to tell me what's going on?"

"Dad—please . . . we were just hanging out . . . things got out of hand," Wren said.

"Hanging out?" He motioned for one of the officers and took him aside to speak to him. The officer looked at Wren and nodded. Wren's mom came into the cottage, her face grim as she took in the scene. Our eyes met. I had to look away. Mr. Caswell called Wren over.

"Wren. Go with your mother to the office. Now."

I stole a glance at Wren. Her eyes were wide, sad.

Sorry, I mouthed.

"Don't look at her," Mr. Caswell said to me.

"Dad, it's not Grayson's—"

"Wren. Go."

Mrs. Caswell put her arm around Wren, but she wrestled away and got closer to her father. "No. It's my fault too. Don't send me away."

He gave her a look so forceful, I half expected Wren to crash into the wall behind her. "Take. Her. Out. Of. Here," he said to Mrs. Caswell.

Wren relented, looking over her shoulder at me as her mother led her out.

Her father turned back to us. A half dozen cops were behind him . . . waiting.

"Seeing as my daughter was the only one without blood on her face, it's safe to say she had nothing to do with this damage?"

"Yes, sir," we all mumbled together.

"You're Blake's son," he said, stepping closer. "Can't

imagine he'd approve."

"No, sir."

He crossed his arms again, staring me down. His eyes were the same shade of blue as Wren's but without the openness. This look told me exactly what he thought of me. Not much. Again this was a moment to defend myself, us. My mind went blank.

"There's a couple of hundred dollars' worth of damage here, if not more . . . wanna tell me why you were here?" he asked.

At least the silence part of our original plan was intact.

"Fine then," the officer who found us first on the scene said. "We'll sort this out at HQ."

I'd been to the police station once before, in second grade, to learn about fingerprinting and get my picture taken with McGruff the Crime Dog. Not much had changed. It was the same generic, white-walled office with fluorescent lighting and rows of desks. Except the computers were flat screens and took up less space. Oh, and I wasn't there to "Take a Bite out of Crime."

"Grayson Barrett."

I sat next to the detective's desk on what had to be the world's most uncomfortable chair. Metal-framed with worn, brown cushions. A support bar dug into my ass. The guy taking my information wore a pale orange polo; an ID dangled in front of his chest on a thick, black cord from around his neck. He smiled, held out his hand.

"Yes, sir," I replied, shaking his hand.

"Detective Charlie Preisano. Want anything while you wait for your parents? There's a vending machine outside, got those Pretzel M&M's everyone's raving about."

"No, thank you, sir."

"How about a soda? Water?"

At the far end of the office, I saw Luke slouched in a chair next to another desk, a bottle of Coke next to him. Andy was under arrest and being held somewhere else, thanks to his Baggie.

"Got any Gatorade?" I asked, pretty sure I couldn't swallow it. Not getting anything would make me look scared or guilty. And I wasn't guilty of anything. Not tonight, at least. I had to keep reminding myself of that. No fear.

"Gatorade? Let me check."

Detective Preisano stood up. After a hushed conversation with someone behind me, he came back and sat down.

"Might be a Powerade, is that okay?"

"Fine, thanks."

"Things got out of hand tonight, huh?" he asked, leaning back in his chair. "Must have gotten in a couple of good jabs; the other guy looks worse than you."

I shrugged.

"What were you fighting over?"

"Nothing."

His eyes went directly to my cheek. It still throbbed where Luke had landed a strong right hook.

"You're pretty banged up over nothing. Sure this wasn't, say, drug related?"

"No, sir."

"So the marijuana your friend has? Nothing to do with this?"

"I didn't even know he had it," I answered truthfully.

He nodded slowly, thinking it over. "Three boys and a girl found in a place of business after hours. A fight. Broken windows. Blood. Something's a little off, don't you think?"

Another officer placed the Powerade in front of me. *Sour-fucking-melon flavor.* The night just kept getting worse. Detective Preisano nodded thanks as he undid the cap and handed me the bottle.

"We were just hanging out."

"Why there? No better place to be on a Friday night?"

I took a sip of the Powerade, stalling. My head swam.

"And you had no clue your friend was carrying drugs? No intention to light up?"

"No, sir. I don't smoke."

"Never?"

"I have. Before. But no, it's not my thing."

"So if it's not drugs you were fighting about . . . then what was it . . . the girl?" There was laughter in his tone when he said "the girl." Wren did not need to be dragged into this any further than she already was.

"Sir, if you don't mind, I'd rather wait until my father gets here to answer any more questions."

Detective Preisano exhaled out his nose, nodding slowly. "Okay, fair enough."

As a bullshit artist, one of the things I had to master was shutting down any part of my brain directly wired to my conscience. Sometimes, when I was with a girl and I could feel myself caring, I could talk myself out of it, stuff it down. I'd imagine I was alone in the world. Invincible and above feeling compassion. I'd always be able to step back into my life, my house, and eat dinner across from Pop and Tiff, chatting without missing a beat about the latest episode of *The Walking Dead* or a Chem test I'd aced.

Those worlds collided at the police station.

Pop walked in looking paler than I'd ever seen him, even when he was in the hospital. He wore his long, black dress coat over track pants and a T-shirt. And his hair had that rumpled look, as if he'd run his hand through it a hundred times and forgotten to smooth it back down. Picking your son up at the police station was not high on the list of good things to do in recovery of a not-quite heart attack. When he saw my face, all he muttered was, "Christ."

Detective Preisano rose and shook Pop's hand.

"Hey, Charlie, come here a minute," the detective talking to Luke said, waving him over. Detective Preisano raised a finger to let him know he'd be right over.

"Mr. Barrett, feel free to take a seat. I'll be right back," he said.

Pop waited until he was out of earshot to speak.

"Grayson, what the hell is going on?"

"I got in a fight with Luke, Pop. It just got out of hand."

"Luke?" he asked, running a hand through his hair. "Why?"

I shrugged. He sighed, reached into his pocket, and jammed a piece of gum in his mouth. Just then Luke, being led by the other detective, brushed by us. He wouldn't look at Pop or at me. My stomach fell to my feet. Detective Preisano was behind them.

"Is my son under arrest?"

"No, Mr. Barrett, the Caswells haven't pressed any charges . . . yet. I'd just like to ask Grayson a few questions, make sure this wasn't more than a couple of kids getting out of hand."

Detective Preisano directed us down the hallway to a different, private room. The same shitty chairs lined each side of a long table. The walls were a pale, industrial green. The only view to the outside world was a small, square window in the door. When the door clunked closed, it felt like we'd been sealed into a bunker.

"What's this about?" Pop asked as we sat down.

Detective Preisano settled into the seat across from us. He took his time putting out his leather portfolio and then slid a piece of paper across the table to Pop.

"This is a juvenile-interrogation form, Mr. Barrett. Basically states your son's right to remain silent, to an attorney, and so on. You can stop the questioning at any time, if you wish."

Pop glanced quickly over the paper. "If he's not under arrest, why is he being questioned?"

"Your friend brought up some new information. I want to give you a chance to tell your side of the story."

I put my elbows on the table, turned to Pop. Satisfied, he signed the form, looked at me, and put out his hand, gesturing to go ahead and talk.

"So then," Detective Preisano said, leaning back in his chair and clasping his hands behind his head, "why the banged-up face?"

"It just happened."

He leaned forward, pulling a pen from the clasp in the center of his portfolio, and opened up to a yellow-lined pad with scribbles on it. Pop shifted in his chair.

"Well, your friend, the one who looks as bad as you . . ." he said, consulting the scribbles. "Luke, is it?"

I nodded.

"He told an interesting story about tonight. You sure you

don't have anything to say to me?"

My insides jolted, like that full-body muscle jerk you sometimes get right before falling asleep. For all I knew, Luke could have told the police about the necklace. I doubted it though. That would brew up a shit storm involving Spiro, Lenny, and the rest of their food chain that none of us would ever be prepared to deal with. Luke might have wanted to stir the pot but not deep enough to do the time for all the stuff we had pulled. This was his way of saying checkmate.

"There's nothing to tell," I answered.

"Grayson," Pop prodded, leaning on the table next to me.

"He claims he was there because you owed him something, and when you couldn't produce it, you offered up"—he ran his pen down the notepad and stopped, tapping the tip at a certain spot—"the Marshall amps instead. And when he didn't want those, things turned violent."

"That's a lie," I said, the words pouring out before I could even think.

"Which part?"

"All of it," I answered.

The detective laughed, but there was frustration beneath it.

There because I owed him something? The story began to concoct itself in my head. I didn't want to lie, but I was desperate. And if Luke wanted to mess with me, I'd get him right back. All I wanted to do was deflect as much of this away from Wren as possible.

"Taking the amps was his idea, not mine," I said.

Detective Preisano leaned forward, chin up, ready to take what I had to offer.

"I owed Luke a term paper. Two actually," I said, turning to Pop. His reaction was just what I needed. His head fell back, eyes closed. He ran a hand across his face before looking at me again, shaking his head.

"Term papers?" Detective Preisano's bushy eyebrows drew together. "Am I missing something?"

"Luke is ranked third at Saint Gabe's and has his eyes on Princeton or Penn. He needs to maintain a certain GPA and needed a little help. He paid me. I'll admit that, and I thought about doing it, but I decided against it after getting in so much trouble last year."

"What kind of trouble?" he asked, writing something down.

"I was expelled from Saint Gabe's, sir. I had a pretty extensive term-paper business there for a while, but I got sloppy, got caught."

"Grayson," Pop said, "the school dealt with this the way they saw fit. It's over."

"I know," I said. "Luke asked me for help and offered me the money up front. But I reneged, even though I did spend the money. I do owe him that. He said he'd take the amps and sell them to make up for the loss, but I really think it was just a threat. I threw the first punch."

Detective Preisano's face remained cool, but I could see in his eyes that I'd just diffused whatever bomb Luke had dropped. He nodded.

"Must be some damn good term papers."

"I was the best, sir," I answered. "But it's not worth getting expelled again. I didn't think it was worth it for Luke either."

"What I'm still not getting is why you were at the Camelot?"

I looked down, closed my eyes.

"Wren Caswell is my girlfriend," I said, keeping my face lowered. "We were there to, um . . ." I hesitated, not knowing if what I was about to say would help or hurt, but I was pretty sure it would get the heat off all of our backs. ". . . be alone."

Detective Preisano's eyebrows raised in understanding. Pop let out a long, slow breath next to me.

"Are we finished here? He's not being held, correct?"

"You're free to go," Detective Preisano said, standing up. He held out his hand to me. *No fear.* I shook it, giving him a small nod before Pop led me out of the room.

The air in the hallway was cooler and a relief after being held up for so long. I wasn't even sure how much time had passed, but it suddenly felt like hours. On our way out of headquarters, we ran into Mr. Dobson.

Decked out in a dark, tailored suit and traveling in a cloud of scent that was a mix of spicy cologne and a hint of alcohol, he looked like he'd been called away from a dinner date. His eyes gleamed when he saw us, a slow grin crossing his face.

"Grayson," he said, embracing me, then backing up to gawk at my injuries.

He looked at Pop. "Hell, Blake, what trouble have our sons gotten into now?" He gave Pop's hand a hearty pump. He didn't seem to notice that Pop was not amused.

"It's been too long; we should all get together. Tell Tiff that Izzy said to call her," he said, waving us off as he continued into the station. Neither of us had said a word to him.

"Asshole," my father hissed. Truth was he didn't know the half of it. Mr. Dobson seemed like a happy drunk, but Luke had told me otherwise. For a moment I felt bad for Luke, for what he was about to face when his father walked into the room or, later, when he got him home.

Tiffany was parked out front, sitting in the driver's seat of the Mercedes. I'd never been so happy to see her. Pop settled down into the front seat. I slid into the backseat, ignoring Tiff's plea to put on my seat belt, and promptly passed out across the length of it, thinking of Wren.

I WAITED ON THE BENCH OUTSIDE OF MY MOTHER'S office while she spoke to the glass guy about the damages. Without a party going on, the Camelot showed its age. Sir Gus was a sorry, dusty knight with nothing to preside over. The wood paneling and burgundy curtains—which usually added a homey, secluded air—made me feel like I was sitting in a dated medieval-theme-park ride. Even the portrait of my great-grandfather looked a little corny in the plain light, without the glow from the fireplace. The place truly was a relic from another time. And soon a wrecking ball would dash right through it. The thought was thoroughly depressing.

A half hour had passed since the police cars had left, and I was still burning with anger at the way my father had dismissed me so forcefully from the scene—even more embarrassing was that he'd done it in front of Grayson. I couldn't imagine what Gray was going through at the police station, but whatever it was, it couldn't have been good. I was tortured enough just anticipating my own private, Dad-led interrogation.

Eben pushed through the front door in jeans and a dark coat, unraveling his scarf as he came farther into the lobby. Sadness overwhelmed me. Everything I'd been stuffing down since the police had arrived bubbled to the surface. He softened when he saw my face.

"Wren."

I threw my arms around him, putting my cheek to his shoulder. He smelled so good, like oranges and spicy black pepper.

"Baby, why the tears?"

"What are you doing here?" I asked, wiping my tears on my sleeve.

"Ruthie called me in to wait for the glass guy . . . and since I have no social life to speak of, here I am."

"I totally screwed up, Eb," I said. "The cottage is . . . wrecked."

"So I heard, but *you* were involved?" he asked, taking off his coat and hanging it up on the rack near the office. He waved at my mom, who was still on the phone.

"And Grayson . . . and two of his friends . . . and I'm in deep doo-doo. . . . My dad isn't even speaking to me. He's been out there cleaning up the cottage all this time," I said, sitting down on the bench again. Eben sat next to me.

He patted my hand. "Darlin' . . . you and three boys in the love shack? That's not what I meant when I said go hang there with Grayson."

My skin flushed; I leaned my head on his shoulder. He put his arm around me.

"Daddy-O will come around. He probably just needs to breathe a little, I bet."

"The way he looked at me? What he said? I'm—"

My dad steamrolled through the front door with a broom and dustpan in hand. Eben and I both sat up straight. He gave Eben a quick, mechanical smile, once again ignoring me. Eben's eyes widened.

"Oh, my."

"See?"

"Wren, I don't mean to sound like a total wuss, but um," he said, lowering his voice, "you didn't tell them where you got the key . . . did you?"

I mimed locking up my lips. He swiped his forehead dramatically and mouthed, *Whew.*

"I don't even get why they are going to so much trouble . . . the place is going to be dust in a couple of months. Why even fix it?"

My mom breezed out of the office. "Eben, thank you so much for coming in."

Eben stood up and gave her a quick hug. It was odd to see

Mom in jeans and a casual tee at work. Then I remembered it had been date night for her and Dad. Guilt from interrupting their night gnawed at my insides.

"You haven't told her the Camelot news?" Eben asked

"Something else you're not talking to me about?"

My mother held up her hand. "Wren, it's a new development. One that . . . well, is a solution I feel better about."

"So we're not closing?" I asked.

"Yes, yes, we are closing. It's time, but someone gave us a different offer. Someone who's not going to knock it down."

I looked wide-eyed at Eben. "You?"

"Oh, hell no, well, indirectly yes, but no, I'm not the proud new owner. My culinary school will be. In February they start renovations to get ready for the summer semester. This is going to be a satellite campus. It's perfect, good location, parking, kitchens."

"We're going to finish out the last few weddings and then turn it over," my mother said, smiling.

"I think I even convinced them to keep Guinevere's Cottage. Give it a fresh coat, slap on a historic-landmark plate, and turn it into a boutique restaurant. The students can hone their craft while the school charges an exorbitant amount of money for tiny food. So yes, the glass guy is definitely not a waste."

"That's, like, the best news ever," I said, "and no little hot dogs."

"Oh, *mais oui*, Mademoiselle Wren, but we shall call zem *cochons en couvertures*," Eben said, bowing dramatically. I laughed, a genuine feel-good laugh, until my father returned to the lobby. His sullen presence vacuumed up all the cheer. My mother grabbed her coat off the rack.

"What would we do without you, kiddo?" my father said, tossing Eben the keys. "The heat is on low, but there's a space heater in the office if you get cold waiting." Dad finally looked at me.

"Let's go," he said, making a slicing motion with his hand.

"The glass guy should be here within the hour. If there's any trouble, don't hesitate to call me," my mother said, shrugging on her coat.

"Will do, Ruthie." Eben smiled and gave me a sympathetic look.

I hugged him.

"Sure you can't come with me? As a buffer?" I whispered.

He squeezed me tighter. "Baby Caswell, you are fierce. No worries."

At home my father rocketed upstairs to shower. My mother put on a pot of coffee. I sat at the kitchen table and tried not to hurl from nervousness. I wondered if Grayson was still at the police station . . . and what version of the truth he had told. Everything happened so quickly once Luke and I had arrived at the cottage. There was no way I was going to tell my parents the real reason we'd been there.

My heart surged, fearful, when I saw Dad's socked feet padding down the stairs. He'd changed into jeans and a maroon pullover, his hair freshly tousled and wet from the shower. My stomach dropped when I saw his stern face. He came to the table and pulled out the chair across from me.

The three of us sat. Quiet. This had been our dinnertime ritual since August, when Josh had left for school. Except there was no dinner. Just us. No paper, no banter, nothing to hide behind. I wished Josh would explode through the front door, weekend laundry in hand, brimming with some wild story to make my father laugh and to deflect whatever I had coming my way. For a moment my father studied me. Then he spoke.

"Why?"

The disappointment in his voice cut into me.

"I . . ." I began, but stopped. How could I explain? *I organized a faux revenge hookup so Grayson could talk to his friend about getting out of their con game* didn't seem like it would fly. I decided to keep it simple.

"We were just hanging out, and things got out of hand," I answered.

My parents shared a look.

"We, as in you and three boys?" my father asked.

"Um, well, not really."

348

"Did we not just find you with three boys, two covered in blood and one with drugs, at our place of business after hours?" he continued.

"Yes . . ." I said, looking at Mom.

"Wren, you told us you were going out with Maddie. Why did you lie?" she asked.

"I . . . well . . . I . . ."

I had no answer to that one. My dad's face reddened.

"Please, it just happened . . . an accident . . . I'm sorry," I said, trying to tamp down the tears that were finally coming.

"Sorry? *What were you doing there?*"

I wanted to crawl under the table and disappear. There was no easy answer for this.

"I was there to be with Grayson . . . alone."

He ran a hand across his face and got up from the table.

"Jim," my mother said.

"Ruthie, don't."

He walked over to the coffeepot and poured a cup. He brought it over to my mom before pouring another one for himself. "Do you want something, Wren?"

His tone had changed slightly, lightening even. The gesture was encouraging.

"No, no thanks."

He sat down again, hands clasped around his mug.

"You're . . . seeing . . . the Barrett boy?"

"Yes."

He nodded. "Let me guess, you've been seeing him about a month now?"

"Well, yes, seems about right."

"*Hmm*, now imagine that, because I've noticed some changes in you this last month. . . ."

"Dad."

"Am I wrong, Ruth?"

"Wren, you have been more . . . animated lately," she said.

"Animated? What are you talking about?"

"It's like this, Wren," my father began, "ever since you were in kindergarten, I've barely had to raise my voice to you. Every parent/teacher meeting your mother and I have ever been to could have been scripted. They would tell us we didn't even need to be there, but if they had one complaint, it was that you should speak up more. That's a complaint I can live with."

"And that's a good thing?" I asked.

"After Josh? Yes, it's a very good thing," my father continued. "You've never once been late to school, and then we get a call you cut your last period. You've lied about where you were going and who you were with. And now we find you with three boys, and your hair . . . is . . . blue . . . all since you've been seeing this boy."

"You think all of this happened because I met Grayson?"

"Wren, we're just concerned," my mother said.

"To hell with concerned," my father said. "I don't think he's the kind of *friend* we want you to have."

My first instinct was to storm away crying, but I stopped myself. What would that solve?

"You're wrong, Dad. All of this happened because of me. *Me.* I'm tired of being the quiet one. The kid who teachers don't have anything to say about—you really think that's the way I want to be remembered? How I want to go through life? I cut class . . . because . . . well, that was wrong, and being at the Camelot and breaking the window, all of that was stupid, but I didn't do it because of some boy."

"Wren, calm down."

"No, Dad, because you know if Josh did this, you'd already be laughing about it, probably swapping stories—"

"That's not true—"

"And if Brooke did this—"

"Brooke wouldn't do this," both my parents said.

"No, because Brooke is perfect and pregnant—"

"Wren, stop," my mother said.

"No. I won't stop. For the first time I'm making my own mistakes, doing my own thing. You guys are just going to have to deal with it. And Grayson is the kind of friend I want to have, because he likes me for who I am, Dad. He's a good person—we made a mistake tonight, a huge one, but . . . you don't even know him—so don't tell me he's not the kind of

351

friend you want me to have because . . . I . . . I love him."

My words rang out through the kitchen, filling the empty house. Had I actually told them I loved Grayson? I took deep breaths, getting my anger under control. My mother reached for my father's hand. He seemed reluctant at first but then wrapped his fingers around hers.

"Fine," my father began. "You won't be seeing him for a very long time, because I'm not sure you'll ever leave the house again for anything other than school or work. And we can be sure you won't work the same shifts; I know the owner."

"So . . . you're not going to fire him?" I asked, looking between them.

"Wren, I'm not happy about what happened tonight, but no, I'm not firing Grayson," my mother said. "He's a good worker. If he wants to stay on through January, he's more than welcome. And you can certainly work the same shifts; don't listen to this guy."

"But any and all keys to the love shack shall be given to me," my father added. "I don't want you there again unless it's for an event. Do you understand me?"

"Yes, Dad," I said. "Could I, um, get myself some hot chocolate now?"

He nodded. "Grab us some Oreos while you're up."

I turned on the kettle, grabbed the Oreos, and arranged some on a plate before returning to the table. I slid back into my chair and put the cookies in the center. My dad and

I reached for the same one. He mock-scowled at me, and I smiled, letting him take it. He twisted the cookie apart and gave me half.

"Wait a minute. . . . Dad, who told you the staff calls the cottage the love shack?" I asked, raking my teeth across the Oreo cream.

Mom stifled a smile and squeezed my dad's hand. They shared a playful look that seemed to transform them into teenagers again, and suddenly I felt like I was the one interrogating them. My father chuckled, and this odd realization came over me, one that made my skin crawl just a little. . . .

Was my father actually blushing?

"Who do you think named it that twenty-three years ago?" my mother said.

I swallowed my cookie and pushed away from the table to check on my boiling water. Maybe the three of us being quiet and going off to our separate spaces without talking wasn't such a bad thing sometimes.

"Guys . . . that's just . . . wow . . . TMI."

I LIE ON MY BED, STARING AT THE ACNE-VULGARIS ceiling and attempting to send telepathic messages to Wren, since I was banned from all technical/electronic devices. This was a new one for Pop. Even when I was expelled, he'd let me keep my cell phone. I felt like I was under house arrest.

Not that I would have called Luke or Andy, but I kept wondering what sort of story they'd told about last night. Did Detective Preisano go back to Luke with my term-paper explanation? Did Luke deny it? When all was said and done, I felt like I'd put a pretty positive spin on it. And if Luke and Andy were smart, they'd just go along for the ride.

But Luke was vindictive and smart.

And Andy . . . well, just, shit.

My stomach lurched with a weird twinge of hunger or anxiety; I couldn't tell the difference. I hadn't eaten a thing since lunch the day before. Had it only been the day before? A school day? Friday. Christ, it felt like I'd lived a week in one night. I folded my head into a pillow burrito, rolled to my side, and groaned. When I let go to breathe, Pop was standing in the doorway. I sat upright. He looked like he wanted to smile, but it passed. He had two mugs, and he handed me one. Black coffee. I leaned against my headboard. Pop sat in my desk chair, placing his mug in the space my laptop usually occupied before he had confiscated it.

"Last night was not my proudest moment," he said.

"Not mine either, Pop," I said, sitting up and putting the mug on my side table. "I'm sorry."

"I just thought we were past all this, Grayson. You seemed to be gettin' on again, things looking up in school and with Wren. What happened? Why would you even think about writing those term papers? That's all this is about—you were telling the truth last night, right?"

More or less, or less.

"Yes, Pop. It was dumb. I'm done with the term-paper thing."

"Good."

"Does Mom know?" I asked.

"A week and a half before Christmas, ya think I'm gonna

355

saddle her with this shit? Nah, it can wait," he said, taking a sip of coffee. "You know, maybe we don't need to tell her at all. As long as we're handling it."

Pop deciding *not* to tell my mother something? That was new. "I say we let this one slide."

We sat for a few minutes in thick, thoughtful silence. Pop leaned on his elbow against my desk.

"Have I let too many things slide?" he asked.

"What?"

"You think any of this would have happened if you went to live with her?"

"Pop, what are you getting at?"

"Grayson, I'll admit I was happy you chose to live with me. I'm not sure if it had to do with feeling like I'd won something over your mother or the fact that I'd have you with me. Both, I guess. I never doubted I could take care of you, or us, but sometimes I wonder if you might have been better off in Connecticut."

"Don't say that. I could have gotten into trouble anywhere. Could have been worse."

"Could have been better."

"It is what it is," I answered. "I didn't start my term-paper business because of something you or Mom did or didn't do. And last night . . . that was just . . . me, Luke, and Andy being idiots. All of this is my fault. Me."

"You will pay for that window. You. Luke. Andy," he said,

lifting his coffee mug at me for emphasis. "You have to do the right thing."

"Of course."

Tiff knocked on the doorjamb. "Luke's at the door."

"What part of grounded are you not getting?" he asked me.

"I didn't call him."

"I invited him in, but he said he can't stay. Blake, I think you should let the boys talk."

My father stopped midsip. "So that's it, we're playing good cop, bad cop now."

Tiffany clucked her tongue. "I'll tell Luke you'll be down in a minute, Grayson."

Pop sighed and took a slug of coffee.

"When you're done with Luke, take a shower. You look like a greaseball," he said, standing up and tousling my hair. "And leave that screw out of your eyebrow; you look better without it."

"Sure, Pop."

I waited until he left the room to get up. What could Luke possibly want? As I pulled a fresh T-shirt over my head, I thought of at least one thing: the necklace. I grabbed it out of my desk drawer, where it had been since the day Wren gave it back to me. Whether he really wanted it or not, Luke was getting the last lingering trace of a past I wanted to forget. I tossed my jacket on and went outside.

Luke was on the porch, hands in his pockets, waiting.

When he turned around, I saw the damage I'd inflicted. It looked like he'd smeared a deep-purple shade of eye black from the corner of his right eye to the outside of his cheek. I thought for sure that when I saw him again I'd want to finish what we'd started, but I felt strangely calm. His face split into a grin. And for some reason we cracked up, laughing for a long minute.

"I did that?" I asked, inspecting his injuries. He had another bruise on his cheek and a cut on his bottom lip.

"I got three inches and twenty pounds on my old man. Think he's going to mess with me these days?"

I crossed my arms and leaned against the porch railing. "You're not in trouble?"

"With him? Nah, I think he got off on going to the police station. Gives him something to complain about on his next corporate golf outing. Term papers? Nice spin, Barrett."

"I thought so. You went along with it, then?"

He hunched his shoulders, squinted up at the sun. "I didn't want to . . . I was going to take us down, you know . . . big, fiery exit and all that, then I thought, what's the point? I got in, Barrett. Princeton. Early action. Got my letter yesterday."

Luke had set his sights on Princeton freshman year. It was a huge achievement. I should've been happy for him, but it stung. After all the crap he'd pulled, he still got what he'd wanted the most. Where was his karmic payback?

"Congrats. That's . . . that's awesome news, Luke," I said. I knew I should have shaken his hand, or clapped his shoulder, or given him some gesture of bro-love, but I couldn't bring myself to do it. Maybe this had been his sole purpose for coming here—to gloat.

"Why would I screw around with that, right?"

"Right."

Luke gripped the railing with both hands and watched a few cars pass down the street before speaking again. "You want to hear the most messed-up thing? Since you got kicked out of Saint Gabe's, everything is easy. No one challenges me. Nothing drove me like competing with you."

"Dude, c'mon, I was ranked tenth; you were always above me. No competition there."

He laughed. "Don't you get it? You're my friggin' barometer, Barrett. Not even getting into Princeton feels as good as I thought it would without you to measure it by."

I didn't want to admit it, but I understood what Luke meant. I'd felt the same way about being in Bergen Point. The classes were fine, maybe not as specialized as what I'd been used to at Saint Gabe's, but interesting enough. The fact that I didn't have any close friends to challenge me in class or on the lacrosse field was what made it dull.

"Here," I said, pulling out the necklace and offering it to Luke, "consider this your congratulations present."

"You shouldn't have, Barrett," he said, taking it from me.

"What do you think you'll get for it?"

He shrugged, studying the necklace in his open palm, as if he actually did think of it as a present. "I think I only paid, like, eighty bucks for it. It's gold-plated silver."

My mouth dropped open. "What are you talking about? You gave that to me for Spiro to fence."

He closed his fist around the necklace, wound up, and threw it toward my neighbor's house, where it disappeared into the thick evergreen shrubs surrounding the front yard.

"Dude?"

Luke shoved his hands in his pockets and leaned against the railing. "I wasn't lying when I said it was my property," he said. "I bought it last year for Ava as a birthday present. I don't know why . . . maybe hoping it would . . . make her . . . whatever. After that night I caught her—with you—things were never really the same. That's why I gave it to you for Spiro. You've got some set giving it to Wren."

I grimaced. "Yep, I'm living with that one every day. You know I was blitzed out of my mind that night with Ava. I never led her on. I wouldn't have done that, you know."

"I think that made you more of a challenge for her. Sick, right? Chick's got some issues. Maybe that's why I liked her so much," he said. "But I'm done with that. Riding out senior year, clean, unattached, and getting outta here, for good."

"So I know you didn't come here to shoot the shit about Ava. What's up?"

He pulled a white envelope from his pocket. "Here, for the window."

It was filled with twenties, probably close to five hundred bucks. There was only one place this money could have come from.

"What about Amsterdam?"

"Do you really have to ask?" he said, shaking his head, laughing. "Think I want to go to a foreign country with Andy after last night? He probably pissed himself in the holding cell."

Impossible as it seemed, I laughed. "Oh, I'd bet on that."

"Could you picture him overseas, without his parents to bail him out? Christ. Just you know . . . pass it on for the damages. Tell the Caswells it's all from you if you want. I don't care."

"What's the catch, Luke? Are the bills marked? Am I gonna give this to Mr. Caswell, then get caught for something?"

"No, dude. No catch, just . . . time to man up a little. Have you talked to Wren?"

Luke's voice softened when he said Wren's name. I shook my head, ignoring the sudden jab of irrational jealousy I felt. "Not sure when I'll be able to do that."

"Well, that might help," he said, nodding toward the envelope.

"Anything happen with her last night that I should know

about? You know, on the ride over?"

"Nah," he said, shoving his hands in his pockets again. "I knew what she was trying to do. I didn't screw with her . . . well, not too much. She's pretty cool, Grayson. Genuine. Too nice for my taste but, like I said, the kind of girl to get serious about. And you should. Get serious."

"Yeah, maybe . . . we'll see," I said, keeping my cards close to my chest. Luke may have appeared to be sincere about manning up, but I wasn't going to take a chance, especially not with Wren.

"Gotta fly. Heading over to Foley's for damage control. Wanna come?"

"You're serious?"

He shrugged. "Why not?"

"Can't. I'm not sure I'm allowed to leave the house until I'm eighteen. How screwed is that?"

He stopped halfway down the stairs and looked back up.

"It would have been fucking epic, you know. Us. In Amsterdam."

Maybe there was some parallel universe, where all of our different paths played themselves out. One where I was with the guys, experiencing the endless party we'd thought cruising the *rosse buurt* could be. I tried to put post–term-paper-pimp Grayson in that vision, the way I'd imagined myself the year before. How much I'd wanted it, that goal, the freedom, that time fooling around with my friends before getting serious.

Could have been legendary, for sure, but this path I was on with Wren, uncertain as it was . . . made me feel more alive and aware, than that one ever had. That was something Luke would never understand, something he'd never be able to measure against.

I smiled. "Yeah, would have been epic."

TWENTY-SEVEN

WREN

"WREN, NEVER WOULD HAVE PEGGED YOU AS THE Caswell to leave the biggest mark on the Camelot," my brother, Josh, said, raising his glass to the table.

Brooke, Pete, and Eben applauded. I resisted the urge to look down, instead sticking my chin out and bowing slightly. Once word had gotten out that the Camelot was closing, the intimate Christmas party my mother had planned for the staff turned into a good-bye party that filled half the Lancelot ballroom with current and former employees.

My parents had even pardoned my sentence for the evening, and both Mads and Jazz were set to arrive at any minute. The mood in the room was festive, but there was one staff member noticeably missing. At least to me. It had only been a week, and I still hadn't spoken to Grayson about anything that had happened. I'd been anxious to hear his version of the night.

"Yes, the story of 'How I Took Down the Love Shack' . . . Wouldn't that be a stellar college essay?" I said, raising my ginger ale. It felt weird to joke about the love shack in front of everyone. Being the center of attention was still a position I wasn't comfortable with, especially when it was for something that was semiscandalous.

"That would be a page-turner. Give the admissions people a little thrill for a change," Josh said.

"Please don't turn her into the female version of you. She's Hoya material," Brooke said, giving my hand a squeeze.

"Ha. Hoya material. I have a feeling I'd be majoring in babysitting if I went to Georgetown," I answered, patting Brooke's small but newly rounded belly. "We'll see."

"Love shack? Why haven't I heard about this before?" Pete asked. Brooke waved him off.

"Just a nickname for the cottage. I have no clue how it got that name."

"Brooke, darling, didn't you coin that phrase?" Eben asked, tipping his Corona to her.

"Reeeally . . ." Pete said.

"Nope, I think it goes back much farther than that," I said, remembering my parents and the way they'd acted at the kitchen table the night of the love shack incident. I shivered and took a sip of my ginger ale while the others looked at me expectantly.

365

Eben beamed. "Ooh, do tell, Miss Wren."

"Nope. I'm a vault."

"See, it's the quiet ones who know all the good secrets," Josh said.

"Oh. Look. Saved by the text," I said, waving my phone.

We're here!! Meet us in the lobby!! xoxoM&J

I raced across the parquet dance floor in my riding boots, nearly knocking into Mom and Dad, who were slow dancing near the edge of the dance floor. The prospect of actually hanging out with Jazz and Mads made me giddy. My parents had all but banished me to the highest tower in the kingdom, and my week had consisted of going to school, coming home, and—well, that was basically it. I was fiending for some fun with my girls.

"Hey, why didn't you just come in?" I asked, rushing into the lobby to meet them.

"Oh, you know, we wanted to make a grand entrance with the lady of scandal," Mads said, taking off her coat. She was rocking her red minidress and ankle boots. Jazz wore a black mini too, with a pair of sparkly heels. Neither of them needed me for a grand entrance.

"You guys look awesome," I said, taking their coats.

Maddie smoothed down her skirt. "I was promised some hot college guys to flirt with, so I hope this party delivers."

Jazz was silent, standing there with a goofy grin on her face.

"What?"

"We brought you an early Christmas present," she said, motioning behind me.

I pivoted around. In the corner, standing near Sir Gus, was Grayson.

He was wearing the blazer from that first day in the park with a gray CBGB tee underneath, and a seductive smile that made every nerve in my body crackle to attention. My heart swelled standing there; all I wanted to do was tackle him, but I wasn't even sure he was supposed to be at the party. The coats dropped to the floor. A grin I could hardly contain broke across my face as we drifted toward each other. Grayson caught me, and we spun, my feet barely touching the ground. I clung to him, burying my face in his neck and inhaling the earthy scent of his hair.

"You feel soooooooooo good," he whispered in my ear. His grip loosened as his hands wandered the length of my body. Maddie cleared her throat.

"Guys, you know you have an audience."

"That was so adorable," Jazz added, clapping. "Westley and Buttercup have nothing on you guys."

I stepped back and peeked into the ballroom. The slow song had ended, and my parents were speaking with Chef Hank by the bar. I turned back to Grayson. "What are you doing here?"

"I was invited," he said.

"Really?"

"Hey, hello, still here," Mads said, grinning. "Just point us in a direction, and we'll leave you two to catch up."

"Oh, sorry," I said, collecting their jackets from where I'd dropped them on the floor and bringing them over to the coatroom. "We're sitting with Josh, Eben, Brooke, and Pete—over there, see."

"C'mon, Jazzy," Mads said, grabbing her hand. "Holla if you guys need a fire hose!"

"Mads!" Jazz said, shaking her head and following her into the ballroom.

The doors snicked shut behind them, and Grayson pulled me toward the corner again, by Sir Gus, out of view of the ballroom for a proper *Haven't seen you in a week* greeting. I wrapped my arms around him, still in disbelief that he was actually in front of me. Our lips touched, and I was swept away in the warmth of his kiss. I hadn't realized we were moving until I felt the cross-guard of Sir Gus's sword jab into my back. We nearly knocked him off his pedestal.

"Who invited you?" I asked when we stopped for a breath. Our arms remained loosely around each other, neither one of us wanting to let go. I leaned back to take in his face.

He looked toward the ballroom, then back at me. "Your father."

"Um, what?" I asked, breaking our hold.

"Yep, went to his office during the week," he answered,

smiling. "I gave him some money for the damages."

"You paid for the window? He didn't tell me that," I said.

"Well, it was from me, Luke, and Andy," Grayson said, taking both my hands in his and drawing me close to him again. "Wren, sorry doesn't even begin to make up for the other night. I don't know why I let you be part of that crazy plan."

"Grayson, that crazy plan was partly my idea. I *wanted* to be involved. The consequences weren't . . . well, they don't suck as bad as I thought. Especially now."

"You must have gotten into some serious trouble with your parents," he said, brushing his lips across mine.

"I think the thing that bothered my father most was when I told him we were at the love shack to be alone," I said.

He tossed back his head. "You told him that? Snap. If I'd known before, I don't think I would have gone to see him. I'm surprised I got an invite."

"Did the crazy plan work at least? Did you talk to Luke?"

"He's over the Amsterdam thing, if that's what you mean."

"So . . . that means . . ."

"It's over."

"And that means . . ."

The ballroom doors flung open.

"Hey, you two, it's a party—get in here," Eben said, grabbing my hand. Maddie was right behind him, swaying to the beat of the music that pounded over the sound system. She seized Grayson by the arm and they led us into the ballroom.

Everyone, young and old, staff and their guests, were crammed onto the dance floor, doing the "Cha Cha Slide." Eben and Maddie hopped right back in without missing a step, waving us to join them. Jazz had her high heels off and was next to Josh, demonstrating how to take it back. Josh bumped into a few people when they turned to the left, then gave up the proper steps altogether and took Jazz by the hand and spun her around.

Grayson and I stood on the edge of the dance floor.

"Wanna dance?" he asked.

"You can't be serious; no . . . I don't do the group thing," I said, shrinking back from the crowd.

"C'mon," Grayson said, "this is my jam."

"Your jam?"

"Yeah, isn't it about time we just had . . . fun . . . you and me?" he said, bending his knees and bouncing along with the beat. He swayed his hips in a way that made me laugh. I inched a little closer.

"You and me, I love that."

He grinned and stepped into the throng of partiers.

"Then what are you waiting for?" he asked, extending his hand.

There were so many ways to screw this up. I could trip . . . knock into someone and cause a domino effect of fallen dancers . . . make a complete ass of myself. As I stood there, surrounded by the people I loved most, I knew no one would laugh at me even if I took a nose-dive onto the parquet floor.

And in the center of them all stood Grayson.

Waiting.

For me.

A promise . . .

I grabbed his hand.

It was time to dance.

ACKNOWLEDGMENTS

Most of the time writing is such a solitary activity: hours at a desk, staring into space and living in the world inside my head. But the truth is, this book would not have been possible without the following amazing people:

Tamar Rydzinski: Quite simply, one phone call after a dreary day at the DMV changed my life. I could not ask for a better champion of my work. Thank you for believing in my writing, pushing me to make it sing, answering questions both significant and mundane with the same calm assurance, and for helping me keep my stiletto in the door.

Donna Bray: I have only dreamed of working with an editor as kind, down-to-earth, and savvy as you. Thank you for loving Wren and Grayson as much as I do, and for making me dig deeper in the story than I ever thought I could. (And thanks too for introducing me to *Veronica Mars*. Not sure how I made it this long without watching!)

Viana Siniscalchi: Thank you for your enthusiasm—your emails always feel like a smile delivered to my in-box.

Infinite thanks to the extraordinary team at Balzer + Bray and HarperCollins. I'm still pinching myself that there are so many talented and dynamic people working on this book. Thank you for making me feel like part of the family. Truly, I'm honored.

Erin Fitzsimmons: Thank you, thank you, thank you for such a gorgeous cover.

SCBWI, especially the regional chapters of NJSCBWI and SCBWI Carolinas: Thank you for all you do in creating a safe and welcoming haven for writers both new and seasoned.

The Bruegger's Group: Thanks for encouraging me (and straining your voices over the cappuccino machine) when I only had a handful of chapters and doubted my ability to write from a boy's POV. Thanks also for putting up with my Style Savvy obsession, and for the laughter.

Writer buds extraordinaire Meg Wiviott, Gale Sypher Jacob, Judy Palermo, Cindy Clemens, Laura Renegar, Niki Schoenfeldt, Kelly Dyksterhouse, Pat Enright, and my online Paper Wait family: Thank you for getting me, for loving my writing (even when I didn't), and for calmly talking me down from the ledge during the "Why am I doing this again?" moments. This journey would not be the same without each of you, and I'm forever grateful for your friendship.

My parents, who provided countless hours of babysitting (and so much more) so I could attend my critique group. In a chaotic world, your quiet and unwavering support is my anchor.

My family and friends: You've all touched my life in your

own special ways. I'm blessed to have you in my corner. Special shout-outs to my sister, Ruthanne, whose regular phone calls keep me sane; Dave, big brother and fiercest fan; Jerry, for blue sangria and for answering all my lawyer-type questions; and my mother-in-law, Mary, whose gentle encouragement and newspaper clippings buoyed many a day when I was down. For Denise, Beth, Kathy, Mil, Sue, and Jack, our friendship is pretty much the backbone of my life and the inspiration for everything. And many thanks to Rob, who speedily and thoroughly answered all of my police questions without thinking twice.

My own promises of amazing: You know who you are . . . This is what I've been doing at the computer. Thank you for being mostly patient, but thank you more for always being you. You keep me on my toes in the best way. Hugs and love.

And to Jim, my best friend, muse, and partner in crime who always makes me feel like Samantha Baker at the end of *Sixteen Candles*. I love you. Let's get a cupcake.